WRESTLING
WITH DESIRE

D.H. STARR

Featherweight Press
www.featherweightpublishing.com

Copyright 2010 by D.H. Starr

Published by
Featherweight Press
3052 Gaines Waterport Rd.
Albion, NY 14411

Visit Featherweight Press on the Internet:
www.featherweightpublishing.com

Final Cover Art by Deana Jamroz
Cover photo by Dan Skinner
Editing by Lindsay Ketchen

ISBN# 978-1-60820-220-1

Issued 2010

To my sister for believing in me.

Chapter 1

Derek Thompson pulled his Honda Civic into the parking lot reserved for seniors at Brampton High School. *Yeah, that's right,* he thought. *I'm a senior.* Just that was enough to make this the first day of a very good year. He hopped out and ambled toward the main entrance where the jocks always hung out until the final bell, and where the guys on his wrestling team were screwing around, patting Josh Dibbling on the back like he was some kind of hero. Probably screwed another cheerleader or something.

"Hey, Thompson! C'mon over man, you gotta hear 'bout J's summer fun."

Derek pasted on his fake smile and headed over. Like he wanted to hear about Dibbling screwing another *girl.* He was just about to join the group when he was stopped in his tracks by a loud shriek from behind him.

"Derek, you rotten bastard! Where the hell have you been for the past week? I swear, I ought to kick you straight in the nuts right here and now." Derek's mouth pulled up at both sides into a wide, sincere grin as he faced his best friend Rebecca Stoltz. Rebecca was short with brown hair styled in a bob and a body as robust as her personality. As part of the drama club, she tended to bring her flare for drawing attention with her wherever she went.

I owe you Beck. Derek sighed, having been saved from the torture of listening to Josh's bragging. He simply gave the guys a knowing shrug and turned to walk over to Beck. "Hon, um, did you forget that you were in California for the past week? I called you every other day but you didn't call me back. Shouldn't I be threatening to kick you in the nuts right now?"

Rebecca dismissed Derek's explanation with a wave of her hand and began monologuing about the classes they would be sharing, the teachers they were fated to suffer, and worst of all, the fact that her arch nemesis, Malinda Bines, had called her the previous night telling her about the audition piece that she had been rehearsing for the winter musical. "I know that bitch doesn't think she is going to ruin my senior year by stealing the best roles." Allowing Beck to grab him by his arm, he was half dragged into the school where kids were greeting each other excitedly.

When they got to their lockers, they shoved their stuff in, only taking enough time to grab what they needed for first period English. If they didn't get to class early, they ran the risk of sitting in the front. For the past three years, they had always secured seats together in the back of the class so they could keep out of the eye-line of the teacher and more importantly, had perfect vantage points for watching the rest of the students in the class. After the first bell rang, students started to filter into the room. By the time the second bell rang, most of the seats were taken, except for a few in the back row. The seats on either side of them were empty, which suited Derek just fine.

Once seated, Beck took a moment to look at Derek. He was wearing a new pair of blue Levi 501's, a form-fitting white t-shirt, and squeaky clean new white Adidas sneakers. Beck shook her head. "Stand up for me." Derek simply stared at her. "Stand up and turn around."

"Uh, why?" Derek hated drawing attention to himself and did everything he could to fade into the background. He had lots of friends and was popular, but he preferred being the good guy who everyone could talk to.

"Just do it." Beck's voice was dripping with annoyance.

With a glare pasted on his face, Derek obeyed, stood, turned once, and then sat down as quickly as he could.

The few kids that had turned to watch him had already returned to the conversations they were having. "Ok. Satisfied? Now you want to tell me what that was all about?"

Beck shook her head and sighed. "You have such a great body; I don't know why you have to hide it by making yourself so generic." She ruffled his neatly cropped brown hair. "Like this. It's perfectly boring. Standard cookie cutter hair. And your clothes. You're wearing the standard first-day-of-school outfit that all American boys are probably wearing today. At least the jeans and shirt fit your body well. Your ass is still a huge attraction and you show it off beautifully in those jeans."

Derek felt his cheeks warm and was sure that he was beginning to blush. Although he worked hard to blend in, he did love his butt. It was the perfect bubble butt. Nicely toned mounds of muscle pushed his jeans out in perfect proportion to his tapered waist and broad shoulders. "Alright, enough!"

Beck shook her head, and then moved on to a new subject. She leaned in close to Derek so only he could hear her. "So, dish, did you find any hot man meat to play with this summer? I have to know."

"Beck, you know that I didn't. I spent practically every day with you this summer and you travelling with your parents for the past week hardly gave me enough time to…"

"Oh. My. God." Rebecca's mouth dropped open and she grabbed Derek's wrist, digging her nails into the soft under-skin. "I can *not* believe that she is in this class. It's bad enough that I have to deal with Malinda during drama, but to have to suffer that primping little tart's face in class is too much for me to…"

Derek sighed with relief. He knew it would only be a matter of time before Beck became the center of her own universe once again. He nodded and made the appropriate sounds of listening, but his attention had suddenly been diverted to a student who he had never seen before. Derek's pulse quickened as he tried to stare at the newcomer without being noticed. He had unkempt blonde hair which made him look sexy and defiant. His legs were covered by bulky cargo pants, but his upper body caused Derek to gasp. He was wearing a worn, long-sleeved, white cotton shirt with a faded picture of the Tasmanian Devil on the front. It fit him tightly around his chest and Derek immediately noticed the outline of firm pecs and just a hint of nipple pushing at the fabric. The rest of the shirt fell along his body, creating folds which suggested a long, trim frame, but leaving to imagination whether his abdomen was smooth or cut. Derek wished that he had x-ray vision to get a glimpse of the hidden legs and butt, but he could tell that the guy had long legs.

Derek took in a deep breath and remembered to nod and make a sound of affirmation at whatever Rebecca was saying, then continued his surveillance. He noticed that the boy's shoulders were square and that he stood with confidence. Slender muscles rose from the neck of his shirt leading to a sharp jaw line. His lips were pink and his bottom lip was plump and extremely kissable. And his eyes. They were ocean blue. Not the kind of ocean blue like you see along most of the eastern or western coast, but more of a bluish-green like what you would see in the Caribbean.

He walked over to the teacher, Mr. Carlton, and handed him his slip, indicating that he was a new student and was assigned to this class. The teacher nodded and then introduced him to the class.

"Class, first of all, I would like to welcome you to Senior English. We will, I am sure, be having many wonderful discussions about topics of great interest to you. Please know that I am trusting that you can handle the many themes that we will be discussing this year, which are of particular interest and pertinence to your age group, with maturity. I would also like to introduce you to a new student here at Brampton." Mr. Carlton looked at the slip again and then continued. "Scott Thayer is joining the senior class having moved here from Monroe, Iowa. I am sure you will all make him feel welcome and at home. Is there anyone who would be willing to help Scott through his first day at Brampton? I am sure he will need directions to classes and someone to have lunch with today." Scott looked towards his feet at this request and Derek was sure he could see his cheeks flush slightly. *What the heck was wrong with Mr. Carlton anyways? Didn't he realize that being a new senior was bad enough without singling him out on his first day?*

From where he was sitting, Derek could tell that most of the girls in the class were staring bug-eyed at Scott and, most likely, longing to be his appointed buddy but terrified of the rumor mill should they actually volunteer. Most of the boys seemed oblivious or uninterested in the new arrival, likely more interested in what was being served for lunch. It didn't hurt that the only empty seats were in the back row either. Derek raised his hand, "Uh, Mr. Carlton, there are some empty seats back here."

"Great, Derek." Turning to Scott, Mr. Carlton continued, "You can take a seat with Derek and welcome to Brampton." Scott looked up and glanced at Derek. As he worked his way to the back of the room, he maintained eye contact and Derek swore that those sea-blue eyes were saying *thanks for getting me out of this embarrassing situation.* Through his peripheral vision, he could see Rebecca staring at him with a huge grin on her face. Quietly, so that only he could hear, she said, "Careful baby, you might fall in love." He reached into his pocket and took out his cell. Deftly selecting Beck's name from his call list he texted four simple words in response. *Shut the fuck up.*

Scott took his seat next to Derek. "Thanks man. I swear, being the new kid sucks".

Derek felt a thrill of heat run through his body as Scott addressed him. "No problem. I wouldn't want to be standing up there any longer than I had to." He then motioned to Beck. "This is my friend Rebecca," Derek said, leaning back in his chair and allowing Beck to extend her hand across his chest to shake Scott's hand. As she did, she gave Derek a meaningful glance which said *you've got the hots for this one*. Derek returned the look with a penetrating stare which said *if you don't cut the shit, I'm gonna kill you.*

Mr. Carlton took a stack of papers from his desk and handed them to each person sitting in the front row. "If you could please pass these back, we will begin by reviewing this year's syllabus and the required books you will be reading."

At the end of class, Derek looked at Scott's welcome sheet which gave him basic information about Brampton and had his assigned locker number written in the space provided on the front. It turned out that his locker was near Derek and Beck's. *Nice.*

"You must be pretty bummed out. Changing schools in your senior year sucks." Derek tried to make his comment sound casual, but his heart was racing as he walked next to Scott. He faced forward, but was beginning to give himself a headache with the strain he was placing on his eyes through the sideways glances he was giving Scott every five seconds.

Scott's shoulders sagged slightly, but his voice remained cheerful. "Yeah, it does. But I'm used to it. My family has moved around a lot." Derek gave Scott a questioning look and Scott continued. "My dad works in Human Resources for Target and has moved up the corporate ladder. He was manager of the Des Moines area stores and just got promoted to oversee the northeastern regional stores. It was a pretty big promotion and difficult for him to pass up. I understand and all, but it's not the first time that my dad has had to move in order to accept a promotion with his job."

"Wow. That sucks. I've lived here in Cambridge my whole life. I can't imagine what it would be like to up and move my whole life to someplace else. Plus, I have a lifetime of friends here and my wrestling team which I love. I just couldn't imagine it." Derek realized that he was prattling on with someone he hardly knew and suddenly felt uncomfortable. Opening up and volunteering information did not fit nicely into his low-profile comfort zone. He continued walking towards Scott's calculus class to show him where it was. It was in the same direction as his pre-calculus class anyways.

The tone of Scott's voice pulled Derek out of his momentary retreat into his head. "You wrestle?"

"I absolutely love it. It's one of the only sports I know where you are part of a team but it's still an individual sport. Whatever you do helps your team succeed, but when you are on the mat you have to depend entirely on yourself. When you're on the mat it's you, your opponent, and the will to win." Again, he couldn't believe how much he was sharing with a total stranger. *I wonder why that is.*

"You wrestle! That's awesome." Scott's body language shifted and he was suddenly smiling broadly and speaking with animation. "I wrestle as well. I was on the varsity team back in Monroe and was even elected captain for senior year. I actually wrote a paper for a local contest last year about how a wrestling match is like facing major life challenges. It's about your attitude. If you believe you can win and commit yourself to giving your all, then win or lose, you come out of it having grown in some way. How is the team here?"

Most people, at least those who didn't wrestle, usually thought of wrestling as a gay sport where guys rolled around on the mat together. Derek was impressed that Scott not only got the sport, but saw it as more than winning and showing how tough you are physically. He got that it was a sport that required mental toughness as well. "Our team has been getting better and better over the past few years. When I was in 9th grade we sucked and barely won anything. But a core group of us have been on varsity for the past three years and now we are in the top three in our division. We actually have a good chance of winning this year. I usually run throughout the fall to get into shape for the winter season." Derek hadn't noticed that he had moved closer to Scott until their arms brushed together. He quickly took a step back, feeling slightly dizzy as he registered the fresh scent of fabric softener coming off of Scott's shirt.

As they turned the final corner to Scott's calculus class, Derek felt his chest grow a little heavier. He wasn't exactly sure what caused it until they reached the classroom door. Then it hit him. He wanted to keep talking to Scott. *What's going on here? I never just meet someone and start talking to them.*

Needing to get away so that he could clear his head, but wanting to make sure that he was going to see Scott again later, Derek quickly made plans before it was time to head to their second period classes. "Hey, all seniors have fourth period lunch. If you want, I could meet you at the cafeteria and introduce you to Brampton's infamous beef stew. It's got to be on the list of top ten most toxic food items for high school lunches in the country."

Scott laughed. His smile was wide and Derek noticed how one side of his mouth curled up a little bit more than the other, revealing strong white teeth and a dimple which immediately drew his attention. "Sure, I may as well eat the toxic stuff right away. Maybe I can build up a resistance to it before it can kill me."

"Cool." Derek felt tension he hadn't realized had been there fall out of his shoulders and his breathing suddenly came more easily. He needed to get a grip, and fast. "So, you know where your next class is?"

"All set, it's just down the hall from here, right?"

"Yup. I'll see you at lunch." Derek turned and headed towards his pre-calculus class a little more abruptly than he normally would have. He and Beck had most of their classes together this year and he needed to see her. Sitting in the back of the class with her would calm his strained nerves and help him to get his thoughts back in order.

When Derek got to class, he rushed to Beck's side and sat down in the seat she had reserved for him. "Beck, I need to run something by you, and I need to get it out before you start one of your stories."

Beck flashed an indignant look of pure offense. Then her mouth curved up at the sides. "Sure babe. No need to get prissy. I know I love to be the center of attention, but every once in a while I am capable of listening to someone else." She paused, as if she were waiting for Derek to confirm the statement. When Derek said nothing, she huffed and settled into her seat so she was facing him. "The way you were staring at that new kid today, I bet I only need one guess to know what this will be about."

Derek let out a chuckle. "You see, Beck, that's what I love about you. You always know what I need to talk about." Already, Derek felt more like himself. "Ok, so I just walked him to class and I couldn't shut up. I mean, I was babbling on and on and barely let him get a word in edgewise."

"Hang on, I want to hear which part of him you are obsessing about right now. Is it those amazing eyes, his crazy sexy hair, his…?"

"Beck, I said I needed to talk without your interruptions."

"Right, sorry. Do go on." She flashed him a sheepish grin.

Derek sighed and rolled his eyes. "Ok, so it was none of those things. We actually talked about wrestling." Beck shook her head. Derek didn't need her to speak to know that she was getting ready to suffer through a sports oriented-conversation, which she occasionally tolerated, but never enjoyed. "So anyway, he wrestled in Iowa and was apparently pretty good. His team elected him captain for his senior year. But what got me was the *way* he was talking about wrestling."

"What do you mean the *way* he talked about wrestling? You guys all talk about it the same way."

"Beck! No interruptions." Derek gave her a half-serious look which told her that he wasn't annoyed but wanted to finish. Beck's face took on a brief look of offense, and then softened as she meaningfully closed her mouth, using her fingers to lock her lips and throw away the key. Derek placed his hand on her arm. "I mean, he gets that wrestling is more than learning new moves and showing everyone how tough you are. He gets that it's also about drawing from within yourself and facing an adversary with courage, head-on."

Beck never quite understood Derek's passion about the sport, but she did admire his perspective on what it meant to him. Sure, sports helped boys to blow off energy. It made them popular and defined their bodies, something she enjoyed as an effect of athletics for men. But none of the boys talked about sports the way Derek did. She thought it was interesting that this new kid would. "So, what exactly are you asking me, Derek?"

"Well, let's look at the facts. I just met him, yet

immediately felt comfortable telling him things about myself. He shares my passion for wrestling and in the same way I do." As he was speaking, Beck noticed that he was becoming more animated and a sparkle was beginning to dance in his eyes.

"Hey, slow down a minute. What I think is that you need to be careful. You're out to me, but you have been careful to ensure that no one else even suspects that you're gay here at school. You haven't even kissed another boy..."

"That's not true. I kissed..."

Beck cut him off. "Billy Fullan doesn't count. That was in kindergarten and you only kissed him on the cheek because he gave you that retarded transformer you had been dying to get in your McDonald's happy meal box."

"Hey!" Derek retorted, giggling a bit and realizing she was right, "That transformer rounded out my collection and I would have done anything to have it."

Rebecca rolled her eyes and stared at him. "May I continue?" Derek remained silent and gave her a demure look through his eyelashes. "Thank you. All I am saying is that you should be careful. You don't know anything about this guy and as long as I've known you, you have been private and guarded. You're one of the most reserved friends I have ever had. I know we live in Cambridge, Massachusetts, liberal center of the universe, but we're also in high school and I would hate to see you ruin your senior year by moving too quickly and letting something out that you may regret later. I'm not saying that I don't want you to be happy, because you know I do, but I don't want to see you get hurt either. And you hang out with jocks. They aren't notorious for being gay-friendly."

Derek knew she was right. "Ok, so I'm semi-closeted..." Beck's lips thinned into tiny lines. "I mean,

I'm only out to you. Is that better?" Beck's lips relaxed into a self-satisfied smile. "So, what do I do with this feeling like I can't wait until lunch to see Scott? How do I prevent myself from being totally obvious or from making an ass out of myself? If this is what it feels like to like someone, how the hell can anyone handle it?"

Beck took in Derek's behavior with unusual silence. She had never seen him like this before, with his emotions unhinged. A part of her felt warm and fuzzy. She knew how wonderful Derek was and wanted so badly for him to find someone. Here he was, finally showing interest in someone. At the same time, she couldn't help but feel concerned as well. *Who is this new guy Scott Thayer and will he be receptive to Derek?*

There was only one way to begin figuring that out. "You said you are having lunch together right? Well, I'm joining you."

Derek's eyes lit up. "You've just moved into detective mode haven't you?"

She turned to glance at him and blinked her eyes rapidly. "Who me? I have no idea what you are talking about. Today is beef stew day and I certainly don't want to miss the chance to watch a newbie try that toxic waste."

Derek shoved Beck's shoulder then kissed her cheek. "Thanks Beck. You're the best."

"I know. They don't make them better than me."

Just then the second bell rang signaling the beginning of class and Ms. Ritter, their pre-calculus teacher, started calling off names from her attendance record.

Chapter 2

Class dragged as Derek's mind focused on lunch and seeing Scott again. He had crushed on guys plenty of times before, but this was different and it bothered him. The guys he had fantasies about were friends who had girlfriends. They were unattainable and made for good masturbation material. But this excitement was different. It was a nervous anticipation that caused him to squirm in his seat, fidget with his pencil, and gaze around the room, most frequently at the clock. Third period science was no different, but finally the bell rang at 11:20. Derek bounded out of his seat, knocking his chair over in the process.

Beck, who shared Derek's third period class as well, got up and turned to Derek with a look of amused annoyance. "Hon, it's lunch, not a date. You were moving around so much during class, I thought I was going to get motion sickness just sitting next to you. Calm down or you're gonna make an ass of yourself." She smiled a sincere, warm smile and hooked her arm inside his, leading him out of the class. The simple act calmed Derek. He was relieved to have her with him. "By the way, smooth move back there knocking over the chair."

"Shut it, Beck!" They walked to their lockers in silence, dropped their science books off and grabbed their books for Latin, the class they shared after lunch. Derek looked down the hall towards Scott's locker, but he wasn't there. "I told Scott I'd meet him at the cafeteria. He might already be there."

"You think he went to the *cafeteria* for lunch? Good thinking, Derek. Don't know why that idea didn't cross my mind." Derek laughed, his nerves loosening up even more. *What's wrong with me? I never get like this.* He shook off his nerves, trying to rid himself of this unpleasant, new sensation.

When they arrived at the cafeteria, Scott was waiting for them by the entrance where most of the senior class had already convened and formed a line. Smiling broadly, Derek could feel his gut clench and his knees wobble. *Get a fuckin' grip*. Approaching Scott, Derek was able to take in his full physique. He was taller than Derek and leaner, not quite as athletic, but still nice to look at.

"Hey Derek. And Rebecca, right?"

"Yes, but please call me Beck. All my friends do." She placed a hand on his arm to direct him towards the end of the line. "So, how is your first day going?"

"'S not so bad. The classes seem like they're going to be interesting. No repeat stuff of what I've studied before. That is a problem sometimes when you move around. Different school systems cover things at different times. The teachers seem cool and none of the kids have appeared to be overly interested in staring at the new kid, which is a relief." Scott fell into an easy and comfortable conversation with Beck as if they had been friends for years. Derek admired Scott's complete lack of reserve, something that he himself struggled with.

Beck listened attentively, something that Derek was sure required a bit of energy on her part. When there was a brief lull in the conversation, she commented, "So, Derek tells me that you were on your wrestling team in, where was it, Idaho?"

"Iowa, actually. Yes, I was on the team. Derek was telling me that the team here has been getting pretty good. I hope I have a chance to make the varsity line up. Derek, do you know if the 167 pound weight class is open this year?"

It took Derek a minute to realize that Scott had asked him a question and then another couple of seconds to register what the actual question was. *Come on Derek, don't make a complete ass of yourself on the first day.* "Um, the 167 weight class spot was Dylan Chase, who was a senior last year. There are a couple of guys on the team who are vying for the spot, but it's open. Once the season begins, coach will begin the process of lining up challenges for the team to secure spots. We don't automatically get our spots each year though. We have to earn them through inter-team challenges. I wrestle at the 135 pound weight class and I know for a fact that Bobby Dean is planning on challenging me this year."

"Cool, we did it that way in Iowa as well. I guess most teams do. But I'm glad that the spot is currently unclaimed because it doesn't help you make friends if you uproot someone who has already had the spot on the team." Scott's mouth curved up in the same crooked grin that Derek had noticed earlier and the sight sent his blood south of the border. If Derek didn't get a grip on himself, this was going to be a very long and embarrassing lunch.

Derek's attention was suddenly jerked from studying Scott's profile by a subdued gasp from Beck. "Look at who that cow is having lunch with." She was referring to Malinda. "She's sitting with Bryce O'Neill and George Davis." Turning to Scott, she gripped his arm and began to fill him in on the drama. "Bryce and George are in the drama club as well. They are constantly vying for the lead male roles. The drama club faculty sponsor, also the drama teacher, tends to look at the chemistry between the students when casting for parts. I think that is totally unfair since casting decisions should be based on whether a person's personality, look, and abilities match the role, not whether two students seem to get along well. Malinda has never eaten with them before. What is she playing at? I swear, if she thinks she's going to steal my thunder in my senior year when I have put up with three years of waiting my turn while upperclassmen came and went, she has got a serious ass-whipping coming her way."

During her outburst, Beck's normally fair-toned cheeks became cherry red and her typically round, sweet as pie eyes, had become two slits ready to shoot lasers. *Oh boy,* Derek thought, *Scott is getting a taste of Beck in heat, and not the good kind of heat either. Maybe this was a bad idea.*

Scott seemed totally unaffected by her outburst. In fact, a sly smile crossed his lips as he turned to look where Beck was glaring.

"Is that who you are talking about over there? That girl with the stringy, unfortunate, shoulder-length hair with the two guys sitting directly across from each other?"

"Yes, that is the harpy I am talking about. Why?" Beck's tone was sour and cutting.

"And you say that you think she is trying to get in good with, what are their names again?" Scott asked.

"Bryce and George" she replied acidly.

"And you say that your drama teacher tends to cast people based on their chemistry rather than their appropriateness for the role? Something which I have to say is seriously fucked up." Derek wasn't sure where Scott was going with this, but he noticed that Beck's shoulders, which had nearly been squeezing her ears in tension, had lowered a bit.

"Yes," she said with only a hint of venom remaining in her voice.

"Well, I don't think you have anything to worry about then." He said confidently, staring Beck directly in the eyes.

Beck blinked, opened her mouth as if to protest, closed it, then asked, "Huh? Why do you say that?"

Scott laughed, showing his shining pearly whites and Derek was sure he saw an actual dance of light cross his

Caribbean blue-green eyes. "Well, if you look closely, that girl, Harpy was it?"

Beck laughed, "Malinda. What about her?"

"Well, she is talking non-stop *at* them. Look at Bryce and George; they are giving each other side-glances, which, if I'm not mistaken, look like they would rather be chewing on glass than listening to that girl. That means they are either annoyed by her personally, annoyed by her intrusion on their lunch, or both." Scott gave Beck a moment to assess his observation and then asked, "So, which do you think it is? Annoyed by her or annoyed by her intrusion?"

Beck turned to Scott, surveyed him for a moment, then replied, "Both I think. You are quite the observer aren't you? You picked all of that up from a one-minute glance at them?"

"Like I said, I'm used to being a new guy. It teaches you to read people pretty quickly and accurately. I would bet you that in a week she either gives up eating with them or they begin to have conversations with each other and tune her out completely. Either way, it will only help your chances of beating the bitch when you audition for roles this year." Scott crossed his arms over his chest and nodded his head, then refocused on Beck. His assessment of the situation was complete. Derek was awestruck.

Beck slid her arm around Derek and drew him in close so they were both facing Scott. Derek noticed that Scott's eyes briefly glanced at her arm around his waist and then back to Beck. "I *love* him!" She hooked her arm inside Scott's and led both boys into the cafeteria. "You are definitely a keeper. Let's hurry and get the delicious beef stew. I can't wait for you to try it."

Scott laughed and Derek shook his head. "I already told him the stuff was poison, Beck."

Beck blushed, "Oh, whoops. Nothing personal, Scott, it's just fun to watch the reactions of those who have never had the pleasure of eating the stuff before. Since you are forewarned, I would go for the mac and cheese or for a sandwich. The beef stew really is toxic."

Scott thanked her for the suggestion as they entered the kitchen area of the cafeteria to buy their lunches. Once seated, Derek next to Beck and both of them across the table from Scott, Derek settled in to observing the two of them as Beck prattled on about the various students in the room, the winter musical, and her happiness that she was finally at the top of the food chain in the drama club. Scott seemed genuinely interested, asking question after question, which kept her babbling on for the duration of lunch. Every once in a while, he would glance over at Derek with a short chuckle at something Beck had said, and then return his attention to her.

Derek watched the two as they got to know one another. It was the first time all day that he actually felt like himself. It was most likely because he was able to fall into his comfort zone of observing while others did the bulk of the talking. Since he knew Beck so well, he could spend his time observing Scott. He was a charmer, chuckling when she was relating some of the more embarrassing stories about their classmates or responding with a *No* or *Shut up* when she revealed people's secrets. He maintained direct eye contact with her while she spoke, not allowing his attention to wander around the room and take in what others were doing. This was a skill that Derek had not been able to perfect, mostly because he was so keen on observing others and getting a feel for the whole room so as to know the appropriate response in various situations.

Occasionally, Derek made comments to embellish on points Beck had missed or to cut her off with a jab of his elbow if she was about to reveal something that was better left unsaid. Talking about the trip they took to Six Flags that summer when Derek had to practically beg her to stop at a service area on Interstate 95 so he could go to the bathroom was one such moment. When he nudged her, she let out a short gasp and said, "*What*? You were desperate for me to stop and I wanted to go another 20 miles so we could get through the New York/New Jersey border. You know how the traffic gets there."

"Yes, but I am sure that Scott doesn't need to hear about this during lunch. Perhaps it would be a more appropriate topic of conversation during, oh, say, never."

Beck stuck her tongue out at Derek then turned to Scott and said, "Sorry. He gets all embarrassed when I tell stories about him."

Scott smiled, revealing his delicious dimple. "No worries. I just count myself lucky that my friends from Iowa aren't here to reveal some of my more sordid moments." When Beck directed a scowling look at the table with Malinda, Bryce, and George, Scott looked Derek directly in the eyes and winked at him, turning back to Beck just as she returned her attention to their table. The moment sent chills up Derek's spine. In one small action, Scott had revealed that he understood that Beck had embarrassed him, that it was no big deal, and that he was amused by her antics. It was also the first time a guy had winked at him before. *I can't believe how much I like this guy.*

When the bell indicating the end of lunch rang, Derek was startled from his thoughts and realized he had been staring at Scott. Derek mentally slapped himself for allowing the lapse in control. "Uh, can I take a look at your schedule?" Scott handed it over and Derek busied himself reading through it. "You have French after lunch. That class is downstairs at the end of the hallway to the right. Then you have study hall which is located next to the library. History with Mr. Sellen. I have that class too.

That is actually located near our lockers. Want to meet up before that class?"

"Sure. Let's meet at your locker."

Before leaving, Beck walked up to Scott and gave him a hug. "You're terrific. I'm so glad that you came to join us here at Brampton. I know it sucks to have to start over in your senior year, but we'll make sure you have a senior year you won't forget. I promise." With that, Beck and Scott headed towards Latin and Scott left to go to his French class.

Once settled in the back row of Latin, Derek turned to Beck. "So, he's great, right?" When Beck turned to face him, he could see immediately that Beck looked concerned. "*What?*"

"Yes, he's fantastic. He's outgoing and friendly and I absolutely worship him for his recognition that Malinda is a witch from Hell who should be burned at the stake." Derek cocked his head and raised his eyebrows as he looked at Beck. "Ok, well maybe he didn't say those words exactly, but he implied it. Anyway, I have never seen you become so immediately fixated on someone before. You don't know anything about this guy except that he's nice."

"And cute." Beck bit her bottom lip, clearly trying to hold her comments in. "What?"

"It's just that I'm worried. Promise me you will be careful." Derek sat back in his seat, a slight frown crossing his face. Beck melted at the sight. "Look, I'm happy that you like him. Just get to know him a little bit before you go all head-over-heels. That's *all* I'm saying."

Derek looked at Beck with complete seriousness. Having Beck behind him wasn't just something he wanted. It was something he *needed*. If Beck didn't support him then he wouldn't have the courage to even try to find out more about Scott. "Beck, please be with me on this. Please be happy for me. I've known everyone here since elementary school and not once have I had feelings like I am right now. Sure, I've had crushes, but this is different. I want to get to know him in person, not just in my fantasies."

Beck's eyes widened and began to glisten with tears. "Derek. I'm *always* on your side. You never have to question that." A tear escaped her eye and Derek reached out to wipe it away. "Don't over think this. It's not like you don't know how to make friends. You're one of the most likable people in the school. You're nice to everyone. Just don't let your imagination create things that aren't there. You are so good at reading people and situations. Rely on that and give yourself time to figure him out."

The teacher entered the room and Beck opened her notebook and wrote the date at the top of the page. "Just remember, you have been here all these years and have never met anyone else who is openly gay, or secretly gay for that matter. The chance that this new guy is gay and that he is the man of your dreams is highly unlikely. I would hate to see you put yourself in a position to get hurt. But, I *am* happy to see that someone has finally come along who has created a spark in you. I wasn't sure that spark existed."

As class began, Derek let Beck's words sink in. It made sense that she would want him to be careful. He had spent his entire school career making sure that he never did or said anything that cast him in a negative light. Whenever there was something unknown, he always proceeded with caution. *I can handle this. This is no different than any other situation I have faced.* Derek opened his notebook and wrote his name and date on the top of the page. As the teacher took attendance and began to write a few notes on the board, his mind wandered to Scott. He pictured his smile, slightly lopsided and accentuated by that cute little dimple. He pictured those sea-blue eyes. *Yeah, right. Fat chance this is no different. This is completely different.*

As Ms. Dhillon, their Latin teacher, reviewed the syllabus for the year, Derek started doodling in his notebook. As he continued to think of Scott, he became more and more stressed, wondering how he could manage to keep himself reined in until he knew more about him. If he could just behave like he always did, things would work out like they always had. *But how do I get to know him and keep my head screwed on straight at the same time?*

Considering what he knew so far, Derek began to create a checklist of things he could do to get to know Scott without being obvious. Scott wrestled so he could introduce him to the other guys on the team, but he wouldn't be able to figure out if Scott was gay if they spent all their time around the guys on the team. Maybe he could pretend that he didn't understand the history content and ask to be Scott's study partner. *No way. That is pretending to be something that I'm not and I don't do that.* Racking his brain, reviewing the few things they had spoken about after first period and during lunch, Derek couldn't think of anything else that the two of them had in common.

Feeling frustrated, he looked down at his doodles and saw that he was drawing pictures of the bridges along the Charles River which ran past the school and connected Cambridge to Boston and the adjoining towns to the west. *Running would be a good way to calm my nerves and maybe then I can come up with a plan to get to know Scott.* Suddenly it came to him. He would invite Scott to run with him. It was perfect. He ran to get in shape for wrestling and was sure that Scott would be happy to join him. It was something they could do alone, but it wasn't something that could possibly be mistaken as anything but a friendly gesture. He looked around the room to make sure no one was watching, then took his cell phone out of his pocket and flipped it open under the desk and sent a text to Beck. *Running after school. Will ask S to join me.*

A few seconds later, his phone vibrated in his hand. *What, R we in 2ⁿᵈ grade? So what? You always run.*

Derek shot her an exasperated look. Don't B a bitch. I can spend time w/ him without being obvious.

Beck glared at him. Don't get mad @ me. Ur plan sounds good.

With Beck's approval, he spent the rest of Latin thinking of the best way to ask Scott to go running with him without sounding stupid. Once again, class dragged and the same restless feeling from before lunch plagued him until the bell rang.

Sixth period study hall was no better. Study hall was required for all lowerclassmen, but only for upperclassmen that were failing or getting a D in a subject. Since it was the first day of school and there was no study hall, Derek decided to head out to the football field bleachers to take in the sun. When he stepped outside, the fresh air helped to clear his mind and when he got to the bleachers, he found several members of the wrestling team. *Bonus!* He headed over to them, happy for the distraction. Josh Dibbling, the team's captain, Sean Roberts, Nick "the Power" Bower, and Frank Greening were in the middle of a heated conversation.

"Allistaire High in Lexington lost three of its varsity members last year, so they shouldn't be as strong this year," Josh said. "But the team I'm worried about is Birmington in Waltham. Those guys have been together as long as we have and they beat us soundly last year. It's gonna take a lot of work and practice for us to be able to bring them down."

Nick "the Power" Bower, so named because he had been the team's heavyweight for the past three years of high school and had never lost a match, spit out sunflower seed shells, spraying several of them on his chin and the front of his shirt. "Well, I've kicked their heavyweight's ass for the past three years so that's one guy down," he said, wiping the clinging seeds away with the back of his hand.

"It's Dylan's position I'm worried about," said Josh. "He was fucking unbeatable and 167 is always a tough weight class."

Sean Roberts chimed in. "Well, I went to wrestling camp for two weeks this summer and learned a bunch of awesome shit. I'm gonna beat Phil Hamford for the 167 weight class spot and that Waltham pussy better watch out." Josh and Power exchanged a glance, and then nodded, although neither of them seemed convinced.

"Hey guys" Derek chimed in, "Talking about Dylan's spot huh?"

"Thompson!" They all turned and smiled as he joined the group. "How the hell are you? We missed you this morning after Beck dragged you off with her."

Power chimed in with his classic charm, "You hit any of that this summer?"

Derek rolled his eyes. *Fuckin' Power.* Without fail, their interest in his involvement with girls would come up in conversation and it always put him on edge. "Naw, she went away a lot with her parents and when she was here, she took those acting classes at Cambridge Community."

Derek turned to Power and gave him a meaningful glance. "I hit the weights a lot this summer to keep up my strength and ran quite a bit to keep the weight down." He then turned to face the rest of the group. "I'm feeling good about this season. Barney Hanger from Waltham won't be able to out strength me this year and Fred from

Lexington graduated."

"Yeah? That's great." Power held Derek's stare for an extended moment before turning back to the topic of the 167 weight class position. "Sean here says he has the 167 weight class spot locked in. Maybe we should put down bets to see whether Sean really has what it takes to beat out Phil." Power laughed and punched Sean in the shoulder. From the wince that crossed Sean's face, it seemed that the punch was harder than a friendly knock.

As much as Derek loved wrestling, he had forgotten how much he disliked the ribbing the team gave each other. "You guys know I won't bet against members of the team. Whoever wins the spot wins." Derek shifted where he was standing. This wasn't turning into a nice distraction at all. Deciding to shift the focus in a more positive direction, he decided to mention Scott. "Did any of you guys notice the new guy this morning? He was in my first period English class and I was assigned to show him around today. Turns out he was a pretty good wrestler in Iowa. He wrestled at the 167 pound weight class." Sean's head snapped up and Derek realized that this was *not* what Sean wanted to hear. He regretted having brought up Scott as soon as had spoken.

Power immediately seized upon the opportunity to razz Sean. "Hold the phone, you mean we have three guys competing for the 167 weight class? Sean, I hope that wrestling camp was worth it." Sean smiled weakly, but it was clear that he was deep in thought, most likely worrying about this unknown competitor.

Josh was genuinely interested. "No kidding. Iowa huh? Wrestling is huge out there and kids from the Midwest get tons of wrestling scholarships to the best Division 1 colleges." Turning to the rest of the group, Josh flashed his captain's smile. "This might turn out to be our year boys."

"Yeah, I know," Derek said. "You guys should meet

him and make him feel welcome before the season starts. Even if he doesn't take the weight class," he shot Sean a conciliatory glance, "he will still be on the team."

"Good idea, Thompson. That's what I like about you. Always thinking of ways to build team spirit and morale. Sometimes I think they should have elected you team captain." Derek knew that Josh was full of shit, but it didn't matter. Derek wasn't interested in being captain. All he really cared about was wrestling and keeping the peace on the team.

There was a lull in the conversation, everyone just sitting there thinking, but not talking and it made Derek uncomfortable. Luckily the bell for seventh period rang and the guys got up from the bleachers and headed towards their last period class. "Catch you guys later," Derek said, and headed toward the side entrance that was nearest the stairs to his locker.

Derek made his way to his locker, stopping briefly to say hello to a few friends he had not seen yet. His breath caught in his chest when he turned the corner of the hall where his locker was. Scott was leaning against *his* locker, one foot crossed over the other, casually looking around. His arm was raised and hooked behind his head and Derek noticed that Scott's bicep filled out the upper part of his sleeve to the point of stretching the fabric. The bottom of his shirt lifted a few inches from the waist of his pants, revealing smooth, tanned flesh. His stomach muscle was clearly visible, creating an inviting v-angle leading Derek's eye towards his crotch where a thin line of blonde hair trailed from the top button of his pants and was hidden by his shirt about an inch below his navel. With effort, Derek dragged his attention away from the magnetic pull of Scott's sensuous midsection and looked at his face. His breath caught once again, but this time heat raced up his spine and into his neck and cheeks. Scott was looking directly at him, a smile on his face. *Busted.*

If Scott noticed that Derek had been staring at him, he didn't show it. "Hey Derek. I figured I would wait by your locker since I got here first. History is just down the hall right?"

"Huh? Oh, uh, yeah. It's down the hall on the right. We better get there quick if we want to get seats in the back."

"Why do you like to sit in the back so much?" Scott inquired.

"I don't know actually. It's just something Beck and I started doing in 9th grade and it stuck."

"Beck is some cool shit. A bit of a talker and certainly dramatic, but fun. I imagine you two have had a lot of laughs together over the years." There was a questioning edge to Scott's voice. "I bet there are tons of stories you two could tell."

"Yeah, Beck is awesome. We've been friends since kindergarten." Thinking of Beck had a soothing effect on Derek and he felt his nerves begin to settle.

"So, you two are really close." Again, Scott's tone seemed inquisitive and he was staring at Derek. "You seem totally comfortable together." Scott's eyes were peering directly at Derek and did not waver after he asked the question.

"Yeah. Beck and I are *really* close."

Scott was peering directly at Derek with unwavering eyes. He stood there, looking at him for a moment, then his features seemed to relax and he sighed. "So, are you two an item? You know, like a couple?" The hallway was not well lit, but even in the dim light, Derek could see a slight pinking of Scott's cheeks after he asked the question.

"Me and Beck?" Derek felt a rush of excitement. *He wants to know if Beck and I are a couple.* His excitement was interrupted by Beck's warning words from earlier in the day. *Be careful Derek. Don't let your imagination create things that aren't actually there.* Derek swallowed, his emotions roiling up and down inside him. "An item? No. We are super close though. She knows everything about me and vice versa."

Scott maintained eye contact with Derek for one more moment, and then shifted his attention to the books in his arms. "Well, she's great. You are lucky to have such a good friend." Scott nodded his head towards their history class. "Shall we grab seats then?"

"Yeah, definitely." Derek felt flustered and his nerves began to rise again. He hadn't expected Scott to ask if he and Beck were a couple. "Listen." Derek said, wanting to deflect conversation away from speaking about him and Beck. "During study hall, I met up with a few guys from the team and told them about you. They want to meet you. Sean wasn't too psyched. He's one of the guys who is competing for your weight class. But the rest of the guys were. Maybe we could have lunch with them tomorrow."

Scott's eyes lit up. "Wow! That was really great of you. I appreciate it, really. I'd love to meet the guys on the team." Derek felt a mix of pleasure that Scott was so happy with him and dismay that he was no closer to asking Scott to go running with him.

"Not a problem." Derek felt the heaviness in his chest from earlier in the day return. *What the hell is that feeling anyways? Just ask him already.* He took a deep breath. "Remember I told you I run a lot during the fall season to get in shape for wrestling? Well I was planning on going for a run after school today and was wondering if you wanted to join me." Derek's pulse began to beat in his throat as he waited for Scott's reply.

"Yeah, that would be great." Derek sat up a bit straighter. "Wait a minute. I don't have any running clothes with me today." Derek felt his shoulders slump, then began laughing. Scott looked at him with a hint of concern. "You ok?

Derek looked at Scott and saw the confusion on his face which only goaded him into laughing even harder. Scott, not knowing what to do, nervously joined him, giggling a little but not knowing why. "You know what? I didn't bring my running clothes to school either." *What kind of an idiot devises a plan that they aren't even prepared to execute?*

Scott smiled and Derek wasn't sure if he was just being polite. When Scott spoke, Derek released a sigh; Scott's words were exactly what he had wanted to hear. "I don't live far from here. I could go home, get changed, and meet you back at the school if you're up for it."

Scott wants to go running with me. The heaviness in his chest evaporated, but his heart rate actually increased at Scott's suggestion. "Yeah I'm up for it." His excitement was a bit too exaggerated. *Calm down.* "I don't live far from here either. School gets out at two-forty. How about we meet up at three-thirty in front of the school? I can show you one of my favorite running routes."

"It's a d...plan." Scott briefly looked down, but then lifted his head so that he was looking Derek directly in the eyes. "You know, I'm glad you were in my first period class, Derek. You wrestle, you introduced me to one of your friends, and you are being really welcoming and cool. I appreciate it. I was actually pretty nervous about starting a new school as a senior, but this is turning out completely better than I could have hoped for."

You're not kidding, Derek thought. "It's my pleasure. I sure wouldn't want to be a new guy in my senior year. I think you'll find most people here are pretty friendly and welcoming." Just then, history class began and Derek tried unsuccessfully to concentrate on what he was going to be learning this year. When the final bell rang, Derek and Scott walked to their lockers and firmed up their plans to meet in front of the school at three-thirty.

Chapter 3

Pacing himself as he walked out of the building, Derek kept repeating one phrase over and over. *Stay cool. Stay cool.* The last thing he wanted was to draw attention to himself on the first day of school. But as soon as he hit the parking lot, he ran to his car. Thoughts of Scott crowded his mind as he sped the short five minutes to his home. Once there, his pace became slow and purposeful. Scanning his drawer, he struggled over what to wear. There were his black, spandex shorts, but those wouldn't do for this run with Scott. *Too revealing.* There were cargo shorts. They were casual, but way too bulky for a run. Settling on a pair of nylon Adidas shorts and a new, crisp white t-shirt, his deliberateness shifted back to haste and he got dressed quickly. Before leaving his room, he checked himself out in the mirror on his closet door. *Nice. You get a hint of ass. My legs look strong. The shirt hugs me in all the right places. Excellent.*

Running back down the stairs, his thoughts centered around Scott once again. *How will he look in his running clothes? Will he even show up? Will he think I look hot in this outfit?* Derek was just about out the door when he was stopped short by his mother calling for him from the kitchen. She was standing by the oven, cutting up onions, carrots, and celery. "Hey honey," she said without turning her attention from her food preparation. "How was your first day of school?"

Derek trudged back up the stairs and walked into the kitchen. "It was fine. Classes seem pretty straight-forward. Beck was in rare form today." Although the words were coming out of his mouth, he wasn't paying any attention. All he could focus on was the clock. The minute hand seemed to speeding towards three-thirty.

His mother turned to face him, a hint of a grin on her face. "Really? And what seems to be the drama of the day?" As soon as she looked at Derek, her tone shifted from curiosity to surprise. "Oh, are you going out for a run?"

"Yeah, I was talking with the guys on the team today and figured I may as well start training to get in shape now." Derek glanced at the clock once again and felt the muscle in his eye spasm for a few seconds. "Also, there was this new kid who started today. He's from Iowa. I feel pretty bad that he had to transfer in his senior year and all." Derek felt his stomach lurch as he listened to the words come out of his mouth. It was unlike him to take even the slightest chance of revealing his sexuality to anyone. Anyone except for Beck. *Thank God for her.* Watching his mother carefully for any signs of concern or suspicion, he continued with as casual a tone as he could muster. "Turns out he wrestles, so I asked him if he wanted to go for a run with me."

"That was very nice of you, sweetie. Not that it surprises me much. You are always such a good friend to others." She turned back to her chopping. "I'm preparing a pot roast for dinner tonight. Dad will be home around five-thirty so don't take one of your extra-long runs today."

Whatever worry Derek had that his mother would be able to see through him evaporated. She was so trusting, always taking Derek at face value. "Sure thing mom." Walking out to the car, Derek felt a slight pang of guilt. He felt like he had just lied to his mother. Shaking his head, he laughed out loud, talking quietly to himself. "And what exactly did I lie about? That I met a guy who I think is cute and I'm hoping he will like me back?" As cavalier as he tried to sound, Derek knew what the lie really was. But he wasn't ready for that discussion yet. Later. When he knew himself better. When he knew if

Scott was someone who could return his feelings. When there was actually something to tell. But he couldn't talk to his parents yet.

Once in the car, he dug his cell out of his bag and hit the speed-dial for Beck. She picked up on the second ring. "You better have a damn good reason for taking off today without so much as a wave."

His typical reaction of annoyance and humor at Beck's dramatic behavior did not kick in. This was what he was used to and the familiarity of their banter eased his nerves. "Sorry Beck, but I had to get home. I asked Scott to go for that run and he's meeting me at school in 20 minutes."

"And you couldn't tell me this at school, *why*?" Her voice dripped with sarcasm.

"Come on, Beck. Don't give me shit right now while I'm all excited and nervous. You know I still love you more than anyone." He counted silently in his head. *One, two, three, four…*

"Well, I'm still mad at you." *It only took a four count. She isn't really mad at all.* "I guess I can forgive you this once. But don't leave me hanging in the lurch again or I will cut your balls off and hang them as ornaments on my Christmas tree. Wait, I'm Jewish so I don't have a Christmas tree. I'll hang them from…I'll burn them in my menorah."

"Ok, first of all, EW! That is totally disgusting. And second of all, that's the second time today you have mentioned manhandling my balls. Is there something I should know about that you aren't telling me?"

"Honestly Derek, the things you say to a lady." Derek had to choke back his laughter when he heard the sincerity of Beck's outrage. "Anyhow, you won't believe what happened after you left today. Bryce and George came up to me as I was leaving school and starting bitching about what a total pain in their asses Malinda was at lunch and that it was all they could do to stay seated and not walk away from the table. That new boy of yours sure slammed that nail on the head."

"And now you are talking about boy's slamming and nailing things. You are seriously twisted Beck." Derek didn't bother to hold his laughter back this time, but even so, he could still hear the string of curses Beck was shouting at him as he started the ignition. Beck continued to prattle on about Bryce and George, and Derek listened to the sound of her voice without really hearing her words. When he got to the school parking lot he cut her off. "Beck. I gotta run! I'll see you tomorrow in school. Love you."

Derek headed towards the front of the school and saw that Scott was already there. He felt all of the nerves and excitement from the day flow through him at once and had to concentrate to suppress the smile that was struggling to break out across his face. When he got close enough to get a good look at Scott, he had to struggle to keep other things from becoming noticeable as well.

Scott was wearing mid-thigh, blue nylon running shorts and a tank-top. Derek noted immediately that Scott's arms and upper body had excellent muscle definition. His shoulders were wide set with rounded muscles which gently curved down over his shoulder blades and created a ridge where they met his biceps. The tank was form-fitting and revealed the strong v-shape of his lateral muscles as they slanted down and inwards towards his hips. His stomach was flat, but there were ridges pushing at the fabric indicating a clearly defined six-pack beneath the surface of the fabric. *Well, I guess that answers the question about whether he has a smooth or cut abdomen.* His thigh muscles were solid and undulated as he shifted his weight from one foot to the other as he stretched. Derek realized that he was staring and quickly diverted his attention to Scott's face. That didn't help him to calm down since he was immediately greeted by Scott's dazzling sea-blue eyes and his wavy, unkempt blonde hair which hung messily over his forehead. Sexy. Everything about Scott flowed smoothly. His body had a natural line that drew your eye in and held it like a magnet.

Finally, Derek remembered how to speak. "How long have you been here?"

Scott shrugged. "Not long, I just swung by my house, grabbed my stuff and came back. No one was home so there wasn't anything to do so I just came back here to wait." Scott's tone didn't match the comfort and confidence that he exuded physically. There was something in his body language which suggested that something was bothering him.

Derek watched Scott as he continued to stretch. He was limber, able to bend his entire body so that it lay snugly against his legs. Looking down at him, Derek could see the muscles of Scott's upper back as they flowed into the cut of his shoulder blades. His eyes continued to travel up Scott's body, following the cords of lean muscles in his neck and his perfectly square jaw. Scott was physical perfection. But there was something dark about Scott as well. He was quiet. His words were weighted, as if he had to work to push a pleasant tone out of his mouth. Thinking about it, Devon realized he had been like that all day, his voice sounding pleasant, but undertones of something else going on under the surface. *Funny, I didn't notice that during the day.*

Shaking his head, Derek mentally slapped himself. It was Scott's first day in a new school. All of his friends were back in Iowa and here he was starting over. Of course he wasn't going to be in the best mood. Derek shook his head and decided to talk about their run. "So there are several routes we could run. Generally speaking, each bridge along the river is about three-quarters of a mile if you count it as a round trip." Talking about running, distances, routines, this was a safe topic of conversation and Derek felt his nerves ease. "I like to run three bridges, one bridge west of the school and then two bridges east of the school. It's about two and a half miles and there's great scenery." Scott had been listening to Derek quietly and seemed content to follow his lead, so they finished stretching and began their run.

Pacing his breathing, Derek started out slow, counting to four on his inhale and to three on his exhale. The rhythmic pattern of his breathing, his feet patting the ground, the wind blowing gently against his face and exposed skin, all of it helped to center him. Within minutes, Derek felt warmth rush through his body. Not heat like he had felt when looking at Scott, but a calming warmth like when he took a shower, and his mind began to see clearly once again.

They ran quietly for about five minutes before Scott broke the silence. "You were right. This really is scenic. We don't have a lot of water where I lived in Iowa. It's weird to be surrounded by so much of it here." Derek noticed that there was a nostalgic tone to Scott's voice in addition to his slightly subdued body language and distant eyes.

"Seeing the sun reflect off the water and listening to the boats and the waves relaxes me. It helps me let my mind wander and to forget my problems." Derek was shocked at how much he was revealing about himself. At the same time, he wondered whether opening up about his feelings might prompt Scott to do the same. "But living by water also makes the winters really cold. With so much open space, there's nothing to block the wind. Even when the temperature isn't too cold, the wind chill can make it feel fifteen or twenty degrees colder. It can get pretty bad in the winter."

A light began to flicker behind Scott's eyes. He picked up the pace a bit before he began talking again. "Back in Iowa, I liked to run down long roads along the wheat and corn fields. After a while, I lost track of how far I had gone or how long I had been running. It's kind of the same as what you described in terms of the lulling sensation. In the absence of knowing exactly where you are, you can focus on other things."

Derek examined the mixture of emotions that were playing out inside his head. On the one hand, he could sense the sadness that lingered behind Scott's words and body language. Especially when he talked about his family or his home in Iowa. On the other hand, Scott was so free and open with his feelings. There was no hesitation or awkwardness as he spoke about the fact that he enjoyed the time to just *think*. Derek decided to chance asking about his mood. "Has anyone ever told you that you seem to be both upbeat and slightly down at the same time?"

Scott's lips thinned into a tight line and Derek felt his gut clench. Mentally kicking himself in the ass, he waited until Scott responded, expecting him to start running in the other direction or worse, not to respond at all.

Finally, the tension in Scott's face eased as if he had made up his mind about something and he seemed more relaxed than he had all day. "No. No one has actually said that to me. But that doesn't mean it's not true. It just means that nobody has paid enough attention to notice."

Watching Scott through his peripheral vision, Derek saw that a smile was creeping across his face. It was a sly half smile and Derek had to concentrate to keep from tripping over his own feet. Scott was like a pendulum, his mood swinging this way then that way. It was enough to cause Derek to feel dizzy.

After a few more minutes of silent running, Scott slowed the pace a little. "You know. That was pretty brave of you." Not knowing what Scott was referring to Derek simply smiled. "You know, coming right out and saying that to me? I know I can be moody, but no one seems to say anything to me about it. Sometimes I feel completely alone; like no one knows who I am or really cares."

The words sank into Derek's mind slowly. He had no idea what it felt like to feel alone. Always surrounded by friends, always popular, always having the support of his parents. It became very clear that Scott had experienced things that Derek knew nothing about. Not knowing what to say, he simply spurted the first question that came to his mind. "So, what are your parents like?"

The silence that followed was thick. Derek wished he could take back the question; go back to some lighter topic of conversation. When Scott spoke, his voice sounded tired, almost resigned. "My dad is away a lot. He manages several stores across a wide regional area. In fact, he's up in New Hampshire right now meeting with the regional HR reps for Target. He won't be home until the weekend. Mom works for an insurance company and keeps a nine to five schedule. She doesn't need to work, but she likes to. She wanted to take some time off so that she could be home for me, knowing I wouldn't have my regular distraction of friends, but I told her that was silly and that I could take care of myself. I knew she wouldn't be happy if she didn't have something to occupy her time, especially since Dad is away so much."

"Wow, you're very understanding of your parents aren't you? I'd probably be throwing a tantrum and making my parents feel all sorts of guilt if they made me move." Hearing his words as they came out of his mouth, Derek winced. In comparison to Scott, he seemed like a brat. He did his best to recover. "But, my parents have always been pretty cool, so I guess I would get over it pretty quickly."

Scott smiled. "Oh, don't think I haven't given my parents plenty of *shit* over moving. I just did most of it before the move. Now that we're here, there's not much I can do, and there's no point to making all of our lives miserable over something that can't be changed."

"Again, very understanding of you." Admiration intensified within Derek as he listened to Scott, but he could also sense a different feeling along with the admiration. It darted about like a butterfly and Derek couldn't quite grasp what the other feeling was. One thing he knew, Scott was unlike anyone he had ever met before. He was able to look at things in a practical way. He was able to put his parents' needs before his own. And, Derek realized, he wants to spend time with *me.* The realization filled his lungs with fresh air. It filled his mind with images of the two of them together. It filled his heart with longing and desire. *Pride.* That was the other feeling he felt along with admiration. Derek felt proud to be someone that Scott wanted to spend time with.

Even though he was still kicking himself for asking about Scott's parents, it did seem that Scott really cared about his mom. Maybe that was a safer topic to ask about. "Sounds like you really care for your mom a lot. You know, worrying that she would be unhappy even when she wanted to put things on hold to be there for you."

Scott's mood shifted immediately, his eyes brightening, and Derek felt his own mood lift with Scott's. "She is one of a kind. Although she works one of the world's most boring jobs, she would tell you that herself by the way, my mom is really quite an interesting person. She is an avid reader, loves crossword puzzles, and we play the meanest game of Scrabble you have ever seen."

Derek laughed at this admission and, after a moment, Scott joined him. Over the course of the run, Scott had shifted. At the beginning, he had been guarded, reserved.

Now he was babbling on about crossword puzzles and Scrabble. "What about your dad?"

Scott's body language resumed the subdued manner it had at the beginning of their run. "He works really hard and takes great pride in providing for our family. I think it bothers him that he has to be away from us so much and I know he doesn't like the fact that his job causes us to move around. I don't really know him as well as I know my mom."

They picked up their pace a little and Derek focused on adjusting his breathing. A whirlwind of thoughts and feelings were spinning inside his head and the run wasn't helping him to sort through them. One thing he knew, without question. He knew it down to the tips of his fingers and toes. He wanted to get to know Scott better. Scott was complex, he was emotional, and he was worth knowing.

After a while Scott broke the silence, his mood brighter than it had been moments earlier. "So, aside from wrestling and running, what other things do you get into?"

When Derek turned his head to look at Scott, he stumbled and almost fell. Scott had a sheen of sweat forming on his forehead and a few rivulets were dripping down his temples and his cheeks. His arms and upper chest were also covered in a thin layer of wetness that captured the sun and reflected brightly off him. Every ridge and bulge of muscle was caught perfectly in the light, casting shadows which only helped to accentuate the lithe form running next to him. It took him a moment before he was able to form words.

Finally, after what felt like an embarrassingly long pause, his brain kicked in. "Well, I love to read, particularly science fiction. But I'd have to say that my favorite thing is listening to and mixing music. I love all music except for country and rap, and even that is beginning to grow on me now."

Scott turned his head towards Derek. "What are you listening to right now in your stereo?"

Once again, the question caught Derek off guard. But this time it wasn't because he was ogling Scott. It was that he was impressed with the question. Most people would just nod or not even pay attention to someone talking about their interest in music. Not Scott. He wanted to know what he was listening to right now in his stereo. Derek cut off his thinking abruptly, realizing that once again, there had been an extended pause before he answered. "Um, last night I went to bed listening to John Mayer's *Continuum*. I love musicians with a sort of folk rock feel to their music. You know, like Howie Day or Gavin Degraw…"

Scott's face lit up. "Or Guster. Or Counting Crows."

Derek's head snapped towards Scott who had a wide grin on his face and was looking back at him. "Exactly like them. Third Eye Blind. Five For Fighting…"

Scott continued the list. "Maroon 5. Dishwalla."

"Wait! You know Dishwalla? I've never met anyone who knows Dishwalla. They're one of those bands who are awesome, but nobody's ever heard of them. I'm seriously impressed with your knowledge base. It sounds like we have the same taste in music." Derek felt a warm tingle run up and down his body at the realization. Most of his friends were into thumpa-thumpa dance music or harder rock bands.

"So you said you like to mix music as well? What kinds of stuff do you mix?" Scott had picked up the pace. Derek's speech was interrupted by slightly labored breathing. "Hold on, the Foot Bridge is coming up. We need to cross over the bridge so that we can head back for the final stretch of the run."

"Why do they call it a Foot Bridge?" Scott asked.

"Because most of the bridges along the Charles allow cars to drive on them to cross the river, but this one is purely a pedestrian bridge. Thus its name, The Foot Bridge."

"Straightforward enough." They crossed the bridge and fell into sync, running on the sidewalk along Memorial Drive heading west back toward the school. "So, what kind of stuff do you mix?"

"I usually mix dance stuff for parties." Derek's father had carved out a space for him a few years back so that he could set up his mixing equipment and music. He had said it was to show support for Derek's passions, but Derek knew that his father was sick of listening to the noise from down the hall. Whatever the reason, Derek loved the attic and spent most of his time there when he was home. "I try to keep a low profile most of the time. You know, at school I don't like to be noticed. But when I mix it's different. I don't mind the attention then." His chest swelled thinking about his mixing and he began to run faster without realizing it.

Scott kept up easily, matching Derek stride for stride. After a while he turned his head and looked at Derek with interest. Derek was still lost in thought, so when he turned and saw Scott looking at him, it caught him off guard. "What is it?"

"Nothing really," Scott said, "Just, you said you don't like to draw attention to yourself. Why is that?"

Derek was glad that they were running because he was sure that if he had been rested the rush of red that flowed into his cheeks would have been obvious. It wasn't like him to just say revealing things about himself, especially things like that. "Uh, well, I don't really know exactly. I've always kind of been like that. Having a friend like Beck sort of necessitates having a back-seat personality. But more than that, I've noticed that kids who try to be popular end up abusing their popularity or alienating themselves. I figure that as long as I am doing things I like to do and I'm doing them with people I like, that's good enough for me." It was a decent response, and the truth. What surprised Derek was how enjoyable it felt to talk so freely with Scott. He had known him for less than a day, yet telling him about the things that mattered most to him, about his thoughts and feelings, seemed natural and easy. "It's helped to prevent me from becoming the center of the gossip mill at school. Does that make any sense?"

"It makes perfect sense. You have to know yourself pretty well to be confident enough to actively try *not* to be noticed." The way Scott said it, the clear admiration and respect in his voice, sent a shiver up Derek's spine. The pride he had identified earlier surged up and filled him to the point of bursting. It was a fleeting sensation and was quickly replaced by another feeling he had experienced earlier. Guilt. He felt like he was lying.

Derek knew that he wasn't nearly as comfortable with himself as Scott seemed to think. Only Beck knew the real reason he kept his personal life personal. With Scott sharing such personal information, Derek felt even worse knowing that he was keeping things to himself. He started pumping his arms faster and picked up the pace. Scott kept up, but they both ran in silence, focusing on finishing the run and their breathing.

Derek felt like scrubbing his brain with soap, cleansing it of the thoughts rushing at him all at once. His gut was telling him to be honest with Scott, to just tell him that he was gay and see how he reacted. His head was telling him to keep doing what he always did, which was to keep a low profile. Keep the secret at all costs. His heart was telling him that he couldn't keep the secret for much longer. He was ready to find someone to share something more with. More than what he was able to share with Beck. He loved her, but it wasn't the kind of love he dreamed about at night. It wasn't *in-love* love.

As they reached the final bridge of their run, Derek picked up the pace even more. With each step, tension drained out of him. His focus narrowed to only his body and his breathing. This was why he loved running. Not just to get in shape, but to clear his head. To calm his typically overactive mind. Running just short of a sprint for the last few hundred yards, they both collapsed on the grass by the bridge across the street from their school.

Gasping to take air into his lungs, Derek stared up at the sky. Once he had caught his breath and his heart stopped racing, he sat up and started stretching his tired and burning leg muscles. Scott did the same. They were facing each other as they stretched and looked up at the same time. Derek first noticed the pulsing of Scott's heartbeat along the length of his now dripping neck. Watching Scott's neck thrum sent Derek's blood rapidly rushing south. There was something incredibly sexy about looking at Scott, shiny with sweat and spent from exertion. Then, without knowing how it happened, they locked gazes and he found himself staring into those blue-green eyes. Scott's look was penetrating, searing, and…something else. His focus was centered directly on Derek and there was no hint of uncertainty or discomfort. Suddenly, Derek saw the quality he hadn't been able to place. It was desire, wrestling beneath the surface, but clearly there. There was something in those eyes that let Derek know that Scott wanted something more from him than casual friendship. What that was, Derek wasn't sure, but he was determined to find out. Scott was someone he wanted to get to know better.

As suddenly as their eyes locked, they faltered and separated. Scott jumped up and offered Derek his hand, helping him to his feet. As connected as they had been just seconds earlier, now Derek felt a distance between them, as if Scott had put up a wall. "Thanks for the run.

I'll see you tomorrow in school." And with no further comment, he turned and started jogging home.

"Sounds good," Derek said to his retreating back. Derek put his hands on his knees and tried to calm the rising adrenaline he felt coursing through his veins. *What was that? I swear if we held that stare for another minute I would have jumped him right here.* He stood up, still winded, but feeling more stable on his feet.

Chapter 4

Dinner was a blur as Derek responded mindlessly to his parents questions about school. His thoughts were focused on Scott. The whole day had actually turned out completely different than he had expected it to. Wrestling was the only thing that had caused him to feel the charge of excitement and nervousness that he had felt all day. But that was because he loved wrestling. He cared about it more than anything else. When he got on the mat, he felt like he was stepping into a world designed just for him. And when the season ended, he felt a sense of loss. *Just like I did when I wasn't around Scott today.*

A piece of the puzzle clicked into place inside Derek's head and he suddenly needed to be alone. Excusing himself, he went to his room and turned on his stereo, playing Gavin DeGraw's *Chariot*, the acoustic version. The combination of the vocals and the guitar penetrated Derek's whirring thoughts and slowly eased his mind. As his tension began to subside, he fell back onto his bed. The same phrase was repeating itself in his head and he had to fight to cut himself off before finishing it. *The only thing I have loved, that has made me feel like this, is wrestling. But now...*

He wouldn't allow himself to finish the thought. Heat rushed up and down his spine, and he wasn't sure whether it was caused by nerves or excitement. He had spent years protecting himself from getting hurt. He had become an expert at blending into the background, keeping secrets, and not being noticed. He had come to depend on his guard, but now it was crumbling before his eyes. Scott was breaking past every barrier he had ever built as if passing through air. And Derek wasn't trying to prevent it. Digging deep, Derek had to admit that he wanted Scott to succeed.

It was too much. Rather than continuing to think, he allowed the music and Gavin's voice to override any other thoughts. Thinking, admitting things to himself, it was all too scary. Music was a constant that he could count on. As he lay in bed, Gavin sang to him, lulling him, until at some point, he drifted to sleep.

It was dark and he was walking along the Charles River. Arriving at the Foot Bridge, he decided to stand and watch the moon reflect and dance over the soft movement of the water. The night was dark and warm and he was alone. Looking around he realized how still the evening was and that none of the street lamps were lit. The only light was coming from the nearly full moon, careening off the water's surface. He looked over the edge of the bridge and could see his shadow reflected on the water and illuminated by the moonlight.

"Derek." The sound was airy, almost sounding like the blowing of a breeze. "Derek." It was a bit stronger this time.

He turned and was facing Scott. Although he was initially startled, his nerves immediately subsided and a feeling of warmth and calm overtook him as he stared into piercing blue-green eyes. "What are you doing here?"

Scott took a step closer to him so that they were standing with their faces almost touching. "Derek" he said, his breath brushing against Derek's cheek, causing the hairs on his neck to rise. Scott reached his hand up and cupped Derek's cheek, gently curving his fingers around the back of his head.

Derek closed his eyes and took in a deep breath through his nose. "Mmm, you smell so good." He felt Scott's other hand, warm and strong, caress his neck as Scott's thumb gently brushed across his lips. Derek leaned into Scott, allowing himself to press against Scott's chest and tilting his head up so that their mouths were merely inches apart. Scott pulled Derek closer and soft lips brushed against his own. Their lips remained connected for sweet, sensual seconds and then Derek felt Scott pull him closer and the kiss became intense. Scott opened his mouth, inviting Derek to lose himself in his scent and touch. Derek explored his mouth with his tongue, basking in the silky, delicious warmth. Scott's desire became more urgent as he pressed his mouth hungrily onto Derek's, wrapping his arms around Derek's shoulders and waist, squeezing him tightly against his muscled body. Derek submitted completely, resting his hands on Scott's hips and surrendering himself to Scott's commanding desire and the secure, powerful feel of his strong embrace.

Derek woke up with a start, sweat beading his neck and forehead. Getting out of bed, he felt something wet and sticky in his boxer briefs. *Holy crap! I haven't had a wet dream in...I don't even remember the last time.* He glanced at the clock which read 5:45. Knowing he would never fall back to sleep and shaken from the intensity of his dream, Derek decided to take a long shower before going to school.

As the water washed over him, he remembered the rushing water of the Charles from his dream; Scott's hands, his lips, his mouth, their kiss. Looking down, Derek was surprised to find that his hand was gripping his member which was quickly filling out and expanding. Leaning against the shower wall, he allowed his mind to replay the dream over and over as he increased the pressure of his hand on his dick.

He pictured Scott lowering his head to his neck and gently nibbling at the sensitive skin, grazing it lightly with a hint of stubble. First, Derek thought it, then could actually feel it, the ticklish sensation sending shivers through his body. He imagined Scott lifting his head and nuzzling Derek's ear. *I want you so bad.* The combination of the hot water pouring over his body and the image of Scott whispering his name, pulling him into a sweet, lingering kiss, made the work short and easy. A few more strokes and his member throbbed in orgasm, sending waves of pleasure pulsing throughout his body.

Before leaving for school, he grabbed his shorts, shirt, and running shoes and stuffed them into his bag. *Maybe Scott will want to go for a run again today.* Derek felt a rush of excitement at the thought, but the thrill also frightened him. He had to figure out how to control his feelings until he knew more about Scott. Until he knew whether or not Scott could possibly return his feelings.

Derek had to admit that it was highly unlikely that all of a sudden, out of the blue, this perfect, gorgeous, friendly, wrestling, Adonis would materialize to sweep him off his feet in his senior year. A voice whispered in the back of Derek's mind. *Fuck being reasonable.* Derek felt himself agreeing with the voice, and then smacked himself. He had to be reasonable. He had too much to lose. The voice called out again. *You have too much to lose if you don't give it a chance.* Derek had to admit, the voice made a good point. But he still wanted some form of security. Something that would help him keep his nerves and his self-control intact.

He decided to introduce Scott to the guys on the team at lunch. Watching people in groups was his strong point, his comfort zone. He could spend time with Scott and figure out whether he was someone he could open up to, but he would also have the safety of numbers to control his tendency to babble when around him. Nodding his head, Derek approved of the plan and his nerves settled as he drove into the school parking lot.

When Derek arrived at English class, Scott and Beck were already in their seats chatting away. For a moment, Derek recalled the way Scott had practically run away from him the day before. *What if he's already decided that he doesn't like me?* As soon as Scott looked up, all of Derek's fears melted away. Scott's face spread into the same crooked grin he had noticed at lunch the day before. It almost seemed as if Scott's face actually lit up. Derek took his seat and began writing the date on the top of a new page of his English notebook.

Scott leaned back in his chair and stretched. He was wearing a Nike shirt and it rode high as he lifted his arms, revealing his bronzed skin and that wispy trail of blonde hair leading from his navel towards...

Derek snapped his head back to his notebook. *Get it together.* Once his breathing returned to normal, he looked up to face Scott. "My legs are killing me after yesterday."

At the mention of sore legs, Scott reflexively reached down and began to rub his thighs. That drew Derek's eyes right back to the place he had been trying to avoid. "Oh, yeah? Mine are a little sore too, but you know how that goes. After a week the pain goes away."

For a moment, their eyes locked, as they had on the grassy bank by the bridge. Peering into those eyes, sea-blue, sparkling with enthusiasm, completely welcoming, Derek felt an invisible rope pulling at him, drawing him closer. It wasn't until Beck broke the momentary spell that Derek realized he had actually begun to lean in towards Scott. The odd thing was, Scott seemed to have leaned in towards him as well.

Beck's voice was shrill, speaking loud enough for the class to hear. "Well, my *ass* is sore from that pain Malinda."

Derek quickly looked around to see whether she was in the room. Although Malinda wasn't, several of her friends were. "Beck, you might want to tone it down. Malinda will hear about this. Do really want an enemy on the second day of school?"

Beck threw her shoulders back, her jaw set and hands clenched. "Honestly, I don't give a rat's ass. This morning she came up to me all sweet saying that she never knew how friendly and cute Bryce and George were and what a good time they had together at lunch yesterday…"

Scott gave him a knowing glance and winked, then leaned over to listen to Beck's rampage. Derek was surprised when he felt his cock begin to lengthen in his pants. *Can a simple wink from Scott really do this to me? And was I about to kiss him in the middle of class?*

They were several minutes into class when Derek felt his phone vibrate. Reaching into his pocket, he stealthily pulled it out and placed it on his leg. There was a message from Beck. *You've been awfully quiet today. Everything alright?*

Derek considered her question. Honestly, he wasn't sure whether things were unbelievably right or terribly wrong. After a minute he texted back. *I can't stop thinking bout S.*

Who? U mean Scott? We talked about this.

B, don't need shit right now.

But you need to be careful.

B, really don't need shit right now.

But…fine, but we R talking l8r.

After English, Derek stopped Scott in the hallway. Normally, he would have walked to class with Beck, but he didn't want to face her right now. "I was wondering if you wanted to do lunch again today. I made plans to eat with the guys on the wrestling team and thought you might like to meet them."

Scott's eyes lit up. "Really? That would be awesome. Thanks." He placed his hand on Derek's shoulder. "I really appreciate how cool you're being to me. It's made things a lot easier than I expected."

Derek felt his muscles tremble as the heat from Scott's hand bore through his shirt and into his shoulder. For the third time in just a few hours, he felt his prick shift in his pants, but this time he was standing and there was no way to adjust without being obvious about it. "I told you I would introduce you to the guys."

"I know. But I still appreciate it. It would have been a lot easier for you to just show me around yesterday and then go back to your normal routine. Not many people would go out of their way to make a new senior feel welcome." His hand was still on Derek's shoulder and the warmth from the touch was radiating throughout Derek's body.

Derek tilted his head toward the math wing of the building. "I really don't mind at all." Scott released Derek's shoulder and it left him feeling cold where the hand had been. They got to Derek's class first. "I'll see you at lunch." He then entered his class and was immediately met by Beck's piercing glare. Steeling himself, he walked to the seat next to her in the back of the class.

At lunch, Josh, Power, and Frank had already claimed a table. Derek noticed that Phil and Sean had joined them, probably because they knew they were going to meet Scott and wanted to size up their competition.

After grabbing their lunches, Derek led Scott to the table and introduced him. "Guys, this is Scott, the new guy I told you about from Iowa. Scott, this is Josh, our captain. Nick is the really big guy over there." Nick stood up and leaned towards Derek menacingly. Derek laughed, flipping him the bird without even glancing at him. That earned him several laughs from around the table. "We call him Nick 'the Power' Bower or just 'Power' for short. You'll find out why when the season begins." Power laughed and gave Derek a hard pat on the back knocking some of the wind out of his lungs. "This is Sean, Frank, and Phil." Josh, Power, and Frank extended their hands immediately and welcomed Scott warmly. Sean and Phil were polite, but far less welcoming. Derek wondered if they would be a problem later if Scott beat them and took the 167 weight class spot.

"So, you wrestled in Iowa?" Josh said with clear approval. "And at the 167 weight class as well. I bet Sean and Phil aren't too psyched that you're here, but the rest of us sure as Hell are. We need to have a strong team to take division this year and the more competition for each spot the better, I say." He gave Sean and Phil a meaningful stare. Although Josh was an arrogant fuck, he was a good captain and Derek appreciated the dig he had thrown at Sean and Phil who were now sitting quietly and looking remorseful.

Derek's only concern was that Scott might feel uncomfortable knowing he was the reason for any tension at all. To his relief, Scott picked up on Josh's lead without missing a beat. "I agree completely. Each year I'm always worried about holding onto my spot. You never know who gained or lost weight to enter your weight class and who trained during the summer and learned new moves to outmaneuver you on the mat." Scott also gave Sean and Phil a meaningful look, but his was completely different than Josh's had been. His look said that he knew where they were coming from and understood why they would feel animosity. The two of them visibly relaxed and even smiled a bit.

Josh appraised his comment with a nod. "That's just the attitude we look for here." Derek let out the breath he hadn't realized he was holding. He was able to fall into his comfort zone of sitting back and observing as the guys fired question after question at Scott about his team in Iowa, the coolest move he had used in a meet, his team's record. By the end of lunch, Scott was one of the guys. Derek shook his head, pleased and filled with admiration.

They were leaving the cafeteria and Derek was about to walk with Scott back to their lockers, when Power sidled up to them. "So, you had to up and leave your school and friends for senior year. You leave a girl behind in Iowa?" Derek's gut clenched when Power asked the question. There was a pause before Scott answered the question and Derek swore that he glanced at him for a split second. *Was that panic in his eyes?*

Whatever the look was, Scott collected himself, turned back to Power and broke into a wide grin. "Power, that's too long of a story for me to answer right now. If you still want to know, ask me again tomorrow."

Power let out a guttural, "Yeah boy!" and clapped Scott on the back.

Josh simply shook his head. "Don't mind him. He was brought up by a pack of wolves and doesn't know how to behave around people." Power laughed, but when he punched Josh in the arm, Josh winced. "It was nice meeting you."

As Derek and Scott walked towards their lockers, Power's question screamed inside Derek's head. He wanted to know the answer, but there was no way he was going to ask the question again. Instead, he made idle conversation. "So what did you think of the guys?"

"They seem cool. I think Sean and Phil weren't too happy, but then again, I wouldn't be either if an unknown came to my school and turned out to be my competition."

"They're good guys. Once the season begins and things settle into place, they'll be cool with you no matter how it turns out." Derek wasn't as sure of that as he sounded, but there was no point in creating tension when the season hadn't even begun.

Scott took the information in and nodded. They continued towards their lockers in silence. Every time Derek looked at Scott he seemed deep in thought, almost troubled. As they walked, the silence continued and seemed to grow. By the time they arrived at their lockers,

Derek's mind was spinning a mile a minute, trying to figure out what he possibly could have done to shut Scott down so suddenly. Collecting the things he would need for the rest of the day, Derek felt his lungs constrict and his eyes began to burn. The day had started so well. Scott had just told him how much he appreciated him. Tears were about to spill from his eyes and he had to blink rapidly to force them back.

It was when he was about to close his locker that Scott finally broke the silence. "Listen, I've been trying to think of a way to say this that won't sound totally weird, but I can't think of one so I'm just gonna take a chance at sounding weird." Scott took a deep breath before continuing. "I've never met someone like you before." Derek lost his ability to breathe. "You're a really great guy and so friendly and..." Scott's cheeks began to turn red as he spoke, "easy to be around." Derek was able to breathe again. "That was really nice of you to introduce me to the guys. You didn't have to, but I want you to know I appreciate that you did. I know I told you that I appreciate that you've been so cool earlier, but..." Again, Scott was struggling with his words and his face had become burgundy. Scott had been shifting from one foot to the other, but when he spoke again, he stopped moving and looked Derek directly in the eyes. "I'm just trying to say that I'm really glad that we are friends. I think we could be better friends than any of the guys I know back in Iowa. There's something about you that is...I don't know what the word is, but I want you to know that I think you are really cool."

No one had ever spoken to him with such raw honesty. Ever. Not his parents or Beck. No one. Scott hadn't been silent *because* of him at all. He had been thinking of how he could tell Derek how much he *liked* him. Derek had worked himself into a state of panic for nothing.

Hearing Scott's words, the intensity behind them,

caused his body to betray him for the fourth time that day. At least this time he could use the motion of closing his locker and leaning against the wall as camouflage for adjusting himself. "I find it easy to do nice things for people." Derek winced internally. That wasn't what he wanted to say and it wasn't even particularly true. "Besides, I like you Scott. I think we have a lot in common." *That* was what he had meant to say and now that it was said he wished he could take it back. *So much for being careful and keeping my guard up.*

Scott's smile returned to his face, one corner of his mouth slightly higher than the other and that cute dimple peering out at him from Scott's cheek. "I'm glad you understand what I'm trying to say. I was worried that I might make you feel…"

"Awkward?" Derek suggested.

A single laugh escaped Scott's mouth. "Yeah. Did it?"

The question took Derek by surprise. *He's as concerned about my reactions as I am about his.* Somehow the knowledge emboldened him. "No, it didn't. I like that you aren't afraid to say what's on your mind."

Scott closed his locker and the two of them headed towards their fifth period class. Scott's cheerful nature had returned and his voice was light and animated. "Hey, I know I'm seeing you in history, but you want to go running again after school today? I brought my stuff with me just in case."

Derek had completely forgotten that he had brought his running clothes to school as well. The fact that Scott had asked first, had been thinking about him the night before and had planned to ask him to go running, sent him soaring. Somehow, he managed to sound casual in his response. "So did I. That would be great."

During fifth period Latin, Derek considered the mixture of thoughts that were circulating in his head. He was stunned at the effect Scott had on people. Meeting others, opening up, fitting in…it was all so natural to him. And Scott had a way of expressing his feelings without sounding like a freak. Derek had tons of feelings, but he never knew how to get them out of his head. Scott put into words how Derek felt but was unable to say. Then there was Power's question about whether Scott had left a girl back in Iowa. That was exactly the question Derek wanted to have answered and Scott had deftly skirted it without making himself look like a jerk and without giving the slightest hint of an answer.

And finally, there was what he had said at the lockers. Derek had never in his life felt so special, so important. That Scott thought so highly of him. Derek pushed his thoughts from his mind and focused on the teacher. There was only one thing that mattered. Scott was a great guy and liked spending time with him. Analyzing Scott to death would not help Derek's nerves and wouldn't give him the answers he needed.

Chapter 5

A month later, Derek felt no closer to figuring things out with Scott than he had on that first day. They had fallen into a routine; a pattern of simple actions and behaviors that they could count on each day. They still ran after school most days, although Scott had taken to working out with the guys on the team a couple days a week. They always ate lunch together, but Derek couldn't get a read on Scott when surrounded by all of their friends.

"So, Bryce and I were rehearsing a dance number for the closing scene. Bryce is playing the part of Link Larkin..." Beck had landed the lead role of Tracy Turnblad in the winter musical, *Hairspray*. Derek was relieved. If the lead had gone to Malinda, his life would have taken an abrupt and significant turn for the worse having to deal with Beck's morose outbursts at the injustices of life itself.

"And you *so* wish that it was really Zac Efron who you got to kiss and smooch and grind against on the dance floor instead of Bryce. We know, you have told us this every day at lunch for the past month." Derek rolled his eyes and patted her arm.

Beck remained still, mouth partially open, then closed her mouth abruptly, tilted her head to the side as she considered how to react, and snapped her head back towards Derek. "Babe, I love you more than my left tit, but if you interrupt me one more time when I am talking about my rehearsals I'm gonna—"

"Rip his nuts off, roll them into perfect spheres, and use them for golf practice?" Scott suggested. Both Beck and Derek's eyes shot across the table at Scott, their mouths twin images of shock. "What?" Scott asked. "You were going to say something like that right?"

Beck's shock turned into a wide grin. "No, I was going to use them as paper weights, but I like your idea much better." All three of them laughed.

Walking back to their lockers, Scott and Beck were talking as Derek followed them thinking. He had always loved routines. They were safe and easy to hide behind. People came to expect that things would happen a certain way each day. Any variation drew attention and Derek hated attention. But wanting to figure Scott out, wanting to make sense of the small things he had noticed about Scott that hinted that he could maybe feel the same way, made the routines torturous. Derek felt the answers pulling further and further away the more entrenched the patterns of the days became. Something had to change. He had to break the pattern or he would never get the answers he so desperately needed.

After school, Derek changed into his running clothes and contemplated which route he would take. On his own today, Derek opted for a long run and headed west. He decided to run two bridges towards Brighton, cross over to the other side of the river, then run to the Foot Bridge and finish back at school. It only added another three miles to the run, but he felt like he needed the extra time so he could think.

Derek could see that his wrestling teammates were impressed by Scott and had high hopes that he may be just what the team needed to take division this year. Oddly, on the days that Scott went to work out with Josh and Power, Derek felt no jealousy or resentment. He was glad that Scott was bonding with the members of the team and he knew, from their frequent conversations, that Scott spent a lot of time alone at home. Perhaps it was because they shared two classes, had lunch together every day, and went running often enough after school, that he didn't feel jealous.

Man, I sound like a girl when I think like this. Derek reprimanded himself and picked up his pace to drum out his obsessive thinking. Pacing his breathing, he focused on the thrum of his feet as they connected with the sidewalk. He ran mindlessly for about ten minutes, watching the rowers on the river practicing for the Charles Regatta.

The day was unseasonably warm, and there were people littered about on the bank of the river listening to music or eating. A few kids were tossing a Frisbee, and a little boy was throwing a stick for his dog to fetch and retrieve. A couple was sitting on a blanket by the water's edge. They were sitting side by side, both staring at the water, their fingers intertwined on the ground between them. The man leaned over and kissed the woman on the cheek and she turned in response to kiss him on the lips.

His dream where Scott had kissed him played in his mind. Sometimes it was triggered by something like the couple on the blanket, and other times it came to him for no reason at all. Each time it did, Derek had to work harder and harder to push the image away. Looking at this couple by the bank, so casually showing their affection, no thoughts or worries...it burned inside Derek like a fire. A fire that angered him and left him feeling hollow. How many times had he wanted to kiss Scott? How badly did he wish that the couple he was watching could be the two of them?

Tension crept into him. His breathing became labored, and a stitch began to form in his side. Concentrating on his breathing, he began the slow process of reclaiming control of his body. It always started with breathing. Measured breaths, in and out. Then, he focused on the rhythm of his feet hitting the ground. He imagined that his legs were driven by pistons, pushing him forward at a steady pace. His arms pumped, propelling him even faster and helping his body flow harmoniously. He concentrated on his running, his body, the mechanics. It always worked to calm him and slowly he felt the stitch dissipate and his tension subside.

When Derek looked around to get his bearings on where he was, he was surprised to find that he had already passed the last bridge and only had a few hundred yards left for his run. He slowed his pace to begin his warm-down process and ended up crossing the street to the school at a slow jog. He was covered in a sheen of sweat and salty drops began to trickle down the back of his shirt, tickling his spine as they rolled over the sensitive skin. Sitting on one of the benches which lined the walkway to the main entrance, he dropped his head into the palms of his hands. *Man that was a good run.*

"Hey, earth to Derek. You ok?" Derek looked up to see Scott standing over him. He had been so focused on his run that he hadn't been paying attention to anything else. Scott walked over and sat down on the bench next to him. "I was just saying that you look like you just had a good run."

Derek looked at Scott. "*You* said that? I thought…" Derek stopped when he saw the confused look on Scott's face. "I mean, I was just thinking the same thing. It *was* a good run." *What the fuck? Now we are thinking the same things at the same time?*

Scott was still looking at him with concern. "You sure you're ok? You're acting kind of weird."

"Yeah, I'm fine," Derek said, wiping his forehead with the base of his shirt, exposing his abdomen and chest. "I just pushed myself really hard today. Don't know why. I just need a few minutes for my brain to start working again." Derek finished wiping his face then dropped his shirt and looked up at Scott. Scott's eyes darted up to meet his and Derek could swear he saw a flush in Scott's cheeks which hadn't been there before. *Was he checking me out?*

"Uh, wow...yeah. Working brains are good." Scott was fumbling for words.

Derek tilted his head and stared at him. "Deep."

Scott laughed, giving Derek a playful shove. "Hey, before I forget, the guys wanted me to tell you that they're planning a party for this weekend and they wanted to know if you could DJ for it." He looked at his hand, and then wiped it on his pants. "You are so totally gross."

Scott seemed to have returned to his normal, literate self and was clearly forming sentences which consisted of a subject and predicate. Derek turned his head slowly to face him and summoned his driest, most sarcastic voice. "You were telling me about some party?"

Scott's eyes lit up, remembering his original train of thought. "Oh yeah. They said you should record a mix ahead of time since you always miss out on the party itself when you DJ live."

"I actually prefer to do the parties live. People come and hang out with me, so it's not like I'm bored or anything, and I can control the music to fit the mood of the party." Derek knew this wasn't the real reason he liked to remain at the mixing table, but the excuse was never questioned. Mixing meant that he was constantly busy during parties and therefore, had a perfect excuse to maneuver his way around advances from girls.

Derek got to his feet and stretched down to touch his toes. When he stood back up and looked at Scott, his eyes darted to his face as they had before, the same flush rushing to his cheeks. *He* is *checking me out.* The tension that Derek had just burned off returned. This was the yo-yo game that they had been playing since the first day they met. *That my mind has been playing*, Derek corrected himself. *Scott is just being Scott.* "Thanks, I'll start picking out music tonight to load into the mixing board's memory."

"Load music into the mixing board memory? Don't you just have, like, a turntable or something? Whenever I see DJs at parties, they have two turntables and headphones and switch between the two."

"Yes, most do, but not me. I like to create the music right then and there with what I'm feeling at the moment. You want to come over and see what I'm talking about?" Derek froze. He hadn't intended on inviting Scott to his house. It just came out without thought or warning.

I'm breaking the routine. As soon as he thought it, his heart went into overdrive. *I'm breaking the* routine! Scott was going to be in his home. They were going to be alone, and he was going to learn about Derek's mixing, the only other thing Derek loved besides wrestling. It was perfect.

Scott's eyes lit up. "I would love to see how you mix music. I've never seen it done before."

Derek beamed, hardly able to contain his excitement. "You can try it yourself too if you want. It's not that hard once you know what to do." He wasn't sure if he was more pleased by the fact that that Scott was going to be in his house or that Scott was so genuinely interested in his favorite pastime. Either way, Derek got the feeling that something good was going to happen. This was the chance he had been looking for to get some answers to the questions that had been torturing him for the past month.

Derek ran into the athletic building, grabbed his bag from his locker, forgoing a shower, and rushed back outside to Scott. He was actually a bit winded when they both got into his car.

Scott was smiling that sly grin that always turned Derek on. "Seriously, man. You stink."

Derek laughed. "Fine. I'll take a shower when we get home."

When they entered the front door, the smell of roasting turkey overwhelmed them and they could hear Derek's mother humming in the kitchen. Derek shed his jacket and slung it over his shoulder, motioning for Scott to follow him up the stairs. His mother was facing the sink, washing and drying some dishes.

"Hey Mom. I want to introduce you to Scott. You know, the guy who just moved here from Iowa."

Derek's mother turned around and leaned towards Derek. He dutifully planted a kiss on her cheek. With a broad smile, she extended her hand to Scott. "It's nice to finally meet you. Derek talks about you so much I feel like I already know you. Welcome to our home. I'm Claire."

Derek felt heat rush to his face for the third time in the last half hour. Damn it, Mom! How could you possibly think that telling him I talk about him is a good thing?

Scott was taken aback for a moment by how warmly he had been instantly welcomed, but quickly took her hand. "Scott Thayer. It's nice to meet you as well."

Claire covered Scott's hand with hers, patting it a couple of times, then turned to the oven to check on the turkey. "We'll be having turkey for dinner. Would you like to join us?"

Scott stood and stared for a moment, not sure how to answer. Derek came to his rescue. "My mom always cooks enough to feed an army. We'll be eating leftovers for the rest of the week. And you don't want to miss one of her dinners if it's offered."

Scott hesitated, but looking at Derek and seeing his smile, he agreed. "I'd love to, but I have to call my mom and let her know I won't be home for dinner. I don't think it should be a problem." He reached into his pocket and pulled out his cell. "Thanks so much."

"Of course. Any friend of Derek's is always welcome in our home." She turned to Derek and gave him a peck on the forehead then wrinkled her nose. "Oh dear, I think you may want to take a shower before dinner, honey."

"Mom, you're embarrassing me." Derek could practically feel the color of his face change. Glancing at Scott, he was confronted once again with that crooked, devilish smile and his dimple staring back at him. He shifted uncomfortably as his crotch began to squirm in his shorts. Panic set in. *These shorts won't hide anything.* "Scott can call his mom from my room. I'm going to show him my mixing equipment."

"That's fine. I'll call you down when dinner is ready."

Derek rushed Scott down the hallway to his room. Scott sat on Derek's bed and shucked his jacket, tossing it on the floor where Derek had dropped his. "Your mom is really friendly. Do you think she was just being nice by inviting me for dinner?"

Derek turned and faced Scott with a sincere look on his face. His cock had settled down so he wasn't worried about what Scott might see. "No, she prides herself on feeding me and my friends. Just wait until wrestling season begins. You're going to find it hard to keep within your weight limit."

Derek pulled off his shirt and tossed it into the hamper next to his closet. Leaning his head down to sniff his armpits he gasped. "Woof! The two of you weren't kidding. I'm ripe. I better take a shower *now*." He glanced over at Scott and saw his head snap down to stare at the floor. *He watched me take my shirt off.*

The realization made him feel sexy. "You can turn on the TV if you like or you can feel free to explore my room. I won't be long." Kicking off his shoes, he leaned against the wall so he could pull off his socks. Although he wasn't looking at Scott directly, he used his peripheral vision to see if Scott had shifted his attention from the floor to him. There was no movement.

Scott flipped open his cell phone. "Ok, well, if you're sure, I better call my mom and see if it's ok."

Still watching Scott though side glances, Derek pushed his shorts down over his waist. They slid off his hips and bunched at his feet. He was only wearing a jock strap now and knew his ass was one of his best features. Scott's head tilted slightly towards him and Derek was pretty sure that Scott was trying to look at him without being obvious. Encouraged, he kicked his shorts to the hamper where he had thrown his shirt and walked directly past Scott to grab his towel off the back of his desk chair which was located next to his bed. Derek lingered there for a moment, taking time to wipe his face and to give Scott a moment to stare. When Derek dropped the towel over his shoulder and looked at Scott, there was no question where Scott's attention had been. His head snapped up and panic played across his eyes.

Derek had no idea what had come over him. He was never this bold. Taking a deep breath, he slid his fingers beneath the waistband of his jock strap and lowered them, first pulling one leg out, then the other. It took all of his self-control not to tremble as he provided this final display for Scott. Once his jock had been kicked into the hamper with the rest of his clothes, he grabbed his towel and wrapped it around his waist. "I'll only be about five minutes. Do you need anything?" Surprisingly, his voice came out steady and strong.

Scott sat perfectly still on the bed. "I, er, uh. N-No. I'm fine. I just have to call my mom is all."

Derek nodded and turned to head to the bathroom. He looked back once more before he left his room and saw what he had been waiting to see for a month. Scott was adjusting himself, completely absorbed in untangling whatever mess had formed in his pants. A wide grin spread across Derek's face as he sauntered to the bathroom and took his shower.

Five minutes later, clean and no longer stinking to high heaven, Derek returned to his room and quickly threw on a new pair of jeans and a threadbare Mickey Mouse t-shirt. He would never wear the shirt in public but it was his favorite and most comfortable shirt nonetheless. "So, you gonna be able to stay for dinner?" It stunned him that he could remain so calm after the show he had just given Scott and the reaction he got from it.

Scott also seemed to have regained control of himself, looking much more comfortable than he had a few minutes earlier. "Mom said it was fine, but not to be home too late."

"Awesome. So, you want to check out my mixing equipment?"

"Hell yeah! Where is it?"

"I keep it up in the attic. I can spread my records and technology out and my dad let me haul the old couch up there when he bought the new one for the living room. No one bothers me, and my stuff doesn't clutter the house. It's pretty ideal actually. C'mon, I'll show you."

Scott hopped up from the bed and followed Derek to the stairs at the end of the hallway which led up to the attic. Derek first showed Scott his records. They weren't the kind with regular songs, but contained all sorts of beats, sounds, instrumentals, and vocals. "What are all these records for?" Scott asked.

Derek knelt beside some records on the floor that he had been using and motioned for Scott to come sit with him. "When you mix, you take the various parts of the song, and put them together however you feel. Actual songs are only one component of the mixing process, and I use my iPod for those. Here, listen to this." Derek grabbed a record that was lying next to his turntable and handed it to Scott.

Derek watched him place the album on the turntable. Scott's eyes were wide with excitement and when he spoke his voice was animated. "Holy shit. I haven't ever met someone who actually has a record player since I was a kid. You use these for mixing?"

Derek couldn't help the giggle that escaped from him. Watching Scott, seeing the music and the equipment through his eyes, electrified the moment. "I don't actually use the record player for mixing, but I do use it to pick out the sounds I want to record digitally and upload to my mixer." Scott was paying close attention to every word. "Here, check out the various sounds on this one. It's all sorts of different beats."

Scott started listening to the various tracks. Some beats were steady and unwavering while others were more complex, varying from slow to fast rhythms.

"I have tons of records that just have beats on them. There are records which contain different vocal sounds or instrumental sounds. They even have records that have random shit like a train engine or a bomb going off." Derek moved closer to Scott so that their arms were touching. He was both surprised and pleased that Scott didn't flinch. "Here." He grabbed an album that was by his feet. "Listen to this one. It's one of the records with random shit on it."

Scott took the record from Derek. "I had no idea that there were records like this." His interest was genuine and pure. Derek kicked himself for having waited so long before inviting Scott to his house.

Derek felt his own excitement begin to expand in his chest. He had never shared his love of mixing with anyone before. Not even Beck. People just knew that he did it and they liked what he produced. He certainly had never invited anyone up to the attic before. Reaching into the pile of records next to him, he pulled out an album with vocal sounds on it.

They sat huddled together next to the turntable on the floor for several minutes. Eventually, Scott shifted his position so that he was facing Derek. "So how do you actually mix?"

"Well, the first thing I do is select the sounds I want to use. Why don't you pick a couple of sounds that you like? Choose a variety of them. You know, beats, vocals, instrumentals. Then we can mix them." Scott listened to the various records for a few minutes and finally chose five sounds that he liked. "Ok, good. So now, I attach this DAT recorder to the player…"

"I'm sorry, a what?" Scott asked.

"A DAT recorder. It stands for Digital Audio Tape recorder. It's how I digitize the stuff from the records so they can be saved in the mixer's computer." He forgot that Scott didn't know any of this. It just felt so normal to have him here in the attic surrounded by his records and equipment. "Sorry, I'll try to break it down a little better. Once the sounds are recorded like this," Derek attached the DAT recorder to the record player and began recording the first beat Scott had selected, "I connect the DAT recorder to the mixer with a USB cable and upload it to the mixer's memory."

"Ok, I get that part. It's like uploading a file to a computer, right?"

"Exactly. So you repeat this process with beats and with all of the other sounds until you have uploaded everything you want. Then comes the fun stuff. The mixing."

"Can we try it?"

The way Scott asked the question, the genuine interest and enthusiasm, caused Derek's breath to catch in his throat. A wave of affection flooded his senses and he had to fight the urge to hug him as tightly as he could. "Heck yeah! Let's start mixing."

Derek spent the next hour explaining the various parts of the mixing machine, how to bring in one sound and then blend a new sound on top of the one playing. His mixer allowed for eight separate tracks to be played at once which could get quite complicated when you figured in balancing the volume, the level of the bass, fades from one set of sounds into a new set of sounds. Scott never became frustrated though. Whenever he wasn't sure what to do, he simply asked Derek how to do it, grinning and laughing with excitement the whole time. They could have continued for hours, but Derek's mother called them down for dinner.

"That was amazing. I can't believe you know how to do all that stuff." Scott was staring directly at Derek with unguarded admiration and his blue-green eyes were dancing. Derek was shocked by how beautiful Scott looked at that very moment.

"I got interested in playing around with my dad's record player when I was younger, and when I discovered the music store that sells these records for mixing in Harvard Square, I guess it all just sort of took off from there. I'm not all that great at it, but I'm passable and it gets me invited to all the parties." Derek didn't know why he had chosen to downplay Scott's compliment when he could have responded with a simple *Thanks*. Especially when Scott's praise made him feel like he was flying.

"Well, I think it's so cool. I can't wait to hear you at this weekend's party."

"Yeah, it will be fun." Derek didn't want this moment to end. He wanted to spend the rest of his life sitting on his attic floor with Scott. Reluctantly, he said the words he didn't want to say. "We should get downstairs before my mom comes up here and drags us to the table by our ears. When she cooks, she wants to *see* her dinners enjoyed." Derek nodded his head towards the door motioning for them to head out. He pushed himself to his feet and extended his hand to help Scott up.

Throughout dinner, Derek's parents questioned Scott about his home in Iowa, his parents, how he was enjoying Brampton High so far, and wrestling. Derek simply sat back and watched as his parents and Scott fell easily into comfortable conversation. He had had lots of friends over before, and his parents were always friendly and talkative, but seeing Scott and his parents together was different. He wasn't sure what it was, but he felt better than he could ever remember feeling.

When dinner was over, Clair hugged Scott and gave him a kiss on his forehead. "You make sure to come around again."

"Thank you so much Mr. and Mrs. Thompson. Dinner was wonderful. I can't remember the last time I ate a home cooked meal." As soon as the words escaped his lips, Scott's mouth clamped shut.

Claire placed a hand on his shoulder, seemingly unaware of Scott's discomfort. "Please call me Claire and call him Henry." Henry stepped forward and shook his hand.

In the car, Scott sat back against the seat, his head turned so that he faced Derek. "You're lucky. You know that right?"

Derek turned to face Scott. "Sure. But what specifically are you referring to?"

"Your parents. They're both so cool. They didn't even think twice about having me join you for dinner."

"They're like that. Always have been. But yes, I agree with you. I have great parents."

Scott yawned. "I'm glad you invited me to your house.

I've been wondering what your room looks like." The statement wasn't loaded with any underlying meaning, it was just a statement, but Derek's mind began to reel. "And the fact that you have that whole set up in your attic. It's awesome."

Derek pulled up to Scott's house and let the engine idle. Turning to face Scott, all of the excitement and closeness of the evening seemed to intensify. Scott was the one who was good at saying things. It had never been Derek's strength. He had always felt safer observing. But tonight had been a night of taking risks. *Why stop now?* "Scott, I'm not just lucky because of my parents. I feel lucky that I met you this year."

Scott let his head roll slowly on the headrest until he was facing Derek. There was no reservation or hesitation when he spoke. "I'm glad you told me that." There was something in the way he said it that made Derek want to reach out and touch him. To comfort him. Scott sat there looking at Derek for another minute, then faced forward, stretching his arms in front of him. "I better get going. I'll see you tomorrow at school."

Derek watched Scott's retreating body as he walked up to his door. Tonight had been a good night. He had taken a risk and broken the routine. Hell, he had stripped in front of Scott, and he was pretty sure that Scott had been interested. But he needed to know for sure.

Chapter 6

The rest of the week progressed as the whole month had with Derek trying to read beneath Scott's surface, attempting to detect signs and scrutinize them until his head hurt. There were plenty of hints: a glance that lasted a little longer than normal, the snap of Scott's head from his body to his face when Derek turned his way, their banter and playfulness. Scott had even come over to Derek's house every day that week, continuing their effort on the song they had been working on. But none of it brought Derek any closer to an actual answer. *Does he like me that way?*

Although Derek, Scott, and Beck had agreed to meet up at Derek's house at 6:00pm to go to Josh's party together, Derek waited until Friday's Latin class to ask Beck to come over a bit earlier so they could talk. He hadn't had much time to spend with Beck since her rehearsal schedule had picked up considerably and he needed to talk.

Beck showed up at around 4:00pm. After spending an obligatory few minutes with his parents, who hadn't seen Beck in ages, they headed up to Derek's room. Beck lay on his bed while Derek took his desk seat and placed it so he could face Beck while resting his feet on the bed frame at the same time.

"So," Derek asked, "How's it going with Bryce and line rehearsals?" It was a lame conversation opener and he knew it, but he wasn't sure how to broach the topic of Scott with Beck yet.

Beck raised an eyebrow and tilted her head so she was staring directly at Derek. "Are you trying to tell me that you invited me to come over early so you could ask me about my rehearsal schedule?"

Derek shrugged his shoulders and widened his eyes giving his best impression of an innocent puppy dog. "We haven't spent much time together lately and I just want to know how things are going with you."

"Bullshit!" He was startled by the force Beck used when she said it. "Something's on your mind and you want to talk about it. So talk!"

"Ok, fine Mrs. ESP Mind-Reader lady." Beck lay back down with a smug grin on her face. "It's Scott…"

"I *knew* it. You are in love with him and obsessing, aren't you?" Beck's statement was delivered plainly enough, but her facial expression was hard to read. Her grimace could have indicated frustration or bemused acceptance. He wasn't sure.

"Well, we've been hanging out for over a month now and I'm not making any headway towards figuring him out. I mean, if there were no signs at all, I would already have assumed he's straight, gotten over it, and moved on. But there *are* signs." Derek paused and stared at Beck for a moment. Now that he was sharing with Beck, everything became real. The problem with real was that it could go either way. It could turn out that his sense was correct and that Scott was also gay. Or, it could turn out that he was seeing something because he wanted to. Something that wasn't really there. Either way, making it real ended the fantasy of what could be.

He was brought back to the moment by Beck's voice. "Ok, I am going to indulge you completely for this conversation, but I want to be frank. I'm worried about you. You are heading straight down the road to Hurtsville and I don't want to see that happen to you." Beck settled into a more comfortable position. "So, what are these alleged signs?"

"*That's* supposed to be indulging me? You sound like you've already made up your mind that I'm nuts."

Beck sighed. "All right, fine! Tell me what you've observed. I'll be open-minded." Derek looked at her through slightly narrowed eyes. "I *promise*. Look," she made a circular motion around her head, "mind open."

Satisfied that Beck was as ready to hear what he had to say as she was going to get, Derek took a deep breath and let it out slowly. The words came spilling out of him. The compulsion to get it out of his head was not simply to prevent Beck from interrupting, but also to cleanse his brain. "Well, on the first day we met, after our run, we locked eyes for longer than you normally lock eyes with someone, then he glanced away and left pretty suddenly. The other day I had him over here and was showing him my mixing stuff upstairs and we were having an awesome time. He was really getting into it and we locked eyes again, but this time he didn't drop his gaze. He's come over every day this week to mix music with me. Also, I think I've caught him checking me out a couple of times and when I look at him, his head shifts suddenly and I swear I catch him blushing afterwards. And then there is his way of talking about his feelings and opening up. None of my other guy friends are like that at all. I know it's weak, and I sound like I'm digging, but..."

"Pro-JEC-tion!" Beck trilled the final syllable of the word dramatically. "Babe! Locked eyes. Furtive glances. Opening up. Come on. You can't really think that adds up to him being gay and into you, can you? First, you don't have open conversations with guys because your guy friends are Neanderthal jocks." Derek began to protest but Beck lifted a halting hand and he promptly closed his mouth. "Second, Scott is from Iowa. People are different from different places in the country. For all you know, everyone in Iowa sits around and pours out their innermost feelings at the dinner table just before saying *Amen* and digging in." Derek laughed out loud at that one. "And finally...glances at each other? You have to do better than that."

"Ok, well, let me explain the glancing part. Most of what you just said, I would agree with, but the other day, when he was over here, I got undressed in front of him."

Beck shot up into a sitting position. "You what?"

"Calm down. I was just taking a shower because I smelled like the living dead after a long run."

"Oh," Beck relaxed and laid back down.

"But, I did notice when I looked at him after I took off my shirt that his eyes darted to the floor as if he had been staring at me. So, I decided to test him out and I dropped my pants and walked across the room in my jock strap to get my towel and…maybe I'm imagining things…but I swear he was checking out my ass. When I turned to look at him, he shot his eyes towards my face and was definitely blushing. Then, I took off my jock and he didn't know *where* to look." Derek stopped talking and replayed the scene in his head. "That was the most embarrassing thing I have done in a long time. Anyhow, just before I left the room I turned to look at him and he was engrossed in readjusting himself." Derek finished and waited as Beck pondered this new bit of information. He felt the tension build up inside him as he waited for Beck to respond. After another minute or two he couldn't take it any longer. "Uh, Beck, you still there?"

Beck sat up, turned her head slowly to face Derek, and placed a hand on his knee. The way she looked at him and then sighed, he feared that she was going to crush his hopes. That his fantasies were about to come to an end and she was going to explain to him why he was wrong. After another moment, she slowly shook her head, and then burst into a wicked grin. "You little TART! I had no idea you were an exhibitionist. That was a well-played maneuver my friend. I wish I could have been here to witness it. You know how partial I and the other girls are to your ass. Thank goodness you don't wear all those baggy, hang to your knees pants like the other boys hiding that precious gem of an asset of yours, pun intended. And then you stripped that off as well. I *love* it."

"Beck, thanks, but totally not on point right now!"

"Right, sorry." Beck collected herself. "So, you say he was adjusting himself. What, like changing positions or something?"

Derek rolled his eyes. "Sometimes I forget that you're a girl."

"Thanks."

"That's not what I meant." He gave her a knowing glance. "He was *adjusting* himself."

Beck's eyes widened in understanding. "Ok, I'll give you that one. Guys don't check out other guys' asses and if they do it certainly doesn't cause them to have to… adjust themselves. Honestly, I don't know how you guys walk around with those things between your legs. They are so ugly and they must get in the way."

"Beck. Still not on point."

"Right." Beck flashed him a weak smile. "I still don't think you have a lot to go on though. But it certainly does seem that you aren't just allowing your imagination to run wild either. Let's keep our eyes peeled and see what happens."

"So you think that there might be something there?" Before Beck could answer, Derek's cell phone vibrated on his desktop. He flipped it open. "Hello."

"Derek, hey, it's Scott."

Derek covered the receiver with his free hand and mouthed *Scott* to Beck. Her eyes widened a bit.

"So, I thought maybe you could use some help getting your mixing equipment into your car and was wondering if you wanted me to come over a little early."

Derek smiled into the phone. "Yeah, actually, I could use the help. Beck came over early too. We could hang out together before the party."

"Oh," Scott paused for a moment. "Ok, that sounds great. How does fifteen minutes sound?"

Derek wasn't sure, but he thought that Scott sounded a little disappointed. "Come over whenever you want. We'll be here."

"Great, well, I'll be there soon. Later." Whatever emotion Scott had been feeling, he had regained his cheerfulness.

Derek hung up and placed his cell back on his desk. He looked at Beck who was staring at him open mouthed. "What?"

"Derek, I'm seriously impressed. You've been obsessing for the past half hour. By any normal measure, you should have been a blubbering mess on the phone just now. Instead you were calm and collected. You've definitely got game my friend." She looked at him with clear admiration as they both headed down to the kitchen to grab a snack and wait for Scott.

They arrived at Josh's house about an hour before the party was to begin so that Derek would have time to set up his equipment. Scott offered to help and the job got completed much faster than Derek was used to. Grateful for the extra time before other people started showing up, Derek walked over to Josh. "So, who's coming tonight?"

"Actually, looks like it's going to be a friggin' bash. Originally it was just going to be about thirty of the core group, but last minute my parents told me they were heading out of town so now it seems like most of the senior class is going to show up tonight. Should be awesome!"

Scott had remained with the mixing equipment, checking out the connections and testing the speakers. He was hooking up the final wires to the mixer when Derek walked back over. Looking up, his eyes sparkled with excitement. "I can't wait to hear you mix tonight. Now that I have an idea of how it's done and have seen you at work, I know the music is going to kick!"

Derek smiled. Although low profile was his usual MO, he didn't mind that everyone recognized him as a *must* at parties. Nor did he mind that people talked about his music for days after a party. "Yeah, I'm pretty hyped up for it. I actually kind of lose focus on the party itself and concentrate on what people are doing and the vibe so that I can mix to that. It's kind of a power rush actually. I can control the crowd, bringing them up, keeping them there as long as I want, and then letting them down."

Scott considered that for a moment. "You know, I wouldn't have pegged you as someone who got off on controlling others."

Derek furrowed his brow not sure what Scott was implying.

"Wait, I didn't mean that like it sounded." Scott smacked himself on the head. "I meant, music is supposed to take you someplace else, right? It's supposed to create a mood and an atmosphere that wouldn't exist in its absence. You create that mood. I think that's awesome that you like being the one who can provide that for others. It's just opposite of how you normally are when you are around other people."

Derek relaxed, understanding that Scott was expressing admiration and not distaste. Being honest, Derek had often questioned his comfort with being the center of attention when mixing as well. It *was* completely opposite to his normal behavior. *Scott recognized it though. He paid enough attention to see the subtlety of my...* Pushing the thought from his mind, he focused on what Scott had actually said. "I have noticed that you are really good at putting things into words. You say things that I think, but don't know how to say. Have you always been able to do that with your friends?"

Scott face took on a slightly demure look. One that Derek hadn't seen before. "No, actually, I usually keep those thoughts to myself, but with you, it seems like, well, it just feels like you are the kind of guy who can understand and appreciate what I'm trying to say." Scott was staring directly at Derek as he was speaking and Derek became lost in a sea of blue. Just the simplest of comments, the slightest hint of recognition that there was something special between the two of them, sent Derek soaring.

It took serious effort for him to regain his concentration. "Yeah, I've told Beck a million times that you seem different than the other guys around here."

Scott's face took on a stunned look for a moment, but he quickly regained his composure. "Wh…what do you mean?"

"Shit, that sounded stupid." Panic crept up Derek's spine as he scrambled to explain himself. "What I meant is that it's refreshing to have you to talk to. I can't talk to the guys on the team about wrestling the way I can talk to you. With you, I can say what I think as opposed to keeping my mouth shut so that I won't embarrass myself…like I am right now. Fuck." Derek's heart was thrashing in his chest, trying to get as far away from him as possible. "Forget I said anything."

Understanding spread across Scott's face as his mouth curved up into a smile. "No, I think I know what you mean now. I could never talk to my teammates about why I love wrestling either." He put an arm over Derek's shoulder. The contact sent chills through his body and it became difficult to focus on Scott's words. "You don't ever have to worry about being embarrassed with me. I like that I can tell you anything." The chill changed to heat as it moved towards his cock. "I know I haven't known you very long, but you have been a great friend to me and made me feel like I'm welcome here. I was really worried about moving and thought I was going to have a crappy year, but you're turning out to be one of the best friends I have ever had."

Derek barely heard the last words Scott said as his prick surged in his pants, lengthening and pushing uncomfortably at the seam of his jeans. Luckily he didn't have to respond because the team and several other guests arrived, bursting through the door in a loud uproar. "Well, I guess that's my cue to begin." Reluctantly, Scott removed his arm from Derek's shoulder and Derek quickly stepped behind his mixer so that he could shift the tangled mess in his pants.

"Yo, Scott, come over here. There are some guys I want you to meet from the team," Josh called from across the room. Scott seemed to hover for a moment in indecision, glanced at Derek, then lowered his head and turned to join the group of students who had just arrived.

Derek kept the music fairly subdued. Most parties picked up later in the evening, so starting out fast and furious was never a good idea. Although people continually came by to offer him food and drinks, his attention was focused on his conversation with Scott, which played through his mind over and over. *I feel like you are turning out to be one of the best friends I have ever had.* That was a good thing. Derek wanted Scott to feel close to him. *I feel like I can tell you anything.* It was statements like that that caused Derek to feel like he was on a see-saw. None of his guy friends had ever talked about being glad they could say anything to him.

Glancing to the corner of the room where Scott was standing with the guys on the team, Derek felt acid burn at his throat. Susan Chamberlain had latched onto him. A beautiful girl outwardly, Susan's inner traits left something to be desired. Last year she had slept with at least three of his teammates and two of them had girlfriends at the time. She threw her head back and laughed obnoxiously, tossing her hair over her shoulder, and then returned her gaze to Scott. She then placed her hand on his bicep and it seemed that she said *so strong,* although Derek couldn't be sure since he wasn't very good at reading lips.

Derek felt his stomach twist and when Scott glanced over at him it took all of his concentration to ensure that he had a smile plastered across his face. Despite the turmoil going on inside Derek's body, his natural instinct was to project confidence, ease. Seeing Susan on Scott's arm. Knowing what she was probably thinking. *Not* knowing what Scott was thinking. He could feel the acid rising higher and higher in his throat. There was something else, another feeling along with the nausea. He couldn't quite put a finger on what it was, but it was very unpleasant.

Turning his focus to the music, Derek chose a fast, heavy beat, and slid the control for the bass up to increase the reverberation. He then weaved in three vocals to form the foundation of the dance tune. Each time the vocals repeated, he increased the volume slightly until he could hear and feel that the balance between them and the bass had equalized. Next, he mixed in tribal drums. The groove he was creating was rustic and masculine. It had an edge of anger to it, but more than anger, there was a raw, natural feel to the sound. It was a good dance song and more people started to hop around and cheer.

Derek searched for Scott once again, but couldn't find him. It was then that he realized that he couldn't find Susan Chamberlain either. The feeling he couldn't put a finger on earlier reared up inside him. This time there was no question what it was. Jealousy. Jealousy and anger. Scott was *his*, not that slut Susan's. He wanted to be doing whatever she was doing with him. He wanted to find Scott and ask him how he could lower himself to fool around with someone as disgusting as her.

Refocusing on the music, he increased the volume and then began the slow process of increasing the speed. He took deliberate care to make sure that there were no abrupt shifts in the sound and tempo, wanting the music to drown out any thought. Any feeling. All he wanted was to be filled with the thrumming of the sounds in the room. At least that didn't hurt. Finally he mixed in siren sounds. They blared at full blast and then slowly faded as he lowered the volume steadily for that track each time.

Each time they sounded, they mirrored the questions screaming inside Derek's head. Why couldn't his senior year have happened the way he expected it to? Why was he so obsessed about Scott? Why did he keep so many secrets? Why couldn't things go back to the way they were before Scott showed up? The questions flew through his mind at a fever pitch as the music swelled to even louder heights.

As the song reached its climax, Derek realized the one thing he hadn't wanted to admit. Beck had been right. He should have listened to her. He hadn't been careful, and this was the price he was paying for it. Once the confession had been made, his senses began to return to him and he realized that the music had been at a frenzied, rave-like tempo for far too long. He began the process of fading out each of the components until the vocals and beat were all that remained. Once they had been faded out as well, Derek was rewarded with a screaming cheer from the crowd. Everyone waved their hands in the air, wiped the sweat from their brows, and began mingling again.

Derek had to admit that it was quite a satisfying feeling to know that he was responsible for that moment in time. The feeling was quickly replaced by a different, far worse, feeling. Emptiness. Loss. The feeling of hopes dashed. He didn't know if the hurt was in his chest, his heart, his head, or all over, but it was inside and now that the music had stopped, it was all he could feel.

"That was *fucking amazing*!" The voice had come from directly behind him and Derek jumped and whirled around bumping directly into Scott, tripping over his foot. Scott wound an arm around Derek's waist to stabilize him and left it there. It took Derek a moment to register what had happened.

"How long have you been behind me?" Derek tried to control the thumping of his heart as he stood closer to Scott than he ever had before, held in place by Scott's arm. The hand at his side burned, filling the emptiness, replacing it with something else…something feral. Nothing else existed in that moment except for him, Scott, and Scott's hand touching him.

"Well, I was dancing with that Susan girl. And then the music started to, I don't know, it got inside my head. She was grinding against me but all I could think of is that I wanted to come and watch you mix the song, so I ditched her. I was actually standing right in front of the mixing board for a while, but you were so focused on what you were doing that you didn't notice me standing there. It was amazing to watch. So I decided to get out of the way of the dancing and lean against the wall over here to watch you."

Scott removed his hand from Derek's waist, sending a wave of panic through him. He didn't want the emptiness to come back. But Scott touched him again, this time placing his hand on Derek's shoulder. *Don't ever stop touching me.* When Scott continued talking, Derek was only half listening. "You are incredible. I see what you mean now by controlling the crowd. You totally brought everyone up into that place you created and then brought them back down. It was like magic. You could make some serious money doing this you know."

Derek was glad that the room was dark. The heat from his face promised that he was most likely crimson at this point. "Like I said, the mixing is a way for me to get out what I feel."

"So what were you feeling then? It must have been pretty intense."

Scott's hand touching him. The whirlwind of anger and despair he had just experienced. The ups and downs. It was all too much. He couldn't continue with the guessing and wondering any longer. The time had come for taking a chance. He had taken a chance the other day in his room and it had paid off. He had to do it again. He had to know once and for all what Scott might be to him.

Everything inside of Derek screamed for him to stop. To think about what he was doing before it was too late. But the time for thinking had passed. The time for caution was over. What could be between them was worth whatever price he might have to pay.

"Uh, Scott, would you like to get a drink? People seem to be socializing now and I am pretty hot. I wouldn't mind stepping outside for a breath of fresh air before I begin again." Derek wasn't sure how he was going to handle the next few minutes with Scott, but one thing he knew for sure. If he didn't step outside he was going to pass out.

"Yeah, I actually grabbed you a bottle of water. I had it when I came over before, but you were lost in that song." Scott handed Derek the bottle of water. It was still cold and Derek ran it over his forehead, and then held it against the heated flesh of his neck. Scott's eyes followed the bottle where it touched Derek and he had to jerk them back to Derek's face. "Josh has a back yard right? I've noticed others going in and out through the kitchen sliding door."

"Yeah, he does, let's go." Derek popped a mix tape into the stereo and then followed Scott through the kitchen and onto the patio where a few students were hanging out and chatting.

"Derek, that was amazing." It was Power.

"Uh, thanks." Derek shifted uncomfortably. He wanted to be alone with Scott. "Listen, I left something I need in my car. Scott and I are going to go and grab it. We'll be back in a few minutes."

Walking down the steps, they headed around the house and stopped in the shaded driveway. The breeze outside felt soothing and cleared Derek's head.

Scott leaned against a car. "So, what did you forget?"

"What? Oh, uh…" Derek's mind was spinning. There was only one thing that he could concentrate on and the topic was standing in front of him. Adrenaline pulsed through his veins as he worked up the courage to begin speaking.

"Everything alright?"

Derek looked at Scott. "Yeah. No. I'm not sure. Being outside feels good." He repeated the fragmented statements he had just uttered in his head and laughed out loud.

"You sure you're ok?" Scott's eyes narrowed and he placed his hand on Derek's shoulder once again. The warmth of Scott's touch brought Derek back to the moment.

"What I meant to say is, yeah, I'm fine. That last song was intense and being outside feels good right now." It was the truth, although it had nothing to do with what he wanted to talk about or why they were standing together in a shaded driveway.

Scott accepted the comment. "So, what were you feeling when you mixed that song?"

Derek considered how he should answer. The same voice that had spoken to him earlier in the week, spoke to him once again. *This is your last chance, Derek. Once you take this step, there's no going back.* Questions raced through Derek's mind. Could he tell him? Should he? The voice spoke once more. *You've kept this to yourself all these years. Why change now and risk everything?*

Once the question had been asked, the answer became clear to him. The obviousness of why he needed to take this chance now caused him to laugh once again. It wasn't a nervous laugh, but one of surprise and relief. The simple fact was that everything *had* changed for him when he met Scott. Now, he was risking everything by *not* telling Scott the truth. What was the worst thing that could happen? Scott would be disgusted by him, tell everyone that he was gay, and he would be a social outcast for the rest of his senior year. That was only a few months and then he'd be off to college. But to *not* take a chance, to *never* know if Scott could accept him as gay or, dare he hope, feel the same way, was simply way too big a risk. It was becoming harder and harder to maintain his guard and to play it safe where Scott was concerned. He took in a deep breath and let it out through pursed lips.

"You're acting kind of strange. Are you *sure* you're ok?" There was no accusation or judgment, only genuine concern. Small wrinkles appeared on Scott's forehead.

I can't let him worry. It's now or never. "Scott. I've never been better, but there's something that I need to tell you." Now that the moment was here, he couldn't wait to begin.

Scott laughed nervously and gave Derek an odd look. "Ok."

Derek shifted restlessly where he stood. "Can we walk for a little bit? I think I'd like to move around." Scott nodded and Derek led them to the end of the driveway and began walking down the street. He wanted to take this risk, but he didn't want others around if Scott freaked out.

"Uh, Derek, where are we going?" Although Scott was being an extremely good sport, his voice wavered, revealing his growing tension and nervousness.

Derek laughed, then stopped and turned to face Scott. "You asked me what I was feeling while mixing that song. I'm going to tell you. I just want us to be alone when I do."

The look he gave Scott caused Scott's mouth to fall open as he drew in a deep, shuddering breath. Letting it out slowly, he regained his demeanor. "You look so… you look…" Whatever he was trying to say, Derek felt Scott's eyes bore straight into him where everything that mattered could be found.

Derek saved him from having to continue. "I was feeling…desire." Scott closed his mouth and stood silently, his eyes never moving from Derek's. "I was thinking about how my life had been going along and suddenly everything changed. In a good way, I mean. There is a part of me that I have always known. Something that makes me different. And I've always been afraid that if I let anyone know, if I revealed my big secret, that my life would become hopeless and difficult." Derek replayed the words and mentally agreed that they were accurate. "But this secret is also something that has made me feel special and strong. It's made me know that when I'm ready, I will be able to truly be who I am instead of trying to be someone who I'm not." Derek shook his head. "I'm beating around the bush and I don't mean to."

Derek took a large gulp of water and swallowed hard.

Just say it. Get it over with. "Since I met you, my feelings have become crystal clear. I now have a face and a name to attach to the feelings I have always had." As he spoke, he felt all of the tension and anger seep from his pores. All of his jealousy, hurt, and doubt dissipated into the night.

Scott was staring directly at Derek and it seemed as if he were holding his breath. Derek realized he still hadn't said the most important part of what he had been trying to say. "When I saw you and Susan together, I felt incredible jealousy and…and a sense of loss. You see, I didn't want Susan to be able to have you that way. I know I'm totally out of line by saying this, but I have to say it. I can't stop or I'll *never* say it."

Derek could hear Scott take in a short breath as understanding began to register in his face. Derek didn't care whether his comments were being received well or if they were freaking Scott out. He had to get through this. To get it out. "Ever since I met you, I've been having these…feelings. Ones that I have never had before. And, while it scares me, while I may live to regret telling you any of this, the truth is, I was thinking of you while I was mixing that song and the desire was…"

Derek registered Scott's movement first and then felt Scott's hands on either side of his face. He felt himself being pulled towards Scott and their lips met in a fevered kiss. Scott wrapped one hand behind Derek's head, twining his fingers into his hair and pulling him in deeper. His other hand snaked around Derek's waist and squeezed him into a tight embrace.

Opening to Scott's eager mouth, Derek allowed their tongues to swirl around each other. He felt his crotch stir and harden, uncomfortably constrained within his jeans for the second time that evening. When Scott ground himself against Derek, he could feel that Scott was just as aroused.

After blissful minutes, which felt like hours, Scott slowly drew his head back and stared into Derek's eyes. "I have wanted to do that since the first day I met you."

Derek's emotions flooded through him as his eyes burned and his vision became blurry. It was only when Scott gently took his finger and traced it along Derek's cheek that he realized he was actually crying.

Looking slightly concerned, Scott pulled back and put his hands on either side of Derek's neck, gently tilting his head up so that they were facing each other. "Why are you crying? What's wrong?"

Derek held Scott's stare. "Absolutely nothing." His voice had never been stronger. He had never been more certain of anything in his entire life. "I've dreamed about this."

Scott smiled. "Me too."

"No seriously, I literally had a dream that you kissed me, almost exactly like this, the first day I met you. That night after we went on our first run."

Scott became serious, pulling Derek close into his arms, and whispered those two words one more time. "Me too."

Chapter 7

The next morning, Derek stayed in bed as long as he could. During the night his kiss with Scott replayed over and over and adrenaline had surged through his veins, making it difficult for him to fall back to sleep. He tried to recall the exact order of events. No matter how hard he tried, all he could focus on was Scott grabbing him on the sidewalk and pulling them together into that kiss. Scott pressing their hard-ons together. Scott whispering to him that he had dreamed about their kiss as well.

During the spare moments that their mouths weren't devouring each other in the car outside his house, he and Scott had agreed to go for a run that morning and then hang out in Harvard Square. Finally, at around 7:00am, he got up, threw on some sweats, noticed that they tented out in the front, and headed down to the kitchen anyway since his parents were still asleep. Putting on a pot of coffee, he began preparing some eggs and toast. *I wonder when it would be late enough to call him.*

Leaning back in the kitchen chair, he sipped his coffee and stared dreamily at the ceiling. His life had changed with a kiss. More precisely, he was growing into himself, becoming more and more the person he recognized from the inside as each day with Scott passed. Before this year he would have never taken the risk he took last night. He wouldn't have dared. But Scott made him want to be brave. *What did that Walt Disney song say? Someday my prince will come? Well mine came alright...and I don't think Disney would make a song out of it.*

Fifteen minutes passed and he couldn't wait any longer. Picking up his cell phone, he dialed Scott's number. Scott picked up on the first ring. Derek laughed and choked on a piece of toast he had been chewing.

"Why'd you let it ring so many times?"

"I was already up thinking about you."

Feeling playful Derek decided to give Scott shit. "You were up? There's a picture that I can use later."

Scott whispered Derek's words to himself a few time. *I was up. I was up. Huh?*...When he spoke, Derek could tell that he had pieced together the play on words. "Oh! That took me a minute. You're feisty this morning."

"Well, if I'm going to be fair, I suppose I should admit that I was up as well. I was calling to see when you wanted to get together this morning."

"How about now?" Scott sounded eager and it sent shivers through Derek.

"Now's good. I'll pick you up in about ten minutes. We may as well take the car since we'll be heading into the Square afterwards."

"Great, I'll be waiting." Scott hung up and Derek gathered his dishes and coffee mug, rinsing them in the sink and placing them in the dishwasher. He went upstairs, changed into his running gear, jotted a note letting his parents know where he was going and secured it to the refrigerator with a magnet.

Ten minutes later, Scott was sitting beside him in the car as they headed for the school parking lot. They decided to take a long, leisurely run, following the same route Derek had the day he invited Scott to his house earlier in the week. The weather was getting colder and most of the leaves had already turned to shades of yellow, red, and brown. Many trees had shed their leaves completely. It was a clear day, however, and the sun was shining which helped to subdue some of the chill the wind carried.

They started off at an easy pace and allowed their muscles to warm up. There were no other runners and very few cars, so the two of them had the river to themselves.

Derek wanted to talk about last night with Scott, but wasn't sure exactly how to start. He contemplated several ways to broach the topic, but dismissed each idea with one excuse or another. Deciding the direct approach was probably best he began speaking. "I've been thinking about last night."

Scott let out an amused laugh between breaths. "It's *all* I've been thinking about."

Encouraging, but not surprising. "I've never kissed another guy before."

Scott smiled, "I was your first huh? So how was I?"

Derek blushed. "You were amazing. The way you grabbed me and pulled me to you like that. You totally caught me off guard. It was probably the best feeling I've ever experienced in my life."

"Well, when I know what I want, I grab it. Literally." Scott glanced sideways at Derek and gave him a short wink before returning to face in the direction they were running.

"Have you…I mean, uh…have there been…"

"Have I kissed other guys before?" Scott had a weird knack of knowing what it was that Derek wanted to ask.

"Um, yeah." Derek's voice was subdued. A small part of him didn't want to know. A much larger part of him knew that he needed to if he was going to maintain his sanity.

"Only once, two summers ago at wrestling camp. It was the last night we were there and one of the guys had an older brother who lived locally and bought us some alcohol. There was lots of beer, we got pretty drunk, and it just happened and then we went our separate ways the next day." Derek pondered that, feeling a mixture of curiosity and jealousy. "But it didn't hold a candle to kissing you. *You*, my friend, are a great kisser. Better than any guy or girl I've kissed." Derek felt a stronger pang of jealousy. He had kissed girls too, but after last night, hearing about Scott kissing anyone bothered him.

"So, have you kissed lots of girls? Or have you had a girlfriend?" Derek was pretty sure he didn't want to know the answer to this question, but also knew that if he didn't ask, the *not* knowing would burn at him.

Scott smiled and looked at Derek. It was a soft smile, but a knowing one. "Well, that depends on what you consider to be *lots*. I've kissed about five girls and, yes, I did have a girlfriend before moving out here."

Derek felt a stitch in his side. "Really? How long were you two together?"

Scott didn't answer for a minute, then slowed his pace and turned his head so he was partially facing Derek. "We were together for most of my junior year. All we did was kiss and maybe a little petting, but she was pretty religious and didn't go in for anything heavy…which was the main reason that I chose to go out with her. That and because she was a really nice person."

Listening to Scott talk about his relationship with a girl caused the stitch in Derek's side to intensify. Just thinking about Scott with anyone else filled his mind with thoughts and feelings that he knew were completely out of line. Despite the displeasure eating him from the inside out, he was curious as well. Derek knew he would never have been able to date a girl. Not *really* date one.

Scott slowed down and jogged over to a bench, placed one foot on the seat, and began to stretch his leg. As he stretched, he looked at Derek carefully. "I figured out I was gay in ninth grade. I didn't really know what to do with those feelings and my buddies had only begun dating. They weren't doing much more than kissing and telling. I figured that if I was going to blend in, I should probably date someone too, but knew that I didn't want to lead anyone on.

"Amber, that was her name, was the perfect choice. Her father was a pastor in the local church and I knew that she wasn't going to want me to try anything too serious with her. It provided a reasonable cover and Amber was a good friend." He paused, turning to look at Derek and waiting for Derek to return his gaze. "But I'm wondering whether you want to ask me about girls I've kissed, or if there is something else you would rather know."

His eyes locked with Derek's and for a moment, Derek couldn't think. *Words? What are those again?* "I...er... uh." Scott maintained steady eye contact and patiently waited for Derek to be able to form coherent sentences. After a moment, Scott's face lifted into that sly smile and the way the sun shone across his cheek made his dimple seem more pronounced than usual. Derek felt some of his nerves begin to unwind and wondered why he was finding it so difficult to ask what was really on his mind. Sighing, he allowed his shoulders to drop and let the words flow from his mouth. "What I want to know is whether last night was something that just happened, or if it's something that will happen again." *There, I said it.*

Scott's smile broadened as he switched legs on the bench. "Is that what you're tiptoeing around?" Scott walked over to Derek, looked around to see if there were any people or cars coming, then placed his fingers under Derek's chin and tilted his head up so that their lips were about an inch apart. Derek's heart began to beat like a bird trapped in a cage. "Last night was not something that just happened." With that he closed the distance between them and gave him a sweet and tender kiss. When he pulled away, he wiped the lingering wetness from Derek's lips with his thumb. "C'mon. Let's continue our jog."

Derek, still flushed and trying to control his racing heart, placed an arm on Scott's shoulder. "I think I might need to take a minute to, er, loosen up before we continue."

Scott gave Derek a momentary glance, then allowing his stare to move downward, let out a chuckle. "Damn. That was just a tiny kiss. You must really like me."

Derek knew he had turned beet red, but didn't care. "You have *no* idea. I've never liked anyone the way I like you." He walked over to the bench where Scott had been stretching and sat down. "I guess that's why I want to know about your past relationships. I've never been in one. You're the first person I have allowed myself to feel this way about."

Scott sat down on the bench, watching Derek as he stretched his muscles. "I'm not sure it's something you allow yourself to do. It just happens." He paused for a moment, and then looked at Derek who was deep in thought. The urge to ask Derek what was on his mind was pressing inside him, but he forced himself to wait until Derek was ready to talk.

From a purely rational standpoint, Derek knew that it made no sense to feel threatened by anything Scott had done in the past. But he seemed so much more experienced. He had kissed a boy before. He had been in a relationship for a year. Even so, Scott had been nothing but friendly, open, and incredibly understanding. Why would he behave differently all of a sudden? The simple answer was that he wouldn't. This was Derek's baggage and the realization calmed him. "I suppose that's true. You can't help your feelings. I still don't like that I feel a bit inexperienced next to you. You…you've felt and done things with other people that I haven't. Maybe I could have. I'm *sure* I could have. But I never did. I never really wanted to. Not until you."

Scott looked directly at Derek. It wasn't with the flirtatious, penetrating stare that caused Derek to become incoherent. Scott was completely serious. "I've never felt this way about anyone either. Amber was just a friend. Nothing more. This is a first for both of us."

Although he hated that it did, the admission came as a relief to Derek. He wanted to be the one who made Scott feel more alive than anyone else ever had. He wanted to be Scott's first real relationship, just like Scott was his.

When he looked at Scott, Derek couldn't help but smile. Scott was being so careful with him. So understanding. But now that he and Scott were together, it created a whole new set of problems. As much as he loved the way he was able to let his guard down with Scott, the way he was able to enjoy small moments and feelings more intensely than ever before, it didn't change the fact that he didn't want to out himself to the whole school.

It was as if Scott had picked the thought right out of Derek's head. "So maybe we should talk about..."

"How to maintain a low profile around other people?" Derek finished for him.

Scott looked down at his feet. "I know it makes me sound like a shit. I loved last night and want a lot more nights like that, but I'm afraid of other people finding out." It was Derek's turn to chuckle. Scott turned his head with a slightly hurt look in his eyes. "Why are you laughing at me?"

Derek leaned in towards Scott and used his shoulder to give him a light shove. "I'm not laughing at you. It's just that you're cute when you get nervous."

Scott flushed, but his smile revealed that Derek's words had pleased him. Derek pulled out all the stops. *There's nothing to lose now. He wants you.* "As you were talking about Amber, I was feeling jealous. I know I have no right to feel that way, but you're the first person I want to be with. It makes me feel better to know that I'm kind of your first too."

"Not *kind of*. Amber wasn't really a girlfriend. She

was a friend." Scott paused, a smile pulling at the corners of his mouth. "That doesn't get to my point, though. I like you. A lot. Still, we should keep a low profile."

"Scott, have you noticed me going out of my way to be noticed by anyone for *any* reason at school? Beck says I'm the most guarded person she knows."

"You? Honestly, you don't seem guarded at all. You are a very genuine person and very outgoing. It's one of the things that attracted me the most when I first met you."

The comment caught Derek off guard. After a moment of thinking about it, he realized that he had never put up his defenses around Scott. He had wondered about that often enough, never really allowing his mind to linger on the thought for too long. The fact was that Scott perceived him entirely differently than other people did because he behaved differently around Scott. He was more himself. The only other person that saw the real Derek, the one that he kept hidden, was Beck. Knowing that he had been letting Scott in all along warmed Derek from the inside. "That's fair. But I'm only that way with Beck, and now with you. With everyone else, I tend to keep fairly quiet, observe what's going on around me, and keep a low profile at all times."

He looked at Scott who had remained quietly staring at his feet. He figured that Scott must still feel badly about wanting to keep their relationship a secret. *Ok, I know what I want to know and now this is getting a little heavy.* A devilish grin spread across his face. "So, what I really want to know…" he paused and waited for Scott to look up. When he did, Derek batted his eyes, "…is will you go steady with me?"

Scott shoved Derek and started laughing. Shaking his head, he threw his arm around Derek's shoulder and pulled him in close. "Yes, I'll go steady with you. Now let's get our asses off this frigid bench."

Derek sprung up with military stiffness, uttering a dutiful, "Yes, Sir!" They continued their run making small talk and enjoying the colors of fall that reflected off the river's surface.

Sitting in *Au Bon Pain* a couple of hours later, sipping their coffee and splitting a turkey sandwich, his kiss with Scott flashed through Derek's mind once again. The picture was interrupted when Scott grabbed his hand, pulling at it. "Hey. Where'd you go? You disappeared for a minute there."

It took a minute for Derek to clear his head. When he was able to focus, the sight of Scott sent a shiver up his back. "I was just thinking about last night again. About our kiss."

Scott nodded. "It makes sense now."

Derek was confused. "What makes sense?"

"The fact that you were all dreamy-eyed for a minute. I would get that way too if I got to fantasize about kissing me."

Derek didn't want to give him the satisfaction, but the comment was so confident, so Scott. Derek couldn't have stopped the smile that spread across his face even if he had wanted to. "I really wish you had more confidence in yourself." He knew he shouldn't say it. Scott was already behaving like a cocky stallion, but why not make him feel even more studly.

Scott reached across the table and gently hooked his finger with Derek's. It was a small touch and only lasted a moment, but it said everything that Derek wanted to hear. His contentment was interrupted when he realized he hadn't brought up the topic of Beck yet. He hoped that Scott would be comfortable with him telling Beck about the two of them. Withholding information like this wasn't something he thought he could do. Scott was almost done with his half of the sandwich and didn't seem to be slowing for air between bites. Offering his half to Scott, Derek decided to bring it up. "Scott, I do have one more question for you."

"Jeez, Derek." His mouth was full so the words came out muffled. "I'm going to start charging you per question." As he said this, a small amount of chewed bread flew from his mouth and landed on the table between them. "Sorry."

Picking up a napkin, Derek wiped up the stray bit of food. "Charming." He was unable to keep his grin from turning into a chuckle. *Pathetic. I even find his clumsy eating cute.* "I just wanted to ask you if we could at least tell Beck about us. She already knows that I've wanted you since the beginning of the year. She's my best friend and quite honestly, I am fearful of the fate of my balls if she ever found out that I didn't tell her."

After taking a gulp of his coffee to wash the food out of his mouth, Scott turned to Derek with a grave look on his face. *Shit. He's going to say no.* Scott placed his elbow on the table and rested his head on his hand as if in deep contemplation. After what seemed like an interminable silence, he finally spoke. "Look. I like you. You like me. Beck is great. But seriously Derek…" He looked a little irritated.

Derek could feel heat rising in his cheeks. *Fuck. I pissed him off.*

Scott continued, "…you've liked me from the beginning of the year and made me wait all this time to find out what a great kisser you are. That's just plain mean." A wicked grin lit up his face.

"You bastard! I thought you were upset." Relief flooded through Derek. "Wait, you didn't answer my question."

Scott smiled at Derek. "Do you trust her to keep it

between us?"

"Absolutely. She's known about me being gay as long as I have and hasn't said a word to anyone. In fact, she's the one who keeps reminding me to be careful."

Scott looked at Derek; the weightiness of his gaze was unquestionable. "Then fine. Tell her whatever you want. Everyone needs a good girlfriend to gossip to." Leaning forward, his face and his posture relaxed. "Just promise me one thing."

"Anything."

"Promise me you'll paint me in a good light."

"You can count on that." As Derek pulled out his cell, an idea popped into his head. "Hey, let's go see a movie."

A look of confusion crossed Scott's face. "Um, did you just topic shift from promising you'll paint me in a good light to watching a movie or are those two comments supposed to be related in a way I can't figure out?"

"Sorry. I do that sometimes. But do you want to go see a movie?"

"Sure, I can do my homework later or tomorrow."

With that, Derek hit Beck's number on his speed dial. "I'm gonna call Beck."

"What, you're calling her now?" Derek couldn't tell if Scott was amused or annoyed.

"Heck yeah! This is big news. We're going steady remember?"

Scott shook his head. This was one of those times that he would have to placate Derek. Somehow, he suspected there would be many times like that. Still, Derek's excitement was sweet. "And the topic has now shifted to us going steady. I'm going to get whiplash trying to follow your line of thinking. Ok, call Beck, but could you do me a favor and call us boyfriends instead of saying that we are going steady? It makes me feel like one of us should be wearing a poodle skirt." He gave Derek a meaningful look. "And I'm not wearing a skirt."

Derek shot Scott a playfully annoyed look. "Hey Beck. S'me, Derek."

"What's up babe? You were awesome last night."

"Scott and I were wondering if you wanted to come to see a movie with us."

Beck's voice rose to a piercing level and Scott barely had to work to hear her voice through the phone that Derek had suddenly moved a few inches away from his ear even though it wasn't on speaker. "Oh, movie popcorn! You know how much I love…wait, did you just say *we*?"

"Yup." A wide grin spread across Derek's face.

"And by *we* you mean…"

"Yup."

"So you…"

"I did."

"And he's…"

"He is."

"So you're…"

"*Beck*, do you want to come to the movies with us or not?" Derek rolled his eyes. Scott, who had heard the entire interaction, simply laughed.

"Yes. Where are you right now?"

"Au Bon Pain."

Derek heard a thud on the other end of the line. "Holy fucking Mary Mother of Jesus! Ouch!" Derek moved the phone about three inches further away from his ear. Scott covered his mouth to muffle his burst of laughter. "Give me thirty minutes."

"You ok?" Derek was only mildly concerned.

"I just walked straight into my chair, jamming my toe on the leg. You need to give me fair warning before dropping a huge bomb like that on me."

Derek smiled, "Sorry."

"Well you should be." There was a brief pause before Beck continued. "Oh, and Derek."

"Yeah?"

"I am so happy for you."

"Thanks." He hung up and they ordered another sandwich while waiting for Beck.

Chapter 8

As wrestling season drew closer, new routines fell into place for Derek and Scott. They had been inseparable ever since the night of Josh's party. A serene calm surrounded Derek wherever he went. Just knowing that Scott was his, filled him with a combined sense of pride and happiness and he practically floated through the days.

Although Derek continued his runs, Scott had taken to spending more and more time working out with the guys on the team. The weather had become significantly colder, all of the leaves having long since fallen off the trees. The scenery didn't evoke the same romanticism that it had when hues of yellow, orange, red, and brown had surrounded him and reflected off the water. With naked branches and cold winds, the weather became another obstacle, one that challenged him as he incorporated sprints into his longer and longer runs. Pretty soon he would have to begin to incorporate weight training, but for now, he was pleased with his improved endurance and stamina.

Scott usually came over to Derek's house after school. The attic, which had previously been Derek's solitary haven, became a nest for the two of them to do their homework, listen to music, and explore each other's bodies. Derek had to admit that they tended to spend much more time kissing and groping each other than actually doing their homework, but his grades hadn't suffered, so he didn't waste energy or time worrying about it.

It was during a last period history class that Derek noticed Scott had been quieter than usual. Not wanting to draw the teacher's attention, Derek pulled out his cell and held it under the desk. Finding Scott's name had become an automatic reflex for him.

What's up? U R in Twilite Zone 2day?

Scott jerked into a straighter sitting position when his phone vibrated in his pocket. He took it out, hiding it beneath his desk as Derek had, and looked at the message. His sly grin spread across his face as he cast a sidelong glance at Derek.

Been thinking about wrestling. Getting nervous.

The response caught Derek off guard. Of all the things that could make Scott nervous, and Derek had found very few things that could, wrestling was not one of them.

Why?

Cause I don't know Sean and Phil.

U'll beat them no prob.

How do U know?

Cause I know. Meet me at lockers after class.

Derek shot Scott a meaningful look, one that was meant to calm him. He wasn't sure whether he achieved his goal from Scott's reaction which remained subdued and quiet.

After they gathered their things from their lockers and were heading over to the athletic complex, Derek picked up their conversation where their texting had left off. "So, what exactly is it that is making you so nervous?"

Once Scott started talking, the words flowed out of him in a continuous stream. "I've been thinking about pre-season. I've always known my competition, but with both Sean and Phil gunning for the 167 pound weight class, and with me not knowing anything about them, I kind of feel like I'm at a disadvantage."

"They don't know anything about you either, so they are at just as big a disadvantage." Derek had to hold back the giggle that was struggling to get out. As much as he understood how Scott felt, seeing him reveal vulnerability was both cute and endearing. Scott was typically so self-assured. He had taken the initiative for their first kiss. He had even kissed Derek in public on their run, although he did make sure no one was around first. In fact, Derek realized, Scott also called him out whenever he was talking around issues instead of addressing them directly. It was a surprising relief to see that Scott had a minor chink in that coat of armor. "If you like, I could give you some pointers so that you have an idea of what to expect. I've been wrestling with them since ninth grade, and even though they didn't make varsity, and were in a different weight class, I did get to watch their challenges each week against Dylan."

Scott pondered the idea for a minute. "Do you really know their moves that well? Didn't Sean say he went to wrestling camp and learned new moves over the summer?"

"I may not know some of the new stuff they've learned, but I know each of their basic moves. The mats are in place in the wrestling room. We could go there after school for the next week or so and practice a bit. I mean, you're carrying thirty pounds on me, so you'll probably kick my ass, but I could still show you what to expect."

"You and me wrestling together…" Derek could see Scott's eyes twinkle with wicked thoughts. Thinking about it himself caused Derek's crotch to shift and he felt his pants become constricted. "I like it. Definitely a good plan. Let's start today."

Derek didn't bother to hold back the giggles that erupted from him this time. "You *do* realize that I am proposing to show you the *wrestling* moves I know Sean and Phil will use, right?"

Scott turned to face Derek, wearing a face of pure innocence. "Of course, Derek. What else could I have been considering besides that?"

Derek gave Scott a shove and Scott flashed a shameless grin and winked at him, causing his dick to lengthen even more inside his pants. He became quiet for a moment as he tried to modify his walking to readjust himself without seeming obvious about it.

Scott didn't miss a beat. The sudden lull in their conversation caused him to look at Derek and, once he looked down and saw the sizable bulge that was prominently staring back at him, his own cock began to stir. Scott looked around to see that they were alone, then boldly reached into his pants to readjust himself while staring at Derek. "You were saying something about your focus being on *wrestling*?"

Derek froze, his gaze locked on Scott's crotch. When he looked up he could only summon one word. "Bastard!"

Scott laughed out loud and they continued their walk to the athletic building in silence. Derek flashed a series of images in his mind. *Dead cats. Sunday Mass. Beck naked.* Slowly, the tension that had built up in his pants subsided. Just as they were arriving at the locker room, he noticed Scott furtively grab at the front of his pants, this time trying to be a bit more subtle. The image sent all of the blood rushing back to his groin and he had to start the process of settling himself down all over again.

It wasn't until they had both regained some semblance of control that they headed up to the wrestling room which was located on the second floor. The weight room was next to it so they decided to stop in to see who from the team was working out before heading to the wrestling room. Josh, Power, and Frank were spotting each other on the bench press. Derek was relieved to see that Sean and Phil weren't there. "Hey guys. What's up?"

"Thompson!" Power called out. "You decide to beef up this year? You never come to the weight room. Maybe you can challenge Frank here at his weight class." He then turned his attention to Frank who was struggling with his reps. "C'mon you fuckin' pussy. That's only your second set and you're already straining."

Josh walked over to Derek and put a hand on his shoulder. "Hey, could I talk with you for a minute?" Derek allowed himself to be led to the corner of the weight room. Once there Josh continued. "Listen, I was talking to Coach the other day and it seems like we are going to be having a lot of challenges for spots this year. You are being challenged by Bobby Dean. Paul is planning on challenging me. Fuckin' idiot! No one's challenging Power. No surprise there. But the spot that has all of us guessing is the 167 weight class. Sean and Phil are sweating bullets about Scott, especially since they've seen him on the weight machines and he can bench more than both of them. I was wondering if you could put together a challenge schedule for us. I'm working out our warm-up routines and scoping out the other schools to see when their meets are scheduled so we can do some reconnaissance during the season."

It surprised Derek to be asked to put together the challenge schedule, but the benefits of the task did not escape him. He would be able to orchestrate challenges to give Scott a slight advantage. The thought only caused a small twinge of guilt, one that he was easily able to dismiss. "Sure, I'd be happy to. When are we going to begin challenges?"

"Well, the season begins in a couple of weeks officially. The wrestling room is ready for us to begin whenever." Josh folded his arms across his chest and bit the inside of his cheek, clearly deep in thought about when to begin challenges. *Seriously Josh, they're just challenges, not final exams.* "I was thinking we could start practices with the core team and any challengers on Monday next week. How about you schedule the matches for Thursday and

Friday next week? That way we will have our varsity line up settled for the first official day of practice."

"Not a problem. I'll have a challenge schedule set up by the end of the week." Derek walked over to Scott who was watching Frank struggle with the weights. Frank's face was beet red and his teeth were clenched so tightly that air actually whistled through them as he labored for breath. He nudged Scott with his shoulder. "You ready?"

Scott nodded and the two headed into the wrestling room. Once there Scott sat on the mat and began stretching. "So what was that all about with Josh?" His voice sounded nonchalant, but he stared intently at Derek when he asked the question which, Derek had learned, meant that Scott was actually quite curious about the answer.

Derek sat down on the mat next to Scott and began stretching as well. "He wants me to put together the schedule for the challenge matches. They're going to happen next Thursday and Friday." He grabbed the toes of his right foot and pulled his torso towards his leg. "I was thinking that I might schedule it so that Sean and Phil wrestle each other first so you can watch them and see what their styles are like. Add that to what I already know about them and it should give you a good idea of how to beat them."

Scott spread his legs and reached his hands out in front of him, using his fingers to walk his body closer to the mat. "Why would you do that? Do you think that I won't be able to beat them without some extra help?"

His breath caught in his throat. "No, I didn't, I mean I don't, I mean—."

The corner of Scott's mouth began to creep up his face. "I'm just giving you shit, Derek. I appreciate that you are willing to help me out. Not that it surprises me. You've helped me since the first day I got here...in more ways than I dared hope for." He looked up and allowed his gaze to bore into Derek, but then he averted his eyes before speaking again. It was very unlike him and it immediately captured Derek's attention. "Ok, we better focus on wrestling 'cause if we start staring at each other I'm gonna forget we're not in your attic."

There's that slightly insecure side. Funny, but I actually find it sexy. Derek's focus was always laser-sharp when wrestling, but then again, he had never had such a tempting distraction before. "Sounds like a good idea."

Scott refocused on his stretching and remained silent for a few minutes. When he spoke again, his voice was serious. "I don't want you to make a schedule that will give me an advantage. I want to win on my own merit. Besides, I can think of better things for you to focus on than challenge schedules."

"Enough of that, Scott. We're here to wrestle, not flirt." Derek actually felt a twinge of irritation, but it quickly evaporated. No matter how focused he was, it still wound him up knowing how much Scott wanted him.

"Why can't we do a little of both?" Scott's grin turned wicked as he raised his eyebrows suggestively.

Derek's thoughts wandered towards the various things they could do on the wrestling mat and none of them had anything to do with wrestling. "Scott. Weren't you the one who just suggested that we keep our focus on wrestling?" He jumped up and started hopping up and down, causing Scott to laugh. "C'mon. You talk a good game. Let's see if you can put your money where your mouth is."

It was all the challenge Scott needed. He jumped up and walked to the center of the mat. They assumed the neutral standing position, shook hands, and started circling each other. Derek was not a fancy wrestler, preferring to perfect basic offensive and defensive moves and to use them with precision. As he and Scott circled each other, he watched how Scott shuffled his feet as opposed to crossing them when he moved. Wrestlers who shuffled required one approach, while those who crossed their feet required another.

Getting a sense of Scott's pace, he placed his left hand on the inside of Scott's arm, grabbing his bicep. He wanted to get an inside hold on Scott's arm to see how Scott reacted.

Scott did nothing to shake his arm off. *Bingo!* In a flash, Derek bent his knees, shot his right hand down to grab and lift Scott's left foot while pushing back on Scott's bicep. The combination of losing balance from the push and the lack of stability from having only one foot on the ground gave Derek the momentum he needed for the takedown. Stepping between Scott's legs and hooking a leg behind the foot Scott still had on the ground, Derek used leverage to drop Scott to the mat and spin behind him to the referee's position. "Two points for the takedown." Derek pushed off Scott's back and stood back up.

"Damn, you are faster than lightening. Are you always that fast with your takedowns?"

"Always. And that is lesson number one. Sean is as fast as I am on the takedown. Don't ever watch his face and never, *ever* allow him an inside grip on you like I got. You need to watch his legs. If you focus on them, you'll know precisely when he's going to make his move, then you can sprawl, he'll end up beneath you, and you can spin on his back for the takedown."

Scott raised an eyebrow. "Ok, good note. Care to try again?" As they returned to neutral position in the center of the mat, Derek could see a fixed determination settle over Scott. It was visible in his stance and in his foot movement. Derek saw that Scott was focused completely on his legs. Derek moved in and tried to place his hand on Scott's bicep again, but Scott wound his hand around attempting to secure the inside hold rather than let Derek take it again. *Ok. Good. Sean will find this difficult.*

While continuing to vie for inner arm position, Derek prepared for his next move. He started turning in a circle, forcing Scott to go with him. Careful not to make any big moves, Derek continued to circle with Scott while keeping Scott's focus on the battle for the inside grip of his arm. Finally, he allowed Scott to get the inside grip of his left arm. Using his handle on Scott's tricep, he pulled while simultaneously taking a large step backward, forcing Scott to step forward. Shooting down to the mat, he scooped up Scott's exposed foot, stepped behind the foot Scott still had on the ground, and used his body weight to push Scott over backwards. Scott landed on his back and Derek quickly swiveled over his chest, slid his arm around Scott's head, and tightened his half-nelson hold.

The move would have worked, and probably pinned, an opponent of equal weight, but Scott easily arched his back, pivoted on his head, and pulled a smooth reversal, causing Derek to land on his back. He then dropped his full weight on Derek's chest, trapping him to the mat.

With the full weight of Scott's body pinning him down, Derek was unable to move at all. "Another nice move, Derek. You were distracting me with the battle for arm position and I forgot to protect myself from exposing my legs. You're damn good."

Derek was pleased that Scott had become so focused, but with Scott lying on top of him, his own focus was rapidly evaporating. "Uh, you want to let me get up now?"

"Oh, yeah. Sorry." When Scott stood up, there was no hint of flirtation or pleasure from the position they had just been in. Instead, he was assessing Derek as if for the first time, seeing a worthy and skilled opponent.

Shaking the gratification of Scott's admiration from his mind, Derek got back to teaching. "Sean's best at takedowns. Once you have control of him, he's not much of a defensive wrestler. Let's keep at it." As they continued practicing, Derek used his speed and the various tricks he knew Sean or Phil would use against Scott. Scott was a quick study and Derek found that it became extremely difficult to maneuver into a position that would allow him to make an offensive move.

After about an hour and a half, Derek was ready to call it quits. He still had homework to do and knew that his body would be sore from wrestling. Even though he was in good shape, he hadn't been using his muscles the way he used them during the season and they were going to protest until he had spent a few weeks reminding his body who was boss. "Let's hit the showers and then head home."

Scott grabbed his sweatshirt and mopped sweat from his forehead and neck. Strands of his blonde hair were matted to his forehead. Derek wanted to brush them aside and kiss the salty slickness of his smooth skin. Knowing that anyone could walk in at any time, he restrained himself.

The two went to the locker room. They stripped out of their workout clothes, grabbed their towels, and headed into the open shower room. Each shower head contained four nozzles.

As the hot water soothed Derek's muscles, he allowed himself to glance at Scott. There were other guys showering as well, so he had to soap himself much more than necessary for the excuse of shifting his body position to shoot spying glances in Scott's direction. Derek realized that this was the first time he had seen Scott completely naked. His body was long and slender, the muscles strong and well toned. His butt wasn't as round and tight as Derek's, but it was still pleasant and full. The muscles of his legs bulged and flexed under the skin with each movement, creating a contoured line towards his narrow waist. His back, lateral, and abdominal muscles formed a graceful v-shape, canting up and out from his hips until they merged into his broad, rounded shoulders. It was impossible not to notice and appreciate the masculine angles and perfect line of Scott's body.

When Derek caught sight of Scott's cock, wet and dripping with foam from soap and shampoo, his breath caught in his chest and he felt an electrical surge of charged sensation shoot straight to his groin. Scott's cock hung about a third of the way down his thigh and appeared to be thick, definitely thicker than his own penis. His balls hung loosely in a smooth sack, and swayed back and forth as he moved. His whole crotch was framed by a wisp of hair which crowned the base of his cock and aside from the thin line of hair that ran up to his belly button, his chest and abdomen were otherwise hairless and iridescent as the lights reflected off of his wet skin.

Although Derek had seen each part of Scott's body before, seeing it all at once, exposed and vulnerable, was better than he had imagined, even in his fantasies. He quickly turned off the hot water and faced the wall. The cold water hit him with a shock and he fought to contain the hiss threatening to escape his throat. Feeling the tension and arousal easing from his groin, Derek turned off the water and quickly placed the towel around his waist. Once dressed, he decided to wait for Scott in the lobby. Fifteen minutes later, they were headed to his house.

In the car, Scott was silent. Derek chanced a look in his direction and was surprised to see that Scott was staring at him. "What?"

"I saw you staring at me in the showers." Scott ran

his tongue over his upper lip and then caught his plump lower lip between his teeth. Derek wanted to pull over to the side of the road and nibble on that lip for him.

"You caught that, huh?" Derek was sure his cheeks were crimson. Although he knew that Scott wouldn't be upset that Derek had been staring, it was still unbelievably embarrassing to be caught in the act.

"You shouldn't be embarrassed, Derek. It made me feel incredibly sexy." Although Derek kept his eyes facing forward, he Derek could feel Scott watching him. "I was posing for you. Did you like what you saw?"

His cock began to thicken in his pants and he knew that he would have a serious case of blue balls if he didn't take care of it sometime soon. Derek glanced over at Scott and then back to the road. "Well, since you caught me, I guess there's no reason to deny it. You're incredibly hot. I had to blast myself with cold water to keep from getting a hard-on right there in the shower room."

Scott leaned over and placed his lips right next to Derek's ear. He nipped at his earlobe then whispered in a husky voice. "I was checking you out too. You have got the best ass in the entire school." When Scott's lips sealed onto Derek's neck and he began to gently nibble and suck, Derek's erection stiffened to full mast and he almost veered the car off the road. Scott leaned back to his own side of the car, a look of satisfaction lighting up his face.

When they got to Derek's home, all he could think of was getting Scott up to the attic couch. To avoid arousing suspicion, he walked into the kitchen to greet his mother. The kitchen was empty, but there was a note on the table. *3:45. Went grocery shopping and then going to the hair salon. Dinner will be at six. I'll be home in a couple of hours. Mom.* Glancing at the clock, Derek saw that his mother had only left 15 minutes ago. *Yes! Good form, Mom!* Derek was almost bouncing when he turned to face Scott. "We have the house to ourselves."

Scott caught on immediately and took Derek by the hand, leading him down the hallway to his bedroom. They entered the room and Scott kicked the door shut and pushed him against it, locking their mouths together. The kiss was hungry, filled with the desire that had built up on the mat, in the shower, and on the drive home. Scott slid his hands up inside of Derek's shirt and ran them over the taut pectoral muscles, rolling the firm nipples between thumb and forefinger. Derek let out soft groans into Scott's mouth and reached around to grab his ass, pulling them even closer together. "Such a good kisser." Scott's words were muffled by Derek's mouth. He then pulled Derek's shirt over his head, trapping his hands above him against the door.

The thrill of losing control added to the frenzy of the moment and Derek allowed Scott to keep his hands bound above his head for another few seconds. He then freed his hands and threw his shirt across the room. Taking a tentative step towards the bed, he urged Scott backwards until the back of his knees hit the edge. Derek collapsed on top of him and they rolled and grasped at each other until Derek was lying on his back, his hands running up and down Scott's muscular body.

Grabbing Scott's shirt, he could only work it part way up his torso before he felt hot lips seal against his once again. Somehow, Derek managed to squeak out a single phrase. "Want your shirt off." Scott removed his shirt, tossing it to the floor with Derek's, then cradled Derek's head in his hands, resting his weight on his elbows and upper arms.

After minutes of passionate kissing, Scott pulled his head back. His lips were swollen and his eyes had a dreamlike quality in them. Reaching down between their bodies, Scott placed his hand on Derek's crotch, rubbing his straining member through the fabric of his jeans.

Derek pushed against Scott's hand, groans of pleasure escaping from deep within him. Grabbing Scott's ass, he pulled their hips together and they both ground their straining cocks against each other as their mouths met in a lustful, ravenous kiss. Derek lost sense of where his lips and tongue ended and Scott's began.

Scott undid Derek's belt buckle, popped the first button of his pants, and slid his hand underneath Derek's boxer briefs, wrapping his warm fingers around Derek's erection which was leaking with precome. The sensation almost caused Derek to come on the spot, but he took in a deep breath, trying to control himself and to allow the moment to last as long as possible. Scott reluctantly pulled his mouth away from Derek's long enough to place it next to his ear. "I want to feel your hands on my dick." He then lowered his lips to Derek's neck, having found the spot and technique to drive him into a frenzy.

Without any need for further prompting, Derek freed Scott's cock from the confines of his pants. With one hand he slowly stroked up and down the shaft, while he cupped Scott's balls with his other hand, giving them a gentle tug. Scott let out a heavy breath of hot air against Derek's neck.

Locking lips once again, they both struggled with shedding first their pants, then their boxer-briefs until they were both lying next to one another, skin on skin, pressed together. Scott continued to pull at Derek's cock with a steady and firm motion while Derek used both hands to pleasure Scott. They both started panting as their bodies writhed together on Derek's bed. "Oh, God, Derek, getting so close. You feel so good."

Hearing Scott losing control and knowing that he was the reason why threw Derek right over the edge. Sucking in a breath, his insides begin to quiver as an electric energy surged through his stomach and balls. "I'm…going…to…" and with an explosion, his orgasm burst, the first spray streaking onto his chest. The waves that followed racked Derek's body as his sperm flowed in gushes coating Scott's hand.

Scott's breathing became heavier. Derek could feel the precise moment that Scott lost control, his balls constricting and pulling up closer to his body. Derek jerked mercilessly at his shaft leaving Scott helpless to do anything but bury his head against Derek's shoulder, clamping down with his teeth on the firm muscle just as his shaft convulsed in Derek's hands. Jets of semen coated his chest, mixing with his own, and then seeped out of Scott's cock onto his hand. Derek closed his eyes, sated and utterly relaxed as he felt Scott's body shudder a few times and then collapse in a heap on top of him. They lay there for a few minutes, gently touching each other and not saying a word.

Once Derek regained enough energy to move, he wiped his hand on a clean patch of skin then took Scott's face in his hands, turning his head up so they were staring into each other's eyes. "That. Was. Incredible."

Scott smiled, still looking a bit disoriented. "Incredible." He leaned in and placed his lips over Derek's. The kiss was sweet and relaxed, communicating through touch and feel all of his affection.

During the days leading up to the challenge matches, Derek and Scott continued their after-school practices. Scott had learned how to evade Sean's takedown moves and had become familiar with many of Phil's defensive techniques. With each day, Scott found himself increasingly amazed by Derek's skill, as well as his knowledge of the members of the team. It wasn't until mid-week that he finally asked the question that had been on his mind since they started practicing together. "Why aren't you captain?"

It wasn't the first time Derek had been asked the question. When asked, he had always said that he didn't want to take on that responsibility and no one questioned his decision. Not seeing a point in lying to Scott, he decided to tell the real reason and see how it felt to share his actual reason for not trying for captain. "At the end of last season, the guys nominated me for captain. I turned it down. Josh wanted to spot more than anything, and if he didn't get it I knew that he would be impossible to lead. In fact, he would have probably destroyed the cohesiveness that we have spent so many years building. As much as it would have been nice to be captain, I knew it would be better for the team if Josh was."

Scott looked at Derek with a mixture of surprise and admiration. "So the guys wanted you to be their captain and you turned it down because Josh was going to be a big cry-baby about it?"

Derek was astounded by Scott's bluntness, but it made him feel better. Although he never allowed himself to dwell on his decision, there was a small part of him that resented Josh. "Pretty much. Yeah."

Scott shook his head. "You're something else."

"What do you mean?" Derek had come to terms with his decision a long time ago. Watching the different expressions cross Scott's face, he wondered if he should have just kept his mouth shut. The one thing that he knew would hurt him was if Scott was disappointed in him or saw him as weak.

Scott sat on the mat, facing Derek, and looked at him for a minute. "I have never met anyone who puts their own needs last as much as you do. I don't think I could have done what you did. I knew I wanted to be captain and I went for it. There were other guys who wanted it too, but I didn't think about what *they* wanted. I thought about what *I* wanted. And I got it too." Scott looked at Derek again, causing a wave of heat to pass through him.

"You're really amazing. You would have been a great captain."

Derek was stunned into silence, overcome with a mixture of relief that Scott approved of his choice and exhilaration at the intensity of his admiration. What shocked him was how bright and full he felt after hearing Scott's words. Just as quickly, old instincts kicked in and Derek pushed the feeling of pride away. Not wanting to be the center of attention or to be seen as conceited, Derek shifted the focus back to Scott. "Yeah, but your family moved you around so much, and from what you've told me, you have put their needs ahead of your own. You could have thrown a fit, but you didn't. I *know* I wouldn't have let my parents off the hook like that."

A thoughtful expression crossed Scott's face. "Why do you do that? Why can't you let me tell you how great you are without deflecting it back to me somehow?"

Derek thought about Scott's questions. The truth was, he wasn't really sure why he was treating the moment as if it were a casual exchange of compliments. He knew he would have made a better captain for the team and a small part of him thought about that every time he looked at Josh. Deep down Scott's comments validated every thought he had had about giving up being captain and there was nothing casual about what Scott had said or how his words had made him feel. So why *did* he downplay it? Why *couldn't* he allow Scott to compliment him? *Because I've always kept my guard up? Because I don't like to be the center of attention? That doesn't cut it where Scott is concerned. He's different.* Still, there was a part of him that couldn't let go of old habits. Not yet. Instead, he decided to meet Scott half way. "Well, I know I admire you. If you admire me too, then I guess you're right."

Scott scooted closer to Derek on the mat. "You know how I feel about you." His voice was soft, but there was no hint of humor when he spoke. "And one of these days

I'm gonna put my foot down and insist that you allow me to tell you how fucking unbelievable you are without turning it back around into something about me."

Derek didn't admit to Scott how it made him soar knowing how Scott felt. He wasn't ready for that yet. But he wanted to be. Looking at Scott, seeing the way he looked at Derek with unguarded adoration, wrapped him in warmth and security. Knowing that Scott wanted to spoil him, to make him happy, to make him feel good, was a tough idea to accept.

Examining the various thoughts rushing through his head, one emotion caught hold. Hope. More than anything, Derek hoped that he could get out of his own way and let Scott in completely, without any walls or protective barriers at all. But that wasn't going to be today. Wanting to lighten the moment, Derek leaned close to Scott, a mischievous grin on his face. "I can't wait to get you back to the attic."

Scott shook his head. "Don't think I can't see what you're doing. But I'll let you get away with it this time." Scott stood up and reached down to help Derek to his feet. The two headed out together and half an hour later they were racing each other up the attic stairs.

Pre-season practices began that Monday. Once the team was gathered in the wrestling room, Coach called for attention. "I wanted to gather the players who held varsity spots last year and any team members who wished to challenge for those spots this year before the regular season begins in a week. Although there can only be one person for each weight class, it takes all of us to push each other to be our best. Each week, we will hold challenges, so no one should assume that if they take a varsity weight class now they are guaranteed the spot for the whole season. If one of you can't make a meet for some reason or gets injured, our team will only be as good as our challengers. If we are going to take division this year…and we *can* take division this year…we have to remember that we are a team that works together and not against each other. Are we in agreement with that?"

The team shouted "Yes, Coach!" in unison.

"Good." Coach's stance relaxed significantly. "I can't tell you how proud I am of this team. Many of you have been together since ninth grade, building what has turned into a class-A competitive team. This is your year boys. Practice for the next three days will be grueling. Josh is going to work you guys hard. If you need to puke, use the trashcan in the hallway, but haul your butts back in here afterwards. Challenges will take place on Thursday and Friday. Thompson has made a schedule and it's posted on the bulletin board in the corner over there." With that, Coach turned practice over to Josh and got out his clipboard.

True to form, Josh worked the team hard, pushing them more intensely than the previous season. Each practice began with stretches, followed by sit-ups, pushups, and circuit training in the weight room. Josh had the team doing spins, sprawls, and sprinting in place every fifteen minutes. They reviewed basic moves for the first few days, and ended practices with scrimmage matches. The workouts were exhausting and Derek woke up each morning sorer than the day before.

On Thursday, the guys were buzzing with nervous energy. Each spot on the team, except for Power's, was being challenged. The only spot that had more than one challenger was the 167 weight class, so that was being spaced over two days. Derek had wanted to schedule Sean and Phil to face off on Thursday. That would have eliminated one of them and given Scott an energy advantage for the Friday challenge. When he presented the idea to Scott, he was met with firm resistance. "Derek, I know you want me to make the varsity team and are trying to be helpful, but I don't want to cut corners. You heard what Coach said the other day. We're gonna have to work harder than ever to take division. Let me wrestle both of them. If I lose, that will suck, but if I win, I'll have beaten both of them. Even if they are pissed, the team will have to admit I won fair and square."

That afternoon, the entire team and all of the challengers crowded around the wrestling mat. Three of the four lowest weight classes went to the guys who held the position the year before. There was one upset at the 127 weight class where Carl Horton, a tenth grade student, beat out Kevin Fields, a twelfth grade student who had held the spot for the past two years. Derek's challenge was over in the first period. He took Bobby Dean down in the first ten seconds and had him on his back after twenty. Bobby put up a good fight and escaped a near pin, but Derek took him down a second time and cemented Bobby's shoulders to the mat for the three-count, securing the 135 weight class.

Derek had scheduled for Scott to challenge Sean that day. When it was time for their match, a solemn silence fell over the room. Sean and Scott walked to the center of the mat and took neutral position. Coach told them to shake hands. The second coach blew his whistle. Sean dove for Scott's foot and grabbed his leg taking him down just as Derek had in their practice that first day. The guys on the team cheered.

"Two points, takedown," Coach called out. Derek held his breath. He could see that Scott was pissed that he had allowed Sean's speed to catch him off guard. Scott twisted his hips swinging them out in front of him so that he was sitting on his butt, breaking Sean's grip in one smooth movement, then quickly jumped to his feet.

"One point, escape," said Coach. On their feet again, they started circling each other and Derek prayed that Scott would remember to watch Sean's legs. If Scott kept getting taken down he would lose by technical default even if he didn't get pinned. Sean reached to get the inside grip on Scott's arm. Scott wound his arm to tussle for inside position but Derek noticed he was paying little attention to the arm movements. His eyes were locked on Sean's legs.

Scott waited for Sean to allow him to keep the inside grip, just as Derek had done during their practices. If he remembered correctly, Sean was probably going to try to pull him off balance and grab his leg. As predicted, Sean started forcing Scott to circle, slowly making him step further and further out, exposing his foot and making it an easy target for a quick grab. When Sean finally took a large step backwards, pulling on Scott's arm and expecting his foot to come forward for balance, Scott released Sean's arm, reached between their bodies and grabbed Sean's exposed foot instead. Lifting Sean's foot, Scott had the advantage. He then placed a leg behind the foot Sean still had on the ground and took him down to the mat, quickly gaining control of the referee's position.

"Two points, take down," Coach called out. "Score is three to two. Thayer in the lead." Once Scott had control of Sean on the mat, the match was over. Quickly maneuvered onto his back, Sean attempted to arch his way out of the pinning hold, but each time he arched onto his head, Scott was able to tighten his grip and further restrict Sean's movement. After a few more seconds, Sean was unable to move at all, his shoulders pinned squarely to the mat. Coach counted to three and slammed the mat.

"Pin. Match goes to Scott." An eruption of cheers filled the room as the members of the team patted Scott on the back. Derek was smiling, but held back, allowing Scott to have his moment.

On the drive home that evening, Derek gave Scott the accolades he had wanted to give him in the wrestling room. "I was worried there at first, especially when he started circling you around like I showed you he would. But you did awesome. And it only took you one period. You'll have plenty of energy for tomorrow's challenge."

Scott was beaming. "Yeah, when Sean got that first takedown I was so pissed at myself. I just went into my normal wrestling mode and forgot how you told me to watch his legs. But, when he started circling me, it occurred to me that if he was going to try to make me expose my leg, he would have to expose his leg as well. When he stepped back to pull me off balance, I decided to beat him at his own game. It felt awesome."

Derek was swimming in Scott's excitement. This couldn't get any better. I have this awesome guy as my boyfriend. He's into all the same things I am. And he can't shut up about wrestling.

After a moment Scott turned to Derek. "You know, I have you to thank for everything. You really are incredible. You're a great friend, a sexy boyfriend, and one hell of a foxy little wrestler. This is turning out to be an amazing year."

Derek felt the corners of his mouth pull up. I was wrong. It could get better, and it just did.

The next day's challenge match against Phil was over even faster than Sean's. The varsity team lineup was finalized and Scott had made the team.

Chapter 9

That night after Scott left, Derek stayed up in the attic listening to music and recording sounds onto his DAT recorder to upload to his mixing board. Choosing slow beats, melodic vocals, flutes, violins, French horns, and other instruments which played fluid, romantic sounds, he already knew that Scott was his inspiration and thought of surprising him with a mix created just for him.

He had just finished selecting the various sounds he was going to use in his mix, when his cell rang. Glancing at the caller ID, he saw that it was Beck. "Hey there, stranger. What's up?"

"Can you get together right now? I really need a shoulder to lean on." Her voice was trembling, on the verge of tears, which was highly uncharacteristic of Beck.

"Of course, sweetie. Are you ok? What happened?"

"I don't want to talk about it over the phone. How about Starbucks in ten minutes?"

"I'll be there in five." Hanging up, Derek switched off his equipment and went down to his room to grab his jacket. He stopped by the living room where his parents were watching TV. "I'm meeting Beck at Starbucks."

His mother was flipping through a magazine on the couch. "Okay, hon. Tell her we said hello." She glanced up to look at Derek. "And tell her she should come over for dinner sometime soon. It's been far too long since we've seen her."

"Sure thing, Mom." He scooted over to his mom and gave her a kiss on the cheek. "See you later Dad."

His father turned to him. "Have fun, son."

Derek arrived at Starbucks exactly five minutes later and saw Beck at a small table with two worn cushioned seats in a secluded corner. She sat in the seat facing the wall and was dabbing at her eyes with a napkin. "Beck!" Derek leaned over her shoulders from behind, squeezing her in a tight hug. She gestured to the open seat and a grandé coffee sitting on the table.

Picking it up and taking the seat, he studied Beck. Her eyes were puffy and red. She was sniffling and had one leg curled under her. The hand that she wasn't using to dab her eyes was tightly hugging her chest. Derek didn't think he had ever seen her in such a protective posture. Giving her a moment to pull herself together, he waited until he was sure she was ok. "What *happened*, Beck?"

"It's Bryce. We were rehearsing lines at my place. I thought we were getting really close. We've been laughing and joking and playfully tickling each other. During breaks, we would talk about our hopes of becoming stage actors in New York and discussing how we wanted our lives to turn out. It felt like we had so much in common. That we were connecting." She sniffled and blew her nose in her napkin. Crumpling it, she tossed it onto the table and began dabbing at her eyes with a new one.

"So, tonight I decided I would take a chance and see if maybe he felt the same way about me as I was beginning to feel about him. We were lying on my bed, staring at the ceiling and listening to the musical soundtrack to *Wicked*. He hasn't seen it yet, so I was telling him the story between each song. He was so interested and when the music was over he told me how much he respected my passion and knowledge for drama and music. It was really sweet. So I told him."

Derek was pretty sure that he was following the conversation, but didn't want to assume anything. "You told him what?"

She whipped the napkin to her lap and stared at him

with annoyance. "I told him that I really liked him and was wondering if he might want to go on a date with me."

"Peace, Beck." He put up two fingers in the peace gesture while instinctively hunching protectively into his seat. "I figured as much, but I didn't want to make any wrong guesses here."

"Oh, don't mind me. It's not your fault that I'm a hopeless, silly girl who believes that any of the boys at our school would be even remotely interested in me." She sniffled and tears started rolling down her cheeks once again.

"Beck, don't say that. You are the most amazing girl I know. Any of the guys at school would be lucky to be with you."

She sighed and turned a softer gaze on Derek. "You're really sweet to say that, but you have to, you're my best friend."

"I don't *have* to say it. I'm saying it because I know it's *true*. So, what happened when you…what…asked him on a date? Did he reject you? Was he nice about it?"

"Worse. He told me that I was beautiful and funny and talented and that he would normally be thrilled to go out with me." Now Derek was becoming confused. "But…" She blew her nose again as a fresh wave of tears streamed out of her eyes and her shoulders started shaking. "But, he said that he's gay. It's my worst nightmare come true."

"Uh…ouch!" Derek knew that she didn't mean to insult him, but the comment stung anyway.

Realizing what she had just said, she looked at Derek with wide eyes full of contrition. "No, I didn't mean that being gay is the worst thing in the world. It's just when I like a guy and he turns out to be gay. That's—."

"I get it Beck. No worries. So, what did you do?"

Beck's cheeks flushed. "Well, you know me, and you know how I am always trying to be discreet..." Derek cocked an eyebrow and tilted his head. "Oh shut up! Fine. I flipped. I told him to get out of my house and to never talk to me again. But now I feel horrible because the musical is in two weeks and we are going to have to spend so much time together."

"Well, it is a musical and you guys are supposed to be acting, right?" Derek could immediately tell that his attempt at humor was seriously misguided as her sadness transformed to shock in a matter of seconds. "Sorry, I was just trying to lighten the mood. So what's really bothering you? Is it that you don't want to have anything to do with him or that you feel bad about how you reacted?"

"Oh, Derek. I just feel awful. I wish I could take it back and redo the whole scene." Beck paused, mouthed the words she had just said, and then smiled timidly. "Whoops. That kind of makes me sound a little shallow doesn't it?"

Derek shook his head. Beck was returning to her old self. "And what would you do differently if you could?"

"I'd tell him that I understood and that I was horribly embarrassed and hoped he could forget I ever said anything." A new round of tears began to roll down Beck's cheeks.

"So do that." Beck stopped sniffling and slowly lifted her head to face Derek. "Do it. Call him and tell him that you over-reacted and that you didn't mean what you said, and that you are a silly, silly diva who needs to be spanked." This time Derek's effort at humor was met with a better response.

Beck giggled once, and then said, "Shut up, Derek. You are *so* not funny." Then she laughed again. "I guess I am a bit of a diva aren't I?"

Derek smiled, got up, and sat in her lap. Taking her cheeks in both hands he planted a big kiss on her lips. "You're *my* diva and I love you. Want that spanking now?" Beck shoved him playfully, laughing even harder. "Seriously. Call him. Right now with me sitting here. I want to hear how it goes."

Beck looked doubtful. "You really think I should call him. Right now?"

"Definitely!"

Beck dug in her purse and pulled out her cell phone. "If he hangs up on me I will never forgive you ever. If he is angry with me and makes me feel even worse I will take your nuts and—."

Derek made a talking motion with his hand. "Beck, less threatening, more calling."

She stuck out her tongue and dialed the number. "Hi. Bryce, it's me. No, I'm not mad at you…what?…why are you sorry?…But I was calling to tell you that *I'm* sorry…I know, but you were just telling me the tru…Will you stop interrupting me? I'm calling to tell you that I was a total bit…Bryce O'Neill! If I say that I am a bitch, then *I am* a bitch and you will not tell me differently. Do you understand?" Derek dropped his head into his hands and rocked it gently. *This is her idea of an apology?* "Of course I still love you…tomorrow night? Yes, definitely. Ok hon, g'night." She snapped her phone shut and shoved it back into her purse. "Seriously, the boy doesn't know how to accept an apology. He kept trying to blame himself and wouldn't let me get a word in edgewise."

Derek lifted his head out of his hands. "So, you guys made nice-nice and everything is all better?"

Beck pursed her lips. "Don't get all smart ass on me, Derek Thompson. It's not like you are Mr. Sensible all the time."

"Very true. So, shall I buy us another round?"

Beck nodded. As he passed her chair she grabbed his hand. "Thanks for being there. It's nice to know that I can still count on my favorite best friend."

Derek woke up to the sound of his cell phone ringing the next morning. Reaching over to his desk without opening his eyes, he fumbled for his phone, spilling a pile of papers and a book onto the floor in the process. "H'lo". His voice was groggy and thick with sleep.

"I woke you. Shit." Scott sounded mortified. "Go back to sleep and call me when you get up."

"No, I'm up, I'm up. What's up?" Derek rolled over and leaned on his elbow, rubbing his eyes with his free hand. It was 10:28.

"Nothing, I just wanted to get together with you." Despite the fact that Derek had only been awake for about thirty seconds, he couldn't suppress the smile that spread across his face. Scott had such an innocent way of saying things with sincere honesty that it was impossible not to feel all warm and fuzzy.

Derek stretched while still managing to keep the phone by his ear. "Yeah. What are you in the mood for?"

"I hadn't really thought about it. You have any ideas?"

"Um, yeah. Maybe we could go into Boston and walk around. I have been meaning to go to Best Buy to check out new mixing boards." Remembering his evening with Beck, he thought it might be a good idea to include her in their plans if Scott didn't mind. "Would you mind if we included Beck with us today? She kind of had a rough night last night."

"Really? What happened? Is she ok?"

"Well, it appears that her musical love interest would be more interested in Beck if she was a chick with a dick." Derek heard a smack through the earpiece of his phone.

"You there?"

When Scott's voice returned, it was thunderous laughter that came through the line. "Yeah." More laughing. "M'here. Sorry. I dropped the phone." It took Scott a minute before he could continue speaking as he attempted to catch his breath. "You have got to be kidding me. Bryce, the only guy that Beck spends time with nowadays, is gay? That is priceless!"

Derek wasn't sure if he appreciated Scott's lack of concern, but he began to laugh with him anyways. *I guess it is kind of funny. As long as I never, ever let Beck know I think so, I should be fine.* "Ok, enough Scott. She was upset. Should I invite her to join us?"

"Yeah, definitely. I love hanging out with Beck."

His irritation was short lived, replaced by affection as Scott so easily and quickly included Beck in their plans. A sudden thought crossed his mind and he became momentarily concerned. "You *will* be nice won't you? I mean, you won't make her feel stupid or bad or anything like that? Sometimes, when the two of you get together you both—."

"Oh, come on. Give me a little more credit than that." Scott sounded insulted. Derek held his breath waiting for Scott to continue. "I love my balls way too much to piss her off." Derek started breathing again.

"Ok, I'll give her a call and then let you know the plan." Hanging up, Derek called Beck who was thrilled about the idea of a trip to Boston. They agreed to meet in Harvard Square at noon so they could take the Red Line into the city.

The train was packed, so Derek and Beck sat next to each other and Scott stood holding one of the railings above the seats to keep stable. Getting off at Kendall Square and walking to Newbury Street, they window shopped for about an hour stopping at clothes stores for Beck, a sports gear store for Scott, and a fragrance store that sold reed diffusers and scented soap for Derek. Finally, they made their way to Copley Place Plaza where Derek could check out mixing boards at Best Buy. The mall was packed, but Best Buy was fairly clear of shoppers in the music equipment section. Derek started looking at the various boards while Beck and Scott followed, paying little attention to what Derek was doing.

"So," Beck said, "I assume Derek has told you about last night's fiasco."

Scott flushed and turned to Derek, not knowing how to respond. Derek looked up, feeling heat rush to his cheeks. Glancing at Scott he shrugged, unsure of what Scott should say or do.

"Oh, relax. Both of you. I'm not stupid." She turned so that she was facing Scott. "I know that whatever I tell Derek and whatever Derek tells me, you will know about it. Just so long as we keep things between the three of us, I have no problem with it. Agreed?" Scott and Derek dutifully nodded their heads in assent. Derek was pretty sure he saw Scott's hands begin to move protectively towards his crotch. "Good, so after Derek dropped me off from Starbucks, Bryce called me and we had this long talk…"

Derek tuned out their conversation and began looking at the mixing boards in earnest. He wasn't sure exactly what he was looking for, but he knew that his current mixing board, with eight tracks, was becoming too limited for him. He wanted something with more memory, more tracks, and a dual stereo system so he could blend one song into another without having to stop the music. It would take more upfront time to mix songs before parties, but the result would be awesome.

He checked out several models and finally decided that the TASCAM M-164FX 16 Channel Mixing Board with Digital Effects came closest to what he was looking for. It was reasonably priced at $350 before taxes and warrantee, but more than he was willing to spend at the moment. He'd have to think it through before buying it.

It caught him off guard when Scott leaned against him, wrapping his arms around Derek's waist and resting his chin on Derek's shoulder. "Find something you like?"

"I think so. This model here would give me the capability I want and I could still use all of the equipment I already have. I would probably have to talk to the owner of the record store where I buy my sound albums to see if he knows the model and could give me some pointers on how to use it. It's a lot more sophisticated than what I use right now. But the songs I could mix would be amazing."

Scott gave Derek a quick peck on the cheek and pressed his crotch against Derek's ass. "I get so hot when you talk all technical and shit."

Derek felt Scott's hardness against him, but what excited him more than the evidence of Scott's arousal, was the feeling of being held by him in public. It hadn't even occurred to him to worry about it as he snuggled back into Scott's embrace. Somehow, it just felt right and he didn't care if anyone was watching.

"Ah-hem. Should I leave you two alone?" Beck tickled Derek's side, causing him to squirm. The movement caused his ass to rub against Scott's crotch.

"Mmm…" Scott moaned into his ear. He gave Derek a quick peck on the cheek, took a nip at his earlobe, evoking a high-pitched squeal from him, then released him and stepped back.

Beck, who had been observing, turned to look at Scott with affection. "I know I should be jealous of you two, but you have got to be the sweetest, cutest couple Brampton has ever seen." Swooping between Scott and Derek, she hooked both of their arms and started leading them towards the door.

Scott stopped them. "You guys mind if we hang out here for a bit longer?"

Beck looked at Scott with a puzzled look in her eyes. "Why?"

Scott sidled up to the shelving unit so that it was blocking him from the waist down, then reached into the front of his pants.

Beck's mouth opened in horror. "What the fuck are you doing?"

Scott's face flushed, but Derek came to his rescue before he had to respond. "Remember how I explained about how guys sometimes have to adjust themselves?"

Beck's expression shifted from thoughtful, to understanding, to shock. "You mean—."

Derek smiled. "Yup."

Beck turned to Scott. "You little horn-dog." She walked over to him and swatted him on the nose playfully. "Bad, Scott. Bad!"

Scott started panting and chased Beck up and down the aisle as if she were a bone. Every few seconds he would bark like a dog.

As the two of them tussled with each other, laughing, Derek turned back to the mixing board he had been looking at. He snatched a spec sheet for it and tucked it into his coat pocket.

After a few more minutes of tickling and grabbing, Beck released Scott. "You boys need to take me to lunch now. Let's see. I think I'm feeling like Legal Seafood."

Derek loved seafood, but couldn't resist the opportunity to use his favorite line. "Beck, how many times have I told you? If I wanted to eat fish, I'd be straight."

Scott choked and started coughing. Beck punched Derek's arm as hard as she could. Derek had to admit that it actually hurt. "You are the crudest, most disgusting person I have ever met...It's one of the reasons I *adore* you!" With that, they headed for the restaurant.

Chapter 10

Over the next couple of weeks Derek and Scott became more and more focused on wrestling. Practices had been going smoothly, and the team was able to recover from Josh's warm-up routines much faster, which left them more time and energy to spend on learning new moves and scrimmaging. Their first meet was scheduled for the following Tuesday against Allistaire High in Lexington. Allistaire was one of the two schools they were worried about as serious contenders for the division.

Coach gathered the team in a semi-circle on the mat. "Today, we are going to learn a new move. It's a tough one and takes a lot of guts. Sean said he learned it this summer and thought it might give us an edge against Lexington next week. Let me start by saying that I do *not* want anyone using this move unless they feel extremely comfortable with it. It's called a suplex and you could end up sprawled on your back with your opponent on top of you if you don't execute it correctly. Sean, would you like to come and show the move?"

Sean got up and walked to the center of the mat. "Ok, while you will be doing this move with someone your own weight, I think it would be best if I taught it using someone from a lower weight class so we can focus on the mechanics of the move. It's harder to execute if you have to worry about hauling weight as well as maneuvering your body correctly. I'm going to be flipping someone over my body by arching backwards and we'll both be in the air for a moment, just as a forewarning. Would anyone like to volunteer to assist me?"

Derek jumped up. "Definitely. I mean if you injure me I'll…uh…probably not be able to do much about it. But learning it firsthand will help me to get the mechanics of the move down."

"All right." Sean moved to the center of the mat, motioning for Derek to join him. He spoke to the group while positioning Derek for the demonstration. "This is a move that happens from the standing position. You won't be able to do it unless you toggle for just the right arm position, so it's not something that you can do right off the whistle. What you want to do is to get outside arm control on both of your opponents arms. They won't be expecting it since most moves are executed from inside arm position. However, you need to be careful, because taking the outside arm position leaves you vulnerable until you make your move."

Sean started circling with Derek and tussled for arm position. "The best thing to do is to focus on one arm, and only grab your opponent's other arm when you're ready. Keeping your second arm free will allow you to fend off any offensive moves from your opponent and will keep them thinking that you are preparing to execute something more standard. Derek, just wrestle like you normally would, but don't go for the takedown." Derek complied and continued circling with Sean, allowing him to maintain outside arm control of his right arm. Suddenly, faster than Derek could register, Sean shot his free arm around the outside of Derek's left arm and squeezed, clamping both of Derek's arms in a tight grip. He then bent his knees, shoved his hips forward and up, arching backwards.

He could feel his body being lifted off the mat as Sean continued arching backwards. Then Sean twisted his body to the side, pulling roughly on Derek's arm for leverage. The motion caused Derek to glide through the air so that his back was facing the mat, while Sean used his body weight and motion so that he would land on top of him, chest to chest, on the mat. Once they landed, Sean hooked both of Derek's legs with his own, tightened his grip on Derek's arms, and arched his back. Derek was unable to move and his shoulders were pinned securely to the mat.

Sean let Derek up and was rewarded with a round of applause and murmurs of approval. "Remember, you could end up landing flat on your ass…er, I mean butt… sorry Coach…if you don't do this right. If you don't get your opponent completely off the ground and if you don't rotate your body mid-air, you will end up on your back with your opponent on top of you."

Sean showed the mechanics of the move a few more times, stopping frequently to explain each hold and giving particular attention to the moment when he used Derek's body weight mid-air to begin the turn so that they would both land properly. When the team began attempting the move, most of the guys, including Derek, ended up on their backs each time they tried to throw their partner. A few guys successfully executed it towards the end of practice. As the team headed to the locker room, Sean received numerous claps on the back.

The team continued practicing the suplex for the next few days, and a few of the guys had gotten pretty good at it. At the end of practice, on the day of the school musical, Scott asked Derek to hang back so they could practice a little longer. He had been having difficulty with the suplex and had been bitching about it non-stop since Sean had demonstrated it a few days earlier. Derek wasn't sure whether it was pride at wanting to learn and perfect the move or competitive jealousy that Sean could do something that he couldn't that was causing him to become so salty. Either way, if helping Scott would put him back in a better mood, Derek was more than willing to be a throw doll for a while.

"I don't get it. I'm doing exactly what Sean did, but I can't get my partner onto his back. I don't know which part I'm screwing up." Derek shrugged and said nothing.

He had practiced with Scott enough to know that Scott was working this out for himself by talking out loud and wasn't expecting an actual answer or comment. They began circling each other. Scott secured Derek's arms, bent his knees, and arched, shoving his hips forward and up. Derek felt himself lift off the ground as he had with Sean. His legs swung up, but once in mid-air, he did not feel the twisting motion of being turned towards his back that he had felt with Sean. He landed on Scott's chest. "DAMN! What am I missing?"

Although grumpiness was not one of Scott's more appealing traits, Derek always admired his dedication and commitment. "Can I make an observation?" Derek cringed internally, hoping that his intrusion on Scott's focus wouldn't make him even more upset.

Shaking his head, Scott let out a heavy sigh. "You may as well. I'm not improving at all."

Good. He's willing to accept my help. "When Sean did the move, it felt exactly the same as when you just did it, except for when I was in the air." Scott just listened, placing his hands on his knees and pacing his breathing. Sweat was dripping down the sides of his face and his arms were coated in a damp sheen. Derek had to clear his mind before he continued speaking. His thoughts were definitely not focused on wrestling with Scott looking like that. "What I felt when Sean had me in the air, just at the moment when my feet began to swing up in the air, was a tug on my arm, almost like he was pulling me sideways as well as backwards. Whenever I watched the move in the Olympics, it always looked like the wrestlers were arching completely backwards, but it's not like that. It's more like you begin with the arch and then turn sideways the rest of the way." Scott looked up and bit his lower lip. Once again, Derek lost momentary focus as the image of Scott's plump lower lip pressed against his filled his mind. Scott stood and walked to the middle of the mat. Shaking his head, Derek followed and took neutral position.

Scott began circling Derek, playing for arm control. Once securing his right arm Scott simultaneously bent his knees and hooked Derek's left arm tightly. Shoving forward and up with his hips, Scott arched backwards. Derek felt himself being lifted off the ground. Once his feet began to swing up, he felt a sharp tug on his arm and his body began to twist towards the mat. For a split second, both he and Scott were airborne, and then Derek was on his back, Scott landing on top of him so they were chest to chest.

There was a brief pause as Scott's mind registered that he had successfully executed the suplex. When he looked at Derek his eyes were sparkling and his dimple was pronounced in the center of his cheek. "I did it. You were right. As soon as I pulled your arm, it was like something clicked. Your body weight did all the work and all I had to do was follow through with the motion of the throw. Thank you, Derek!"

Before Derek could answer, Scott leaned down and locked their lips together. Scott's arms still held control of Derek's, so Derek was prone and unable to do anything but receive the kiss. Responding to Scott's excitement, Derek opened his mouth and their tongues intertwined, massaging each other. Derek treated himself to Scott's lower lip, nibbling on it gently. Having his arms pinned to his sides and Scott controlling his body, Derek felt himself become aroused and wiggled his hips to create some friction. Scott's own excitement became immediately obvious. After a few minutes of kissing and writhing, Scott loosened his grip on Derek and sat up. "Thank you, Derek. That was awesome."

Unsure whether he was referring to the suplex or to the kissing, Derek turned to gaze into Scott's eyes and smiled. "I'm here to please."

It was while they were sitting in the middle of the mat that Josh entered the wrestling room. "Hey, what are you guys still doin' up here? Aren't you gonna grab dinner with the team before the show tonight?"

Derek became acutely aware that his cock was stretching at his shorts. Relieved that he was sitting with his back to the door, Derek turned his head. "We were just practicing a little. Scott wanted to get the suplex down right. We'll catch up with you guys in a few. You're headed to the Square for pizza, right?"

"Yeah. See you guys there."

As Josh left the room, Derek let out a deep breath. Scott turned to him and grinned. "That was close." He leaned over, gave Derek a sweet peck on the cheek, and hopped up. "Let's do two minutes of spins each to make ourselves a bit less obvious before we head out."

The auditorium was filling up quickly by the time Derek, Scott and the rest of the wrestling team showed up for the musical. Derek handed two tickets to the ninth grader collecting them at the door and headed with Scott towards the back row. There were two seats in the back corner which were unoccupied and Derek claimed them, removing his jacket and draping it over the back of his seat. The rest of the guys took random seats throughout the auditorium, so Derek had Scott all to himself.

Looking through the makeshift playbill that one of the cast members had designed, Derek began to read the cast profiles to Scott. "Let's read Beck's. She loves writing these." *Appearing in her fourth musical at Brampton, Ms. Rebecca Stoltz is thrilled to be playing the part of Tracy Turnblad in this year's production of Hairspray. A fierce and fiery girl, Tracy gives new meaning to the poignant phrase 'I like big butts!'*

Scott snapped his head towards Derek and grabbed

the playbill. Reading Beck's profile he laughed and gave Derek a shove. "It doesn't say that. I actually believed you though. It's definitely something she would write. Let me read it." Scott began reading out loud. "*Appearing in her fourth musical at Brampton, Ms. Rebecca Stoltz is thrilled to portray the leading role of Tracy Turnblad, a revolutionary high school girl who proves that beauty comes from within. Beck hopes that her performance will inspire the audience to cast aside their fears and doubts and to grab life by the balls.*"

Derek ripped the playbill from Scott's hands, scanning the profile. "It says *cast aside their fears and doubts and go for their dreams.*" Scott shrugged, smiling his crooked grin, and looked at Derek with a sinister twinkle in his eyes. They continued reading profiles until the lights went down and the orchestra began playing the introductory medley.

The shadowy darkness of the audience gave Derek and Scott a great deal of privacy, as music, the colorful set, and elaborate fifties era costumes filled the auditorium. Leaning back, Derek stretched his legs and then crossed one over the other, resting his hands in the space the position created between his legs. The opening medley was a preview of the main songs of the musical and Derek found himself thinking how similar medleys were to the mixing he loved to do.

His reflection was cut short as he felt something brush against his hand. Looking down, he caught his breath as Scott took his hand and intertwined their fingers. Scott's eyes were peering directly into his as he gave Derek's hand a short squeeze and then turned to the stage just as Beck entered. Derek squeezed Scott's hand in return. Sitting in the back row and cast in darkness, their hand-holding was furtive. The excitement was electrifying even if he and Scott were the only two who knew.

Derek had to admit the musical was the best one the school had produced yet. As the cast came out to give their bows, the audience cheered and applauded. When Beck came out, the cheering rose to a roar of hoots and hollers and the entire audience stood to show their adoration. Derek glanced at the cast. Bryce had a huge grin on his face as the whole cast took a bow together. He then pushed Beck out from the lineup of actors and the audience began a new round of rapturous acclaim. Derek saw that Malinda had a momentary look of disgust on her face which she quickly replaced with a beaming grin. *Well, I'll give her credit. She may hate Beck, but she can sure act like she's pleased as punch about Beck's adoring fans.*

As the auditorium cleared out, Derek and Scott hung back to wait for Beck so they could go to the cast party together. Although most cast parties only included the cast and crew, Brampton prided itself on taking advantage of any opportunity to party. As a result, the bulk of the senior class would be present. It was going to be at George Davis' house since his parents were leaving for a weekend trip directly from the opening night of the musical.

About ten minutes later, Beck came into the auditorium, face cleared of stage makeup and wearing black jeans and a bulky sweater. She was beaming. Derek ran over to her and caught her in a bear hug. "You were fantastic!"

Scott concurred and gave her a peck on the cheek. Reaching into his pocket he pulled out a small gift-wrapped box. "I got you something. S'nothing much, but…"

Beck grabbed the gift from Scott's hands and tore the paper off. Opening the box, she pulled out a plastic keychain in the shape of a star with the name *REBECCA* written on it in bold black letters. "Scott, if that isn't the sweetest thing. Thank you, come give mama a kiss."

Scott blushed. "I wanted to get one that said *BECK* but they didn't have any." He allowed himself to be crushed by Beck's embrace and she gave him a friendly smooch right on the lips. Scott shuffled his feet.

"Oh my God, look at him Derek, he's embarrassed. That is too cute." Beck flashed an elated grin at Scott and hugged him again. "Thank you, Scott. I love it." Derek had no idea that Scott had bought Beck a present. The fact that he had didn't come as a surprise and Derek had to fight the urge to push Beck aside so he could take her place hugging him.

The three of them left the school and headed to George's house. Once there, they had to circle around a couple of times looking for a space. Finally they gave up and drove a couple of blocks down Mt. Auburn Street before they found a place to park. Bundled in winter coats, they headed to the party arm-in-arm. They could hear the music three houses before they reached George's house, and when they opened the front door, Derek could feel the bass from the stereo rumbling through his chest. Making their way up the stairs, they were directed to put their jackets in George's parents' bedroom.

The guys on the wrestling team were already there and were congregated to one side of the living room. Derek and Scott made their way toward the group as Beck excused herself to join Bryce and a few of the other cast members in the kitchen. The guys were talking about the upcoming meet with Lexington.

"So, I found out that the team is going to be really strong after all, even though they lost three players—" Josh interrupted his own speech when he saw Derek and Scott. "Hey guys. C'mon over. You'll want to hear about this." They joined the group as Josh continued. "So their three new members are at the 135, 167, and 179 weight classes." He turned his head towards Derek and Scott giving them a meaningful look. "That's you guys and me. Kinda sucks that they're our first meet because it would have been nice to go and watch them before having to wrestle them." The other team members began mulling over how they had performed against the Lexington wrestlers the previous year. Scott, being new and not knowing any of the Lexington team, was very interested.

Derek, not really wanting to talk about wrestling this evening, elbowed Scott. "I think I'll head to the kitchen and hang with Beck for a while. I'm kinda done with the whole wrestling talk for now." Scott smiled and nodded before turning back to the team.

Derek left them and headed to the kitchen. Looking around, he couldn't find Beck anywhere. He walked out onto the porch off the kitchen, where a number of students were hanging out, and she wasn't there either. Turning to head back into the house, he bumped into Bryce, knocking him off balance. "Whoops, sorry, didn't see you there."

Bryce placed his hand on the wall to balance himself. "No problem."

"The play was awesome. It's definitely the best one yet."

Bryce smiled. "It was fun. I have to give the credit to Beck for helping me pull off this role though. I never would have been able to do it without her." Bryce shivered and started to rub his arms. "It's kind of cold out here. Want to head back inside?" Derek followed Bryce back into the house and into the living room where the bulk of students were located. The heat from their dancing bodies made the room comfortably warm.

Derek looked over to where Scott and the rest of the team were standing and saw that they were still engrossed in conversation. Scott turned, catching Derek's eye for an extended second, then smiled and turned back to the conversation he was having. "So you and Beck spent a lot of time together rehearsing. She said that you are about as serious about acting as she is."

Bryce rolled his eyes. "I think so, but there's an intensity about Beck that I don't think anyone could rival. Don't get me wrong. I worship her. She is amazing. But she kind of scares me sometimes too. Do you know that she made me watch both versions of the *Hairspray* movie? The John Waters version with Ricki Lake and the one that just came out with Nikki Blonsky."

Derek laughed, "I'm surprised she didn't make you go to New York with her to watch the Broadway musical as well."

"Oh, she tried. She even said that if I didn't go, and then fucked up, she would take my nuts, put them in a blender, and feed them back to me in a cup." Bryce shuddered remembering the threat.

Derek laughed and patted Bryce on the shoulder. "You should feel complimented. You aren't a true friend of Beck's unless she's threatened some horrific violence against your balls." Derek looked around the living room. "Speaking of Beck, have you seen her?"

Bryce looked as if he had been caught with his hand in the cookie jar. "She told me not to tell you."

Derek looked at Bryce with a combination of confusion and irritation. "Bryce. Where's Beck?"

"She said that she'd—."

"BRYCE! Where's Beck."

"She ran outside to get sick." Derek took a menacing step towards him and Bryce backed away instinctively.

"How did she get sick already? We just got here."

Bryce lowered his head. "A few of us made her do some shots of vodka and maybe a few other liquors."

"You didn't. Bryce. Didn't you know that—"

"That she can't do shots. No. I had no idea."

"How many shots did she do?"

Bryce started scratching his head as he reviewed the shots. "I made her do a vodka shot. George made her do one of gin. Then Malinda made her do one of peppermint schnapps. That's when she grabbed her mouth and ran outside."

"Jesus Bryce. Were you guys trying to kill her? Did she do them all in a row?"

"Yeah. But she should have told us if she couldn't handle it."

Derek shook his head. "We're talking about Beck. Do you really think she would ever admit to any flaw or weakness? You could have offered her liquefied shit and she would have drunk it just to prove a point."

Bryce trembled at the thought. "You're her best friend, right?"

"Yeah. But what has that got to do with anything?"

Bryce shuffled his feet. "It's just that Beck is the only other person who makes statements that are that disgusting without a second thought." When he looked up to face Derek, he had a slight smile on his face and his head was tilted to the side. His eyes were peering directly at him.

A wave of annoyance passed over Derek. Beck was getting sick and, no matter how proud she was, she needed someone with her. "Look, if Beck is getting sick, we need to help her out. Where is she?"

Bryce's entire posture shifted instantly in response to Derek's clipped tone. "I have no idea. I saw her run out the back door."

Derek shook his head. "Come on. Grab some water and a paper towel. We're going to make sure she's ok." Bryce did as instructed and the two of them headed into the back yard.

"I saw her head off in the direction of the cars."

Derek headed towards the cars. Near the end of the driveway, Derek heard what he had been listening for. Beck was retching just a few feet away. "Beck. Beck! Where are you?"

"Go away. I don't want anyone to see me like this." Beck's voice was raspy and hoarse.

Derek worked his way around the car where Beck's voice came from and saw her curled up on the ground next to a tire wheel. "Beck. Why on earth would you come out here alone to get sick? You could have always told someone to get me."

Beck turned her face up to look at Derek. "I don't want anyone to see me like th—" Her words were cut off by another round of heaving as she threw up bile into the snow. Bryce stood in his spot, frozen and not knowing what to do.

Derek stomped up to Bryce. "Don't just stand there. Give me the water and the napkin." He ripped the napkin from Bryce and gently wiped Beck's mouth with a corner of it. Tearing off the dirtied part, he wet the rest of the napkin with some water and pressed it to the back of her neck. "Here, this should help to make you feel a little bit better. Take the bottle of water and take tiny sips. Tiny sips always make me feel better when I'm sick."

Beck crawled to her hands and knees, then lowered her bottom so it was resting on her heels. "Thanks. That does make me feel a bit better." She took the water bottle and obeyed Derek's instructions, taking tiny sips. After a few minutes, she was able to lift herself up to a kneeling position. "I am *so* never drinking vodka again, ever."

Derek laughed. "Why were you drinking vodka in the first place? I thought you were a wino, not an alchie."

She lifted her head and peered at Derek with menacing eyes. "I will drink whatever I damn well please at my own cast party. Who in the hell do you think you a—"

She doubled over once again and began to vomit some more.

Derek laughed, unable to help himself. He knew that Beck was miserable and sick, but the fact that she had been chastising him and was repaid with another round of nausea seemed like good karma. "Maybe you should spend less time using your mouth to yell at me and more time using it to sip the water I gave you."

She glared at him, but continued sipping the water. After about ten minutes, she seemed to be over the worst of it and Derek helped her to her feet. Bryce had remained still and useless the whole time. "Get over here. Help me with her." Bryce seemed to remember how to function and walked over to Beck's other side, helping her to her feet. Slowly they made their way back to the party.

Once they got to the back yard, they hung back for few minutes until Beck was sure she was feeling good enough to go back inside. "I swear to God. If either of you tell anyone that I got sick I will take your balls, tie them together, and push one of you off a cliff, forcing the other one to have to make a choice to fall as well or to allow your balls to get ripped off in order to save yourself."

Derek looked at Bryce. "She seems to be feeling much better now. I think it's safe to bring her back inside to the party." Bryce had a horror-struck look on his face, but helped Derek walk Beck up the stairs.

Once they were safely inside the house, Beck excused herself to go to the bathroom. Bryce leaned against the wall. "I feel like I have just been to war."

Derek looked at him like he was a leper. He had no tolerance for people who completely froze under pressure. Sighing, he thought of the best way to get away from him so he could go find Scott. He had spent the past thirty minutes nursing Beck and, to some extent, nursing Bryce as well. Now, he wanted to be around someone who he could actually respect. Even though he had only been gone for a half hour, he had his fill of Bryce and wanted to find Scott. With very little enthusiasm, he mustered a polite exit line. "Like I said before. You aren't a true friend of Beck's until she's threatened some form of violence against your nuts. I should probably go and check on her."

Bryce smiled, but it was timid and his hands lowered to protectively cover himself. "So you and Beck have been friends for a long time haven't you?"

Shit. The last thing Derek wanted was to continue a conversation with Bryce. "Yeah. Since we were kids. You already asked me that. Remember?"

Bryce ignored Derek's comment. "I guess she probably told you about me being…you know."

Derek looked at Bryce, not sure what he was referring to. Then Derek remembered and the memory hit him hard. "Uh, yeah. She called me that night that you told her."

Bryce stepped a little closer to Derek, leaving only a few inches between them. "You know, I've never seen *you* with anyone." He reached out and placed his hand on Derek's arm. "I've wondered whether…" The words trailed off as Bryce leveled his gaze directly at Derek with unmistakable attraction.

All of Derek's instincts went into overdrive and told him to move slowly, speak calmly. He didn't want to make any sudden movements, but the rage flowing through his veins made that a difficult task to achieve. Behind gritted teeth, Derek managed to speak in a voice that was barely above a whisper. "Bryce. I'm only going to say this once, so listen carefully. Get your fuckin' hand off of me right now. Even if I were interested in this conversation, this is *so* not the place to be having it."

Bryce didn't remove his hand. Derek had to hold his

breath and count to three to calm the fury that intensified inside of him. "But I thought, I mean I hoped, that maybe we could—."

"You thought wrong. Now let go of me or else…" A sudden movement caught Derek's attention and he looked to the entrance of the kitchen. His eyes locked with Scott's. He was standing at the door and had a hurt look on his face. Turning on his heels, Scott walked out of the room.

"Shit!" Derek yanked his arm away from Bryce and rushed out of the kitchen, trying to catch up to Scott who had stormed up the stairs to the bedroom where the coats were. "Wait. What are you doing?"

Scott started searching for his coat. "I'm going home." Derek put his hand on Scott's arm and tried to turn him so they could face each other. Scott jerked his arm out of Derek's grip.

"What's wrong?" Derek knew that he had seen Bryce's hand on his arm in the kitchen, but he found it hard to believe that Scott could actually think that anything was going on between them.

"Nothing's wrong. Why don't you just go back downstairs and hang out with your new boyfriend?"

Scott's tone was sarcastic, but Derek could hear a quivering in his voice underneath the stoic front. Stunned, he opened his mouth and then closed it again. It took him a moment to compose himself before he could speak. "My, what?"

Scott turned on Derek with a vicious look in his eyes. "Bryce, your new boyfriend. I have been looking for you for the past half hour. I couldn't find you anywhere. Next thing I know I see the two of you hanging off of each other like two little…" The quivering became more pronounced and Scott turned away from Derek, continuing his search for his jacket.

Derek was distinctly aware of two warring emotions playing inside his head. On the one side, he was panicking. He didn't want Scott to be upset with him and he was afraid that Scott might pull away from him or worse, break up with him, over a simple misunderstanding. On the other hand, he felt a warm tingle creep up his spine and fill his chest. *Scott is jealous of Bryce. Ridiculous, but sweet nonetheless.* "Scott, I was looking for Beck and Bryce brought me to her."

"And that took you thirty fucking minutes?"

Derek shook his head. He didn't want Scott to be this upset over nothing. "Beck was getting...she made me promise not to tell anyone, but you need to know. Just keep in mind, when I tell you, if you mention it to her I may still be your boyfriend, but I won't have any balls." Scott's glare didn't soften. There was no hint of a smile. Derek sighed, realizing that humor would get him nowhere until Scott calmed down. "Beck was getting sick and I was helping her. Bryce was with me because he had to show me where Beck was."

Scott didn't look at him, but he had stopped looking for his coat. "Let's say I believe that Beck got sick. Then what was going on between you and Bryce in the kitchen?"

Derek had wanted to avoid going into details. Scott was an understanding person, but not as cautious as Derek. If the roles had been reversed, Derek was pretty sure that even if he was upset, he would have waited before making any kind of a scene. Once he let Scott know that Bryce had come onto him, he wasn't sure how Scott would react and he didn't want to be the center of a gay teenage drama with the whole senior class watching. Still, Scott needed to know. If he and Scott were a couple, then there was no room for secrets. Not when a question was asked directly like Scott had just done. "Look. Please. Promise me you won't go bananas when I tell you."

Scott stiffened and turned to face Derek. "Just tell me already. Whatever you have to say can't be worse than what went through my mind when I saw the two of you together holding each other in the kitchen."

When Scott turned to face him, Derek could see his eyes were red and glistening. *Jesus. He's really upset about this.* "Ok, but please at least try not to fly off the handle." Derek took a deep breath. "After we got Beck back inside, she went to the bathroom. After she left, Bryce kind of…" He didn't want to say it. Once the words were out he would have no control over how Scott reacted. "Bryce basically came out to me and then hit on me. That's what you saw when you came to the kitchen. I'm pretty sure he was about to tell me he hoped that I might be interested in him. Fortunately for him, you showed up and distracted me just before I was about to punch him in the face."

Scott stood still. Derek searched his face, but couldn't read any emotion there. Finally, Scott's shoulders sagged as he let out a deep breath. "I guess I was wrong. That *is* worse than what I imagined."

"What?" Derek felt that it was safe to walk closer to Scott without him continuing to pull away. "What were you thinking?"

"I was thinking that the two of you were flirting."

"And how is what I just said worse than that?"

"Because, he was doing something to you that you didn't want and I wasn't there to protect you." Scott sat down on the bed. "And before you say anything, I know, I'm behaving like a shit right now. It's just I saw you with him and…"

"And you thought the worst. I get it. I would have through the same thing." Derek walked over to Scott and sat on the bed next to him. "We're both new to this. But Scott…" Derek tentatively placed a hand on Scott's chest. He waited until Scott was looking directly at him. It was with a quiet voice filled with as much soothing as he could manage, that Derek finished his thought. "… there is only one person that I want and he's in front of me right now."

A tear escaped from Scott's over-brimming eyes and slowly trickled down his cheek. Using the inside of his thumb to wipe the tear away, Derek wrapped first one arm and then the other around Scott's waist and rested his head on Scott's chest. "Mmm," he hummed, "You are really warm."

He felt Scott wrap his arms around his shoulders and squeeze him tightly. "I'm sorry. I saw the two of you together and I became incredibly jealous. I'm not used to feeling that way with anyone. Especially not with someone I…" Scott's abrupt silence caused Derek to look up. The raw, pure affection he saw in Scott's face took his breath away. He tilted his head upwards and kissed him gently on the lips. "Want to get out of here?"

They found their coats, headed out without stopping to say goodbye to anyone, and walked the few blocks to Derek's car in silence. Derek turned the heat to full blast and rubbed his hands together waiting for the car to warm up. Scott hadn't spoken since they left the house. When he did, his voice was quiet and he was staring at his hands. "I'm sorry."

Derek turned to Scott. There was nothing for him to be sorry about. "Don't be. It's kind of flattering in a way, although I do hate to see you upset and I *really* hate the idea that you thought that I could possibly want anyone else."

Scott lifted his gaze from his hands and turned to face Derek. "It's just that I have never felt this way before and it scares and excites me at the same time. I mean, knowing that I'm gay is one thing, but I've never met anyone who made me really understand what being gay meant. Do you know what I mean?" Derek wasn't sure he did so he remained silent. "It's like I knew that I liked guys and that when I kissed girls, I wasn't feeling the things that my buddies were talking about. But with you, when I kiss you, everything in my body starts to race. I think about you all the time and when I'm not with you, I want to be. Seeing you tonight with Bryce scared the shit out of me. Not because you've given me any reason to be afraid that you would hurt me, but I know how hurt I *would* be if you didn't want to be with me anymore."

Scott's lower lip started to tremble and Derek could see his eyes begin to glisten again. Now he understood exactly what Scott was trying to say. As much as it warmed him to hear Scott verbalize everything that he himself felt but couldn't say, it troubled him that Scott was so insecure about how strongly Derek really felt about him. How deep Derek's feelings actually ran. "Would it help if I could show you that you aren't alone with those feelings you just described? If you knew that I feel exactly the same way that you do, would that make you understand that I would be just as hurt if you didn't want to be with me?"

Scott shook his head. "You shouldn't have to do that. Besides, how can you *show* something like that?"

Derek took Scott's hands and brought them to his lips, kissing each one. "I know I don't have to *prove* anything to you, but I also know that I keep a lot of stuff in. I've told you that a million times. I am better at expressing my feelings and emotions through my music and through wrestling, not with words. So, do you want me to show you that you aren't alone with how you feel?"

Scott's body slunk into his seat in resignation. "Ok, show me!"

Derek opened the glove compartment and pulled out a thin gift-wrapped present. "This was going to be one of your gifts for Christmas, but I think now is the perfect time to give it to you."

Scott took the present from Derek and opened it. It was a CD. Written in Derek's handwriting on the surface was *Tranquility. For Scott. From Derek.* Scott ran his fingers over the case then looked at Derek. "You made me a mix?"

Derek was brimming with excitement. He had been imagining what Scott's reaction would be like when he opened this present. The shock and pleasure did not disappoint. "It's a song that I mixed while thinking about you. You could say that you were my inspiration for it. Go ahead, put it in. Listen to it."

Scott opened the case and popped the CD into the car stereo. After a moment, the car began to fill with a soft, primal beat. Derek had dulled the bass so that the beat created a sense of being alive, like a heartbeat. The vocals were high soprano ballad-like *Ahs* which harmonized one another in complex chord combinations, causing the sounds to mix in exotic ways when they struck the inner ear. They were flighty and caused a sense of disorientation, not knowing exactly which direction the song would take you. Male vocals entered the mix next, giving the song strength and foundation. Combined with the female vocals, the music created a sensation of being suspended between the ground and the air, but somehow causing a feeling of stability. Finally as the flutes and violins weaved in, the song filled out with passion. The flute evoked longing and sensual pleasure while the violin formed the heart of the music...the melody that held everything together.

Scott sat in the heat of the car, eyes closed, listening to the music. Derek watched him become lost in the world he had created through sound. Finally, while the music was slowly winding down, Scott opened his eyes and turned to Derek. Tears were streaming out of both eyes. "That's how I make you feel?"

"That and more." Derek leaned over so that his face was only an inch from Scott's. "Do you understand now that you are all I want? I may not have words, but it doesn't mean that the feelings aren't there."

In answer, Scott wrapped his arms around Derek, pulling him out of the driver's seat and laying him across his lap. Cradling him in a strong embrace, he lowered his lips to Derek's and kissed him gently and slowly.

They savored the feel of their lips as their mouths molded together. Derek ran his fingers through Scott's hair while Scott drew him even closer, tightening his embrace around his shoulders. Derek allowed the lofty female vocals to guide his emotions and felt the male vocals come to life through Scott's touch.

When they parted from the kiss, Scott looked down at Derek. "I feel like an idiot now. I'm really sorry I lost my mind there for a minute."

Derek smiled and gave him another short kiss. "It's ok."

"It's just that I am so used to losing people. I've moved so much that I've learned to believe that people will disappear on me, and that I shouldn't rely on anyone being there for me for the long haul." It hurt Derek to hear Scott communicate such a lonely feeling. "And with how I feel about you, it's really scary. I don't want to lose you, Derek."

Derek hugged Scott as tightly as he could. "That's not going to happen. I promise." He slowly climbed out of Scott's lap and back into the driver's seat. "You ready to head home?" Scott nodded and Derek turned on the car. They listened to the song several more times as they drove.

Chapter 11

The weekend following the cast party found Derek and Scott surrounded by books and listening to music in the attic. With midterms coming up, along with the big meet against Lexington, the weeks leading up to winter break promised to be extremely busy. Armed with hearty meals and frequent snacks provided by Derek's mother, they had little reason to go anywhere else. Their fight, if you could call it that, the night of the cast party had served as a catalyst to draw them even closer together. Scott was more secure than ever about Derek's feelings for him and became increasingly affectionate.

Derek sat on the floor, leaning between Scott's legs, reviewing his Latin vocabulary. Scott was unconsciously brushing his fingers through Derek's hair while reading their English book. Letting out a sigh, Derek dropped his head backwards to rest on Scott's lap. "I think I need a break."

Scott closed his book and scooted over on the couch making room for Derek, lifting his arm so Derek could crawl next to him. "I could use a break as well. Any ideas?" Scott winked at Derek with a glimmer of seductive playfulness in his eyes.

"Yes, *that* idea had crossed my mind, but actually I was thinking that I could really use a run." Derek got up and started pacing around the room.

Scott observed the uncharacteristic jitteriness with curious fascination. "Is everything ok? You seem pretty jumpy."

Derek continued pacing, his arms brushing through his hair. He could feel tension building up inside his chest. "It's Tuesday's meet against Lexington. I'm stressing out about it." He walked over to the stereo, started rifling through his CDs, couldn't decide on any that interested him, and turned around with an exasperated sigh.

Scott stood up and walked over to Derek, grabbing his wrists and holding him firmly in place. He was grinning, but his eyes conveyed sympathy and understanding. "Stop. You're getting anxious for nothing. We've been studying all weekend and have been cooped up in here for almost two days. A run sounds like a good idea. I think I left my running clothes in your car. Get changed while I go and grab them."

Scott's calm contrasted starkly with Derek's nervousness as if they were teetering on opposing sides of a see-saw. Allowing Scott to take control of the moment, they descended the attic steps together and Derek went into his room to change. A couple of minutes later, Scott joined him with his running clothes.

They were just about to head out the door when Scott's cell phone rang. Scott looked at the caller ID. It was his mother. "Hey, Mom. What's up? Hang on a sec, let me check." Covering the mouthpiece with his hand he walked over to Derek. "Mom just asked if you want to come over for dinner. She feels guilty that your mom has been feeding me for practically the whole year."

Derek forgot his anxiety over the match just long enough to realize it had been replaced by a completely new reason to feel edgy. He had met Scott's mother a few times in passing and had only *seen* his father once when he had arrived home from one of his business trips. He had never had to actually make an impression on either of them. With trepidation, Derek decided that it was probably a good idea. "Sure."

"Mom, yeah. We were just going to take a study break to go running, but then we could head over after that. What time is dinner going to be?" He nodded at her answer, which Derek could not hear. "Ok, see you then." Scott's face was lit up with a beaming grin when he turned to look at Derek. "Cool, you'll get a taste of my mom's cooking for a change. I know she isn't around much, but when she puts a meal together, it's fantastic. Not as good as your mom's, but still pretty good."

They headed to the kitchen and found Derek's father sitting at the table working on a crossword puzzle. "Hey, Dad, where's Mom?"

His dad looked up, a pleasant smile on his face. "Hey boys, you've kept yourselves caged up all weekend. How's the studying going?"

"It's going fine. We've kept up in class work despite wrestling so this is really more review than cramming. So, where is Mom?"

"She got a call from Philippe at the salon. He said he got a sudden opening so she grabbed it and ran."

"Oh, ok. Well, Scott and I were going to go for a run and his mom invited me to eat dinner over there. That's ok, right?"

"Sure, son, sounds nice. Your mom was worried that she wouldn't have enough time to prepare a suitable dinner for you anyway and you know how she hates takeout. Have fun." When his father turned back to his crossword puzzle, Derek knew that the conversation had ended.

The two boys departed from the kitchen and walked outside. The December air was cold, made even colder by the breeze. Derek breathed in deeply, allowing the chill to enter his lungs. It immediately cleared some of the nerves that had been building up in his head and gut. They started at a slow jog, heading toward the river, which was about a mile away from his home. Once at the river, their muscles had loosened and warmed up enough for them to pick up the pace. They opted for a short run, two bridges, and took it at a fairly fast pace.

Rather than return to Derek's house, Scott opted to run home for a shower and Derek agreed to meet him there around 4:45. That gave him thirty minutes to get home, clean up, and change.

Derek decided to dress up for the dinner, figuring it would be a smart idea since he had never really spent any time with Scott's parents. He wore khaki pants, a white t-shirt and a blue button-down shirt over that. He left the shirt untucked, not wanting to go too far. As it was, he hated wearing button-down shirts for any reason.

When he arrived at Scott's house, Scott opened the door before he had a chance to knock. Derek laughed. "What, were you standing by the door waiting for me?" Derek teased.

"Actually, yes, I was." Scott smiled and grabbed Derek's ass as he passed through the doorway. Derek let out a short *oh* in surprise. "Here, let me take your coat." Scott helped Derek to remove his coat and hung it on the rack next to the door.

They walked into the kitchen where Scott's mother was standing next to the sink. There were four large steaks already cooked. "Hello, Derek. You came just in time. These steaks need about ten minutes to rest and the potatoes are almost ready. Once the water starts to boil, the green beans will only take about five minutes." She turned to face Derek, wiping her hands on her apron. "I am so glad you could come join us for dinner tonight. Your mother has been so generous in feeding Scott and welcoming him into your home. I knew that I would be ashamed for ages if I didn't have you over for dinner soon." She walked over to Derek and extended her hand. "I'm Shannon. It's so nice to have a chance to be able to actually chat with you."

What struck Derek was the genuine warmth that radiated from her. Shannon emanated sincerity. No pretension. No show. It set Derek immediately at ease.

So that's where he gets it from. He smiled and shook her hand in return. "Thank you for having me. Those steaks smell incredible."

"Oh those, it's nothing. Just salt and pepper and voila, it's done. Come, let me get you a drink. Sit down and make yourself comfortable." She ushered him into a seat at the kitchen table. "Would you like juice, soda, water?"

"Water would be great thanks."

She poured two glasses of water, one for Derek and one for Scott and handed them to Scott. She then picked up her glass of red wine from the counter next to the stove and joined them at the table. "So, Scott tells me that you are quite a good wrestler. You must be very excited about Tuesday's meet. I'll be there rooting for you guys. Unfortunately, Scott's dad has to go out of town again, so he won't be able to make it." Derek glanced at Scott who was sipping his water. He thought that he saw Scott's forehead scrunch slightly when his mother mentioned his father, but couldn't be sure. His attention was drawn back to her when she asked the next question. "Are your parents going to be there? I would love to meet them."

"Yes, they come to all of my meets. My mom usually makes stuff to feed the guys, although none of them like to eat until after their matches, which actually works out great for me since I am one of the earlier matches. Our heavyweight is always grouchy because the food is usually gone by the time his match is over." Derek was surprised that he had to gasp for air as he finished talking. He glanced first at Scott and then at Shannon who were both staring at him silently.

Scott handed Derek his water. "Maybe you should drink this. I think you just said at least a thousand words in one breath."

Shannon took a sip from her wine and noticed that steam was rising from the pot she had on the stovetop.

Getting up from her seat, she took the prepared green beans from the cutting board and placed them in the boiling water, generously salting them. "Scott says that your match on Tuesday is a very important one. He says this is one of the teams that you are worried about."

Derek was impressed with her level of interest in Scott's wrestling. "Yeah. Lexington and Waltham are the two teams we are most worried about. Actually, I was stressing out earlier while Scott and I were studying for midterms since I don't know the guy in my weight class. I have no idea how good he is."

Scott rolled his eyes. "Derek is just being panicky. He's an incredible wrestler and he'll beat that pants off of that Lexington guy, whoever he is. He could crush Johnny who wrestled at his weight class back in Iowa."

"You boys put so much pressure on yourselves to win, win, win. Just do your best and I'm sure that you will do fine." Her voice was chipper and bouncy and Derek couldn't help but smile.

After a few minutes, dinner was ready. Mrs. Thayer took the potatoes out of the oven, placing one on each plate along with a steak. She then spooned the green beans onto a platter and placed a healthy pat of butter on top. "You boys get started. I'll just go into the other room to fetch Scott's father."

Derek felt his salivary glands jump into action as Shannon placed a plate heaping with steak and potatoes in front of him. He was about to tell Scott how much he was enjoying himself, but when he looked up, there was a sullen look in his eyes. Before he could ask what was wrong, Scott's father came into the kitchen with his mother.

His father wore slacks and still had on his work shirt and a tie. He wore bifocal glasses and his lips were pressed into two tight lines. Sitting down, he turned to Scott. "Hello, son." He then turned his gaze toward Derek.

"Sweetheart, this is Derek Thompson. He's the boy who Scott has become good friends with at school, and is also on the wrestling team."

Maintaining his grim expression, Scott's father extended his hand to Derek. "I'm Mr. Thayer. Nice to meet you."

Derek was unaccustomed to parents introducing themselves to him as Mr. or Mrs. Whatever. He was equally unaccustomed to the feeling of being appraised so blatantly upon first meeting. Swallowing the stress building up in his throat, he extended his hand. "It's very nice to meet you, Mr. Thayer. Thank you so much for having me over for dinner."

Mr. Thayer nodded then turned to his plate and began cutting his steak.

Shannon picked up the platter of green beans and passed them towards her husband. "Would you like some green beans, honey?" He took the platter from his wife without a word, spooned some onto his plate, and placed the platter back on the table. Shannon's cheeks pinked as she picked up the platter once again. "Derek, may I give you some green beans?"

"Yes, thanks. Mom makes me eat at least one vegetable at every meal. Well, except breakfast. Actually, do potatoes count as vegetables because I do have hash browns quite often? Wait, I think potatoes are tubers right? I keep forgetting." *What the fuck is wrong with me? Did I just question whether potatoes are vegetables or tubers?*

Scott choked on his water then started laughing and coughing at the same time. Mr. Thayer shot him a harsh glance and Scott immediately became serious once again.

Looking nervously from Scott, to Derek, and then to Mr. Thayer, Shannon took a sip of her wine. "Well, you boys have certainly been busy what with studying and wrestling practice." She spooned green beans onto both Derek's and Scott's plates. "What time is your meet on Tuesday?"

Scott finished chewing the food in his mouth then turned to his mother. "The busses leave the school at 4:30. The meet should begin around 5:30. Lexington isn't very far from where you work, Mom. It's pretty convenient for you."

Shannon flashed a sweet smile towards Scott. "Even if it wasn't, I would make sure to be there. It is your first meet of the season after all."

Mr. Thayer placed his fork and knife on the table next to his plate. "You know, at work I hear people going on and on about their kids' sports events, band concerts, and dramatic plays. I just keep wondering what ever happened to a good old-fashioned focus on academics. I never knew anyone who put food on the table because of their sport, musical, or acting abilities. Good honest work and a focus on studies. That's what prepares a man to provide for his family."

Scott's face turned red and Shannon took another sip of her wine, glancing at a red spot that had landed on the table next to her. She took a napkin, wet it on her tongue, and began to wipe at the spot. Derek turned to Mr. Thayer. "You know. My parents say the same thing to me. Well, sort of the same thing. They say that my classes have to come first and that everything else, while they recognize it's important to me, has to come second. They say in the long run that I'll thank them for the advice. Of course, when I complain, they also say that I'll understand when I'm older." Derek smiled, expecting that his witty comment would break through some of Mr. Thayer's icy exterior. This line usually won a laugh from the parents he had met over the years, but had no effect on Mr. Thayer.

Mr. Thayer fixed his eyes on Derek. "Your parents are absolutely right. School is for learning. If your grades aren't up, then you don't have time for the other things that take your attention away from studying."

Derek had a difficult time swallowing the bit of steak in his mouth. "Yes, sir. I guess that is what my parents mean." He didn't think that was what his parents meant at all, but disagreeing with Scott's father seemed like an ill-advised choice.

The rest of dinner consisted of Shannon making small talk and asking Derek questions about growing up in Cambridge, where he wanted to go to college, and other items of a mild nature. Mr. Thayer remained silent. When he finished, he excused himself, telling Derek once again that it was nice to meet him, and then retired to his room.

The heaviness of the air seemed to disappear, leaving the room with Mr. Thayer. Relief seeped into his muscles and he slumped back against his chair. Chancing a look at Scott, it was obvious that he had relaxed a bit as well, but he still had a solemn look on his face. Reading her son's expression, Shannon walked over and took his plate after asking if he was finished. Derek offered his plate to her as well. As she rinsed the dishes in the sink, she began speaking. "He is very tired from all of the traveling he must do with this new job and the expanded regional responsibilities. When he is preparing for a trip he becomes very focused." Derek had a feeling that this was not the first time that Shannon had offered such an explanation.

Derek accepted the comment and poured on his charm. "Thank you once again for the meal, Shannon. It was wonderful. Don't know the last time I had a steak cooked so perfectly."

Shannon turned and cast a smile at Derek. When she did, he noticed that she had the same crooked smile and dimple as Scott and it made him like her all the more. "You are sweet to say so dear." She motioned towards the sink which was filled with dishes, pots, and serving bowls. "I'm sure you boys don't want to sit here and watch me clean the dishes. Why don't you go up to Scott's room for a bit? Or do you have to get home, Derek?"

"No, no. I can stay for a while." He and Scott got up from the table and Scott led him down the hall to his bedroom. Once inside, he walked over to his bed and sat down with a thud. Swinging his legs onto the bed and leaning back against his pillow, he curled his arms behind his head for support.

Not sure what Scott was feeling, Derek walked over to him and sat down on the bed, placing his hand on Scott's chest. "You ok?"

Scott took in a deep breath and then let it out slowly. Reaching for Derek's hand, he clasped it and pulled Derek so he was lying down next to him on the bed. Derek settled in and Scott wrapped an arm around him, spooning him to his chest. "Hmmm. This feels nice." The vibration of Scott's voice reverberated through his chest and into Derek's back. It was all he said and all he needed to say for Derek to understand that Scott just wanted to lay there and hold him. Derek was more than happy to comply.

In English class the next day, Scott was already sitting at his seat when Derek arrived. He had a worried look on his face. Concerned that something may have happened with his father, Derek went quickly to his seat next to Scott. "Is something wrong? You don't look happy."

Scott turned to Derek and the stress was plain in his eyes. "After you left last night, my mom told me that we were going home to Iowa once the term ends."

Derek's stomach tied into a knot. "You're going home to Iowa...like, for good?"

Realizing that Derek misunderstood what he meant, Scott laughed. "No, not for good. Just for winter break."

Derek's stomach untied. "Whew. You just scared the shit out of me." He punched Scott in the shoulder, hard.

"Ouch. What the hell was that for?" The comment was delivered light heartedly, but he rubbed his arm nonetheless.

"For scaring me. Don't do it again."

Scott's smile lit up. He leaned in close enough so only Derek could hear and whispered to him in a teasing, sing-song voice. "You got all scared that you would never see me again, didn't you?"

Derek pursed his lips, deciding whether to give in and be honest or to come back with a sarcastic remark. Although sarcasm was what Scott deserved at the moment, the truth was that he was right. "Yes, actually, I got all scared that I wouldn't see you again. In case you hadn't noticed, I kind of enjoy spending time with you."

Scott's face softened. "Thanks for not pushing me to talk last night. My dad and I…we just don't…we're very different. Just being with you made me feel much better." He made a motion to take Derek's hand, but remembered that they were in the middle of class and pulled his hand back. "I'm going to miss you over winter break."

It suddenly occurred to Derek that he would not see Scott for a week and a half and the thought left him feeling slightly uneasy and empty. "Well, let's make up for the lost time before you go. We still have the rest of this and next week." Derek ran his tongue across his lip and locked Scott in a brief and piercing gaze, allowing the hint of a seductive smile to cross his lips.

Scott leaned in close, a glint of passion in his eyes as well. "You're giving me a hard-on." The words were barely audible, but they didn't need to be to send Derek's mind reeling.

Imagining Scott's prick growing and shifting caused Derek's groin to swell, becoming increasingly confined in his pants. Mentally reviewing the different times Scott had said or done things which had caused him to become hard, Derek was certain that this was the subtlest one yet. "Huh."

Scott turned to Derek, "That's not quite the response I was going for."

Derek hadn't realized that he had said anything out loud. Turning to Scott, he debated once again whether he should make some sort of witty remark but as before, he opted for the genuine approach, even if it was going to boost Scott's ego undeservedly. "I was just thinking that what you just did was impressive."

"Wh…do I even want to know what you're talking about right now?"

Derek smiled and leaned close to Scott's ear. "There are many things that you do which cause me to become excited. I just never imagined a simple statement like *I'm getting a hard-on* would be one of them."

Scott sat back, wide-eyed. "You mean, you…right now…just because I said…" Derek nodded with a sly smile. "Damn, I am the *man*!" He said it loudly. Derek shook his head and laughed. Several students turned around to look at them. Scott leaned in and whispered in Derek's ear. "You are getting *so* lucky after school. You just made me feel like a superhero."

Although he hadn't wanted to boost Scott's ego, the response was definitely a good one. The reward seemed to warrant ego boosting on a more regular basis.

Chapter 12

The day of the Lexington meet generated a great deal of buzz at Brampton. The wrestling team was one of the only teams that year that had a shot at winning a division championship, so the entire school was behind them. The varsity players all showed up for weigh-ins before school started, starving from not eating breakfast and anxious to feed their food-deprived bodies. In each of their classes, the members of the team were given words of encouragement from their peers and teachers. At lunch, they ate together, psyching each other up as students started up chants which circulated the cafeteria. The normally stringent lunch workers turned a blind, albeit highly irritated, eye to the commotion, understanding that it was a day reserved for school spirit.

Derek was relieved that he had last class with Scott. The day had been nerve-wracking and he continually lost his focus worrying about his opponent for that evening. He wished he knew something about the person he would be wrestling. Sitting in the back of history class, his nerves began to set in and he fidgeted with his pencil, tapped his foot, and sighed repeatedly, anything to relieve the excited angst that was building up inside of him.

Scott, on the other hand, was a portrait of calmness. He had seemed to float through the day, becoming more and more tranquil and assured as the day progressed. Derek was amazed at his composure and poise. He had never known a member of the team to remain so controlled before a match. Towards the end of class, Scott leaned over to whisper in Derek's ear. "I want you to meet me in the parking lot by your car after school." When Derek asked him why he gave him a simple look and repeated, "After school."

As soon as the bell rang, he got up, gathered his belongings from his locker, shoved them into his bag, and followed Scott to the parking lot. When they arrived at his car, Scott said, "Get in. Give me the keys." Unable to come up with an argument, he handed over the keys and got into the passenger side of his car.

Scott said nothing as they drove along the river, finally stopping the car at the side of the road next to the Foot Bridge. "Let's get out here." Scott opened the door and walked to the middle of the bridge. Derek followed and stood next to him. Sliding behind Derek, Scott wrapped his arms around him, lowering his chin to rest on his shoulder. "Sometimes I come out here by myself to watch the river flow by. I look over the side of the bridge and tune everything else out. I ignore the cars, people, even the bridge, and just focus on the flowing water. It makes me feel like I've stepped out of time and place into my own little world…kind of like when I was home in Iowa and ran along the wheat and corn fields. During those moments, when it's just me and the water, I am able to focus on myself and what's going on with me."

Derek felt a chill run up his spine and wasn't sure whether it was the cold wind or what Scott was saying. He leaned over the bridge to look at the water. The current was moving rapidly, the surface rippling with angry white froth. Derek considered how much energy went into causing that water to move so quickly. It was a simple law of nature causing the water to flow. No reason, no explanation, just flowing water. "Why are you showing this to me, Scott?"

Scott leaned in close, hugging Derek even closer. "Because, when I spend these moments here alone, watching the water move along its path, I realize that I am the one who has the power to make things happen for myself. Nothing makes the water move. It just does."

He released Derek and stood next to him, looking over the edge with him. "Today, you've been a nervous wreck. Maybe that's how you need to be, although for the life of me I don't know why. But, you'll win today because you're a good and focused wrestler, not because you built up your nerves and have adrenaline pumping through your veins."

Derek considered his words. "I was amazed at how calm you've been today. I've never seen anything like it from any of the other guys on the team." He continued to watch the water as it pushed past the legs of the bridge. "Explain to me how you can remain so confident."

"It's not confidence. It's accepting that I am the one who is in control of what I do. When I feel like things are beginning to overwhelm me or to take over my actions and thoughts, I come here. Like when my dad is around and lectures on the evils of all that is non-academic, I become someone I'm not. I become quiet, passive, submissive, afraid. Then I come here." The two of them stood there, leaning over the edge for a few seconds. When Scott continued speaking, his voice had taken on a dream-like quality. "The water isn't influenced by others. It does what it is meant to do, nothing more, nothing less. And I remember, that is what I'm meant to do. Nothing more and nothing less than what I'm meant to."

Derek understood. He could see the pure logic of it. Why allow things he could not control to influence the way he felt and acted? Why give power to things outside of himself? "You're amazing, Scott. Thank you for taking me here."

Scott hugged him closer, kissed the back of his neck, and then whispered in his ear, "You are a great wrestler. Just wrestle. Stop thinking about the things you can't do anything about." He led Derek back to the car and they drove back to the school. They had only been gone for twenty minutes, but to Derek, it felt like they had traveled to another world and back.

They arrived at Allistaire High at 5:15. After changing, the team took the mat and warmed up. Josh went easy on them, not wanting to expend too much of their energy before the meet. They did a set of sit ups, some push ups, and two sets of spins to get their muscles warm and limber. As the Allistaire team took the mat, the spectators, who appeared to be most of the school, started screaming and cheering.

Derek's parents were sitting on the bottom bench of the bleacher nearest their team. His mom had brought a cooler of Gatorade and was handing it out in small paper cups to his teammates. She also had a large bin of sandwiches for them once they finished their matches. Power walked up to Derek's mom. "Hi, Mrs. Thompson. Glad to see you haven't lost your touch with the provisions."

Claire smiled at Power. "Well, I think I have improved my rationing techniques." She held up a bag containing two sandwiches. "I am saving this for you for after your match."

Power turned to the rest of the team. "This woman is a Goddess." His voice seemed like it had legitimate devotion in it. Derek shook his head at Power's comment, but was proud that his mom was so cool.

When Scott went to get some Gatorade, Claire gave him a hug. Derek's dad clapped him on the shoulder. "Good luck. We'll be the ones cheering the loudest for you."

Scott gave her a hug. "Thanks Mrs. Thompson." Looking up at the bleachers, he saw his mother sitting towards the middle, surrounded by a number of parents. He waved for her to come down. "Mrs. Thompson—."

"Please, call me Claire."

"Uh, sorry, right." He waited for his mother to arrive at his side. "Claire, Mr. Thompson, uh, I mean Henry. I want you to meet my mom, Shannon." Shannon extended her hand just as Derek walked up.

Shannon was dressed in a smart outfit and looked bright and cheerful. "Shannon Thayer. It is such a pleasure to finally meet you. Scott has told me how you have made him feel right at home at your place. I feel terribly guilty that he has to spend so much time without us around. Your son is a pleasure. A real gentleman. I am so glad that he and Scott have become such good friends." Derek was touched by her generous sentiment.

Claire reached an arm out, waving for Derek to come closer. Wrapping her arm around his shoulders she gave him a big kiss on the cheek.

"Mom, you're embarrassing me."

"Shush." She playfully tussled his hair. "That is very kind of you to say Shannon. It's a pleasure to meet you as well." She reached out her arm and waved for Scott to come over, giving him the same hug and kiss she had given Derek. Scott blushed and Derek had to admit that he felt a bit better since he wasn't the only one getting her affections. "He knows he is welcome anytime."

Derek motioned for Scott to join the team. Once out of earshot he said, "Sorry, she gets all motherly at the meets."

Scott smiled. "Derek, it's awesome. You are so lucky to have parents like Claire and Henry. I'm psyched that my mom is going to watch the meet with them. She looked kind of out of place by herself in the bleachers."

At 5:30 the referee called the two team captains to the mat. Each meet began with the team captains shaking hands in the center. The first four matches went pretty much as expected. Neither wrestler pinned his opponent. Allistaire had won three of the matches giving them a nine to three lead over Brampton.

Derek was the fifth match. Walking onto the mat, he surveyed his opponent. He was taller and thinner than Derek, which meant that he probably wouldn't be as strong, but it would be more difficult to gain control of his lanky arms and legs. *Could be worse. I'll call him Slim.* They faced each other in the center of the mat and took neutral position. As soon as the referee blew his whistle, Derek shot for Slim's leg, snatching his foot and standing up. He used his left leg to step in front of the foot Slim still had on the mat and brought him down.

Before Derek could gain control, Slim twisted out of his grip and got back to his feet. *Damn it. I hate long legs and arms.* They continued to circle each other, Slim grabbing at his arms, fighting for inside control. *Ok, think. How can I use his body to my advantage?* As he continued attempting to gain inside control of the arm, he realized that his hand was able to wrap entirely around Slim's upper arm. *Got it. Now I know what to do.* He allowed Slim to gain inside control, carefully watching for any offensive moves that could catch him off guard. Derek used his outside grip of Slim's arm to pull gently and see how he reacted. After two or three gentle tugs, Derek yanked on the arm, pulling him off balance. He used the momentary disorientation to move behind Slim, wrap both arms around him, and step in front of his feet, tripping him down to the mat.

Now that Slim was under control and had no arm leverage, it was fairly easy for Derek to place a half-nelson hold on him and begin the process of rolling him to his back. He found it difficult to maintain the half-nelson because Slim's arms were so long, but eventually he had a secure hold. Derek tightened his grip. When he saw the ref begin to count, he held on with all of his strength. With three waves of his arm, the ref slammed his hand on the mat and the match was over. Derek had won.

Jumping up, he ripped off his headgear and threw his arms in the air. The cheer he received caused far less reverberation in the auditorium since the spectators were largely Allistaire students and families, but Derek didn't care. His team was jumping up and down and his parents were screaming at the top of their lungs. It was Scott who caught his attention last. He had his crooked grin on his face and his blue-green eyes seemed to be glowing with pride. He gave Derek a wink and mouthed *I told you so*. If Derek hadn't just spent so much energy wrestling, he was sure his cock would have become rock hard on the spot. Derek's pin had tied the team scores at nine to nine.

There were three more matches before Scott's. Two of his teammates lost to the Allistaire wrestlers and one of his teammates won setting the score at fifteen to twelve in Allistaire's favor.

Scott's match wasn't even close. He took his opponent down right off the whistle. Derek was impressed, never having seen Scott move so quickly. He had control and quickly locked his opponent in a cradle and the match was over in thirty seconds. Brampton was now up eighteen to fifteen.

Josh's match was disastrous. During the first period, he seemed to be in control having taken his opponent down and gaining points for exposing his opponent's back to the mat twice. In the second round, the two kept reversing each other which maintained their point spread. In his third round, Josh made the fatal mistake of reaching back to try to grab his opponents head in a headlock. He found himself locked in a half-nelson hold. He fought the grip for about forty-five seconds, but ultimately wasn't able to keep from being rolled onto his back and pinned. Allistaire now led twenty-one to eighteen.

Power, true to his name, overtook his opponent,

almost causing a penalty when he lifted him straight off the ground and dropped him to the mat. If he hadn't lowered to his knees before his opponent touched the mat, the move would have been considered a slam, an illegal move in high school wrestling. Using his tremendous weight, Power flattened his opponent, pinning him within seconds.

The Brampton spectators and wrestlers went wild, screaming and hollering. It was a pitiful display compared to the gloomy hush that overtook three-quarters of the auditorium from the Allistaire spectators, but no one seemed to notice or care. Brampton had won. The only person who couldn't enjoy the celebratory madness was Josh who sulked off to a water cooler along the wall.

After the match, most of the team took rides home with their parents. Derek's parents and Shannon had suggested that they go to Uno's in Harvard Square to celebrate the victory against Allistaire. During dinner, Derek and Scott meticulously reviewed each match, move by move, planning to keep solid track of the players and their weaknesses so that their team would be better prepared for the next time they competed against them, which would be at the division championship tournament. When it was time to leave, Scott asked if he could accompany Derek, who had to get his car from the school parking lot. Shannon agreed and Derek's parents drove them. Before leaving they congratulated both boys once more and suggested that they not stay out too late since it was a school night.

Sitting in the car in the darkened parking lot, Derek turned on the radio. He leaned towards Scott. When Scott turned his head, Derek clamped their mouths together, grabbing him to pull them even closer together. After minutes of bruising kisses which left both of their mouths red and swollen, Derek broke away and shook his head to clear his mind. "Scott. I'm…I…You…"

Scott sat there gazing at Derek with an amused look on his face. "Full sentences please."

Derek held up his hand. "No, I have something I need to say, and am determined to use my words tonight." Scott became silent and waited for Derek to continue. Derek's heart began to race and a tingling sensation ran up and down his back. Words had never been easy for him, but he was going to say this. His whole life, he had carefully shielded himself from taking risks and making himself vulnerable to ridicule and gossip. It wasn't until he had met Scott that he realized the price he had paid for his lifetime of maintaining his guard. He had never allowed himself to feel the kinds of things he now felt with Scott.

As much as he knew Scott cared for him, and knew that Scott had opened him up to new feelings, he was scared. He knew that his fear was simply a residual effect from years of keeping everything in and he owed it to Scott and to himself to take a step forward and allow them to become closer. Derek took a deep breath and looked at Scott. Scott's eyes were locked on Derek as he patiently waited. Derek felt his reservations melt under Scott's compassionate and understanding regard. He took both of Scott's hands. "I love you, Scott. I am totally, head over heels, in love with you." Derek let out a huge sigh of relief once he had gotten the words out.

Scott stared at him, stunned. He hadn't expected Derek to proclaim that he loved him, but as soon as he heard Derek say the words, he knew that he felt them too. "I love you, too. So much."

The kiss that followed their declaration to one another was soft, slow, and sweet. As far as they knew or cared, they were the only people in the world.

Chapter 13

The school was an explosion of activity the next day. Students and teachers congratulated the wrestling team. Signs appeared on the walls, prophetically predicting a sure championship for them. At the same time, teachers were churning out study guides for midterms that would be taking place the next week.

Derek, Beck, and Scott used study hall to prepare for their English midterm together, quizzing each other on vocabulary, literary terms, and details about the books they had read. Each felt confident that they were well prepared. After practices, Derek and Scott continued their studying in the attic, particularly focusing on history, which was the other class they both shared. Overall, they felt confident that they would do well.

Scott was sprawled on the floor, reviewing his calculus notes and doing the practice problems his teacher had assigned when he suddenly slammed his book shut and let out an exasperated growl. Derek, who had been lying on the couch diligently answering his science study-guide questions, looked up. "Problems?"

Scott jumped to his feet and walked over to the window, peering out at the heavy flakes of snow that, as the meteorologist had predicted, had begun that evening. It was estimated that six inches would accumulate by morning. "It's my dad. He came home last night and gave me a *talking to.*" Scott punctuated the last words with finger quotes.

Placing his science book face down on his lap, Derek sat up and turned his attention to Scott.

"He started like always. You know, like at dinner that night, saying how academics come first and everything else is a distraction. But this time he actually added an ultimatum. He said that if I didn't pull straight A's like I had in Iowa that he would pull me from the wrestling team." Scott was gripping the window sill and Derek could see the bones of his knuckles pressing tightly against his skin.

"Do you really think he would do that? I mean, you have been doing great in school. Does he really expect straight A's?" Derek wasn't as concerned about Scott not being on the team as he was about how Scott would feel if he couldn't be on the team. He was beginning to really dislike Scott's father.

Scott turned to face Derek. "Honestly, yeah, I do. It's not the first time he's restricted me when I've disappointed him. In the past, if I pulled a B on a paper or a test, he would make me come directly home from school for a week and redouble my efforts in that subject area. He even made me ask the teachers if I could do extra credit work to make up for the grade." Walking over to Derek, Scott motioned for him to scoot over on the couch. When Derek complied, Scott sat on the couch, swiveled his hips so that his feet were dangling over the couch arm, and laid his head onto Derek's lap, smacking it against the spine of the science book. "Ouch! *Shit!*"

Derek gently lifted Scott's head, pushed his book to the floor, and replaced it with one of the couch pillows. "Close your eyes." He began rubbing Scott's temples using a circular motion with his index and middle fingers. "Have you talked to your mom about this? What does she say?"

Scott let out a contented sigh, allowing himself to be pampered by Derek. "She was there when he said it. She didn't agree with him, but she never disagrees with him either. It's like when he's around, she and I become completely different people than when it's just us. I'm sure if he says I have to stop wrestling, she won't fight it."

Derek stopped massaging Scott's temples and placed one arm under his neck, urging him to sit up a bit so he could wrap his arms around him. Scott scooted into a seated position and allowed himself to be cradled. Derek had no idea what to say. He couldn't solve Scott's problems with his dad, nor could he ensure that Scott would get all A's. He could suggest that Scott talk to his mom when his dad wasn't around, but now that his dad had returned from his latest business trip, he was going to be around until they returned from their trip to Iowa over winter break. He could even tell him that it wouldn't be the end of the world if he couldn't be on the team, but that wouldn't make Scott feel better. Instead, he opted to just hold Scott tight, running a hand up and down his back and pulling him closer.

Midterm week flew by faster than Derek could believe. They were given Monday through Wednesday and teachers had to enter their term grades into the school's computer by Thursday night. Friday was the last day before winter break. Students would be receiving their midyear report cards from their last period teacher.

On Thursday, after practice, Derek and Scott decided to drive around aimlessly. Listening to music, they rode down Mt. Auburn Street into Watertown and then Newton, hopping on the Mass Pike and heading west towards Natick. Scott had been restless and moody all week, stressing about his exams.

Derek's midterms had gone well. All except for science. He didn't know what it was about science that eluded him, but it was the only subject that ever gave him trouble. It wasn't *his* midterms that were worrying him at the moment. Watching Scott stare out the passenger side window, he wondered whether he should break the silence or not. "How do you think you did on your midterms?"

Scott started fidgeting with the radio controls, playing with the bass, treble and balance. "I don't know. Guess I'll find out tomorrow. English and history were easy. So was French. Science wasn't so bad. The one I'm worried about is calculus." Releasing the radio dials, he leaned back in his seat and resumed staring out the passenger-side window.

It didn't bother Derek that Scott didn't seem to want to talk, but he could tell his mind was spinning with worry. "Do you really think that your dad is going to flip if you don't get all A's? I mean, what if you got one B." Scott's shoulders tensed. *Wrong question to ask.*

"Yes, I do." Scott's voice was solemn and sure.

Derek briefly glanced at Scott's sulking figure, slouched in the seat next to him. He was leaving for Iowa the following evening and Derek didn't want their last night before being separated for ten days to be tense and troubled. "You know what I think we need to do? We need to go to Dave & Buster's at the Natick Mall. We can abuse the pinball machines and slam an air hockey puck around." They were only ten minutes from the mall and Derek wanted to create a shift in mood as quickly as possible.

Scott shrugged. "Sure, if you want to."

It wasn't the level of enthusiasm Derek was hoping for, but he would work with it. Pulling into the Natick Mall parking lot, he drove past the section with all of the department stores to the side lot where the arcade and movie theater were located. Once they had purchased tokens, Derek beelined for the air hockey table, which was empty. Depositing the required number of tokens, he heard the mechanical whir as the air began to push through the tiny holes on the surface and the clink as the puck landed in the receptacle at the side of the table. They messed around for a while, getting used to each other's styles. And finally they began playing in earnest.

Derek loved to play air hockey, but sucked at it. He had good dexterity and hand-eye coordination when he did things with his body, but when he had to use things like the air hockey pushers or tennis racquets, he was hopelessly inept. Scott, on the other hand, proved to be a very good player and his mood had lightened significantly. Capitalizing on the moment, Derek decided to become comical. "Ok, tough guy, let's play for real. I've been going easy on you so far."

Scott smirked, "Bring it on."

Derek hit the puck and Scott slammed it back, deflecting it against the side of the table. It flew into Derek's goal.

Scott laughed. "I see what you mean. You're gonna kick my ass. I can tell." The corner of his mouth began to creep up the side of his face and he bit his lower lip. Whenever Scott bit his lip, the lip Derek found so sensual and kissable, he became distracted and aroused. "Hey, tell you what. I'll play one handed." Hitting the puck, Scott knocked it directly towards Derek's goal. It slipped in easily.

"Just you shut up." Derek laughed, feeling his ears burn at the jab, but he was pleased that Scott's mood was lightening up. To his utter horror, Scott continued to trample him even with one arm behind his back. When they finished the game, Derek had lost, eleven to zero, but Scott was back in his usual upbeat mood. Trying to salvage the whipping he had just taken, Derek raised his hands in the air in mock victory. "See, I told you I'd whip your ass."

Scott tilted his head back and uttered a single *Ha*. "Right, you put me to shame."

They spent another hour playing different games, and then headed into the mall to grab an ice cream. Finally, they decided to head back home. In the car, Scott's mood remained cheerful. "That was fun. I needed to blow off some steam."

As they drove down Route Nine, heading back east towards Cambridge, Derek felt a warm sense of satisfaction in his chest. He reached over and took Scott's hand in his. Scott twined their fingers together, lifted Derek's hand to his mouth and gave it a soft kiss, then lowered it into his lap, holding it there. They drove, contentedly in silence, listening to music.

The next day, when they got their grades in history class, Derek's heart fell. He had received three A's and two B's. It wasn't his grades that bothered him. He knew that his parents would be happy. It was Scott's grades that concerned him. He had received all A's except for calculus. He received a B- in that class. As they left the school saying their goodbyes to their friends, Scott's mood dampened, becoming as cold as the weather outside. Sitting in his car outside Scott's house, he wished there was something he could do to brighten the moment. He wouldn't be seeing Scott for ten days and didn't want his last moment with him to be like this.

Turning to Scott, he spoke using a gentle voice. "I'm gonna miss you. Promise that we'll talk at least once a day."

Scott leaned over, placing his hand on the side of Derek's face and curling his fingers behind Derek's neck. Pulling him in, Scott closed the distance between them and kissed him with warm tenderness. The wetness from the inside of his mouth slicked over Derek's lips creating a seal between them as their tongues intertwined. Derek loved their slow sweet kisses, but this particular kiss had a feeling of longing and desire that he hadn't felt before. It felt like Scott needed this kiss and wouldn't let it go. After a few minutes, Scott reluctantly drew his head back and held Derek in a silent gaze. "I'm going to miss you too. More than you can imagine."

❖   ❖   ❖

The first few days of winter break dragged longer than Derek could have imagined. Not only did he miss Scott terribly, used to seeing him every day, but Scott hadn't called. Derek called frequently and kept getting forwarded to his voicemail. A mixture of real worry and extreme anger soured his mood. His parents asked him a few times what was wrong, but they had no idea that he and Scott were in a relationship, or that he was gay for that matter, so it would sound odd to start complaining that a boy hadn't called him in a few days. Instead, he just grumpily claimed that nothing was wrong and went to the attic to listen to music.

After dinner on Christmas Eve, Derek was unable to contain the thoughts that kept him in his surly mood and decided to call Beck. Being Jewish, she was one of his few friends who was always free from family obligations around the winter holidays. "Hey Beck. I'm about ready to throw my mixing board out the window. Can we get together?"

Beck had called him each day to find out if he had talked to Scott. Derek's proclamation made the question unnecessary at the moment. "Sure babe. Let's meet up at The Syrian Wrap in Central Square. Half an hour sound good to you?"

"Sure. I'll see you there."

A half an hour later, Derek and Beck were sitting at a table by the window, watching last minute Christmas shoppers trudge through the snow and slush. Derek had ordered a chai tea and a chicken Caesar wrap. Beck had opted for a double mocha and a barbeque chicken wrap with extra hot sauce. Dipping one end of her wrap into the blue cheese dressing that came with her meal, she took a large bite and surveyed Derek. A dollop of blue cheese had pasted itself to the corner of her mouth and was beginning to drip towards her chin. "Okay. Just start talking and don't stop until you get it all out. I will, in my superior manner, sort through your feelings for you when you are finished."

Derek smiled weakly, but was grateful for the chance to vent with someone who knew exactly what was going on with him. "I just don't get it. Everything was going so well. We even admitted that we love each other. We spend all of our time together. He promised me that he would call me every day. And now, nothing. No call. Nothing. I don't know what to think. I mean, I know he was freaked out when he got his report card because his dad had threatened to pull him from the team if he didn't get straight A's, but seriously, could his dad really be upset with all A's except for a B- in calculus? That's not even a required math class in high school. And even if his dad did pull him from the team, wouldn't you think that he would want to call me to let me know? Also, I have been calling him for the past four days which makes me feel like the lamest, most clingy girl in the world." He held up a hand to prevent the protest that flashed across Beck's face. "Sorry, Beck, you know what I mean. It's just not like me to go chasing after people. That's all I'm saying. I keep getting his voicemail. I have left several messages telling him I am worried and that I miss him, but still, nothing. I don't know what to think. Part of me is terrified that something has happened to him. I know his plane landed safely because I made him give me his flight information before he left, but still, I don't know what to think." Derek leaned back in his chair and felt his face become hot and his vision began to blur. A tear escaped his eye and slowly worked its way down his cheek. "Damn it! I hate feeling this way."

Beck had remained surprisingly silent, allowing Derek to get all of his feelings off his chest. "First of all, bravo. I have never heard you string together so many feelings out loud before. Through your music, yes, but with words, no. Good for you. Second, I don't know what to tell you about what's going on with Scott. It could be a million things." Derek's shoulders slumped and he could feel more tears spilling out of his eyes. "Hold on, I said I can't tell you what's going on with Scott. But I can tell you what I think is going on with you."

Derek wiped his eyes and continued to listen as Beck went on. "You have never had to worry about what other people think about you. You have always had friends and, well, have been popular in the traditional sense of the word. Your parents are just the right balance of liberal, but parental, imposing reasonable limits, but trusting you and giving you plenty of freedom. And, of course, you have had me, the utterly fabulous and progressive actor extraordinaire." Derek continued listening, but his expression did not change. "Aw, c'mon, Derek. That was a little funny wasn't it?" When Derek didn't respond, Beck stuck her tongue out at him. "Fine, be that way. What I mean is that you have had me to talk to about being gay. Whatever you have felt or gone through, you haven't had to go through it alone. I have been there every step along the way, still loving you, still accepting you, and still your best friend. So now you are faced with a situation that you have never had to face. You are in love. By the way, have I mentioned that I am quite jealous of how sweet you guys are together?"

Derek reluctantly grinned. "Maybe a few times."

"You've allowed your feelings to get tied up into him, and now that he is unreachable and you can't get a feel for what is going on, you feel lost. You've allowed him to connect to your heart, and the uncertainty of what's going on with him right now is tugging at that connection and making you feel uncomfortable. That's normal Derek. You just haven't allowed yourself to get close to anyone in that way before."

Derek considered her words. They made sense in a logical way. But they didn't alleviate any of the discomfort, fear, and anger he was feeling. "I totally get what you are saying, but it doesn't make me feel any better. I can't stand feeling this way."

Beck smiled and shook her head. "Derek, it's not supposed to make you feel better. When you love, you open yourself to hurt. It's just the way it works. Right now you're hurting and you just have to work through it. There is no quick fix here." Derek's head slumped into his hands and he emitted a loud sigh. Beck couldn't help the smile that pulled at the sides of her mouth. At the same time, she knew that Derek was struggling and it hurt to see him upset. "For what it's worth, I am sure that there is a perfectly good explanation for why he hasn't called you, and when you finally do connect and understand what has been going on with him you will probably feel much better."

Derek considered that and did actually begin to feel a bit better. Knowing what he needed gave him a sense of control over his feelings. The problem was, *when* would he be able to get Scott on the phone? By the time Derek left to head back home, he felt much better. Not back to normal, but much better than he had felt since vacation began.

The next morning Derek woke to the sound of his cell phone ringing. Glancing at the caller ID, he did not recognize the number. He decided to answer anyway. "Hello."

"Derek! It's me." Scott was talking in a whisper and his voice sounded tense.

Derek felt an immediate sense of relief which, almost as quickly, was replaced by anger. "Where the hell have you been? I have been so worried about you. Do you even have the slightest idea what my imagination has been doing to my nerves?"

Scott was silent. After a few moments he spoke. "Actually, yes, I *can* imagine how you have been feeling because I have been feeling the same way and I am so sorry. My dad was furious when he saw my calculus grade and took my phone away from me. My mom woke me up this morning and gave me her cell so I could call you. She said that she's been worried about me ever since we came out here. I haven't really been all that pleasant."

Derek felt his anger dissipate as he realized that Scott had wanted to call him the whole time, but had been prevented from doing so by his father. He also felt a searing hatred towards Scott's father. "Beck figured there would be a logical explanation. I was just too miserable imagining that you…" He couldn't finish the sentence. "Anyway. It's so good to hear your voice. Merry Christmas. I miss you."

"I miss you, too. I wish I were home with you instead of here." As angry as he had been, as stressed, worried, and despondent, hearing Scott call Cambridge his home caused Derek's heart rate to speed up a bit. Scott's next comment brought him back to the shitty situation the two of them were in. "Dad has been…well…difficult."

"Are you going to be able to wrestle when you get back?"

Scott's voice was steady as he replied, "That hasn't been determined yet, but Mom says that he probably won't pull me from the team. She did say that he would probably restrict my activity until I bring my calculus grade up and I won't get my cell back. But I'll still be able to be on the team."

"That's good. At least he's not taking everything away."

"Yeah, I guess." Scott's voice sounded resigned. "But I still feel like I'm being punished harshly and that life will probably feel like a prison, even with wrestling to distract me." Derek felt a slight sting that Scott hadn't included him on the list with wrestling as something that could distract him, but pushed the thought aside realizing that this conversation was not about him, it was about Scott. "Anyhow, Mom said I couldn't stay on the phone long. I really wanted to hear your voice and to wish you a Merry Christmas. I'm sorry that I haven't called. Can you forgive me?"

Derek's heart softened and all he wanted to do was to make Scott realize that everything was alright. "There's nothing to forgive. I can't wait to see you when you get back."

"Me, too. I gotta go."

Derek heard the other end of the phone click. Closing his phone and leaning back in bed, he took in a deep breath. It felt cleansing and he realized that a huge weight had been lifted off his chest. But there was a nagging feeling inside him as well. In this conversation a nervous and subordinated side of Scott revealed itself. It seemed like the self-assured and confident person that Derek had become accustomed to was missing. He hoped that when Scott came back, whatever was missing would also come back.

Chapter 14

Knowing that Scott was back in Cambridge, but being unable to talk to him, made the Sunday night before returning to school the most stressful of the entire vacation for Derek. He wanted to see Scott, away from other students, in the privacy of the attic. He needed to feel Scott's arms around him, to feel their lips pressed together. He wanted to see Scott's eyes, those blue-green windows which were always open to him, so that he could know without any doubt that Scott still loved him.

Listening to music and mixing hadn't helped to distract him. Beck's phone call earlier that evening had only served as a momentary reprieve from his concerns, leaving him feeling even more alone and scared once they hung up. *Please, let things be good tomorrow.* Derek went to bed fretful and unable to sleep. As he tried to fall asleep, Derek began to create scenarios of what their reunion would be like the next day. Some of the scenarios made him feel warm and tingly. He imagined walking to school and seeing Scott waiting by his locker with his crooked grin spread across his face and furtively whispering the things he needed to hear. Other scenarios increased his anxiety, leaving him tense and worried like imagining Scott sitting forlorn and removed, trapped by the weight of his father's unreasonable expectations.

The next morning, Derek, who had slept intermittently, constantly waking up thinking about Scott, was exhausted and drained. With little energy, he prepared for school and headed out. When he arrived at Brampton, the school was already bustling with students. Some had copper tans or peeling faces from their tropical vacations. Others were bundled in new down coats, purchased at ski slopes in New Hampshire or Vermont. There was an air of excitement and newness which shone in the faces of the students. Derek became immediately aware that he shared none of this excitement with his classmates. He had one thing on his mind...seeing Scott.

Walking into the building, he quickly made his way upstairs, holding his breath when he turned the final corner where his locker was located. Scott wasn't there. He blew the breath he had been holding in a slow controlled exhale, the disappointment crushing the last of his hope for a happy reunion. The only thing that cheered him up was when Beck showed and gave him a hug. "You look awful Derek.

Smiling with half-hearted energy, he returned Beck's hug. "Thanks. That's a lot better than I actually feel right now."

Beck placed a comforting arm on his shoulder. "Come on, I'm the one who is supposed to have the bipolar mood swings, remember." She grabbed his arm. "Let's get to class."

Allowing himself to be led to English, which was on the other end of the building, Derek considered his options. He could sulk and be depressed, or he could try to allow Beck to cheer him up. Although depression seemed like the far easier choice to make at the moment, he knew that a sullen mood would only draw attention to him. People were used to him being cheerful and upbeat.

Taking a deep breath, he repeated the phrase he had used with himself for years whenever he felt down and needed to pick himself up. *What would you do if you lost a wrestling match? You would practice harder and win the next time.* Although he was still feeling low, he had to admit that the wrestling analogy did make him feel a bit better. As they turned the corner to the hallway, where their English class was, Derek caught his breath. Scott was standing outside the room.

Seeing Derek and Beck, he started walking towards them. He didn't have a smile on his face, but he didn't look glum either. "Hey guys. You're both a sight for sore eyes." He gave Beck a hug and put his arm around Derek's shoulder. "How were your breaks?"

Beck smiled at him, unconsciously placing a protective hand on Derek's arm. "Break was great. Uneventful, but relaxing. Derek told me that yours was less than stellar. I'm sorry about your dad."

Scott's expression became blank for a moment. Shaking his head as if he had a shiver, he took in a deep breath through his nose, releasing it in an audible exhale through his mouth. "Thanks." He then turned toward Derek with what seemed to be both a pleading and apologetic look. "Could we talk for a minute before class?"

Taking the hint, Beck kissed Scott, then Derek, on the cheeks, and headed into class. Scott looked directly into Derek's eyes, and then allowed himself to drop his gaze to take in the rest of his body. "Come with me. There's no one in the stairwell. I want a minute alone with you." Derek allowed Scott to lead him to the stairwell at the end of the hallway. Once they were safely behind the closed doors, Scott pulled Derek into a tight hug. "Derek, you don't know how good it is to see you. The past ten days have been awful. I thought about you every day. I wanted to call you last night, but…" Scott tensed and Derek could see his lips tighten into an angry thin line. "I'm so sorry Derek. Please believe me. You have been all that's on my mind."

After all the days of stress and the lack of sleep, Derek felt himself crumble with relief at Scott's words. His eyes started to blur and he couldn't control the tears that spilled out of them. Scott pulled him into a tight hug once again. After a moment, Derek was able to speak. "I was so afraid that you felt differently about me since you've been gone. It was horrible and I tried not to let my mind play games with me, but I couldn't help it."

"I know. I'm sorry Derek. My feelings haven't changed. I still love you. It's going to be harder to spend time together, but we'll figure it out. Once I get my calculus grade back up, everything can go back to how it was." Scott lowered his head to Derek's neck and kissed him, gently licking the sensitive spot he had memorized and causing Derek's brain to block out everything but Scott's touch. He clutched at Scott, holding him in a tight embrace. Scott pulled back. "Not that I'm complaining about the hug, and you are even sexier than ever, but you stink!"

Derek pulled back and stared at Scott with shock, then began laughing. He hadn't taken a shower for the past two days and was too tired to really clean himself thoroughly this morning. "Well, I've been a bit distracted and it's kind of taken my motivation for grooming away. You have to keep this a secret because no one knows, but I have this boyfriend here at school whose dad wouldn't let him call me over winter break, and I sort of lost it towards the end there. I didn't sleep well last night and my shower this morning was half-hearted at best. I did brush my teeth though."

Scott laughed. "Your secret is safe with me as long as you keep my secret."

Derek wiped his eyes which had finally dried after his sudden rush of emotion a moment before. "You can tell me, but I can't make any promises that I'll keep the secret."

"Fine, I'll take my chances." Scott was beaming, not missing a beat in their banter. "I also have this boyfriend here at school. Over break, my dickhead father took my phone so I couldn't call him. He wouldn't even let me call him last night even though I was dying to. Guess what?"

"What? Tell me." The last of Derek's tension ebbed from his mind and muscles and all that was left was contentment to be with Scott once again.

"I almost snuck out of the house last night to go see him, but I was worried that if my dad found out, he would make things even more difficult than they already are."

"You should have..." Derek stopped himself and shifted back into character. Now was not the time to make Scott feel bad. "Well, if I were this boyfriend of yours, I know I would have been extremely happy to have you calling at my window in the wee hours of the night. I would probably have been so happy that I would have given you a reward."

Scott's smile widened and a seductive glint shone in his eye. "You know what? I think you just beat me at my own game." Not sure what he meant, Derek stood there with a perplexed look on his face. Reading his confusion, Scott took Derek's hand and placed it on his crotch. Derek immediately felt his engorged cock straining against his jeans. "I guess I'm not the only one who gives someone a hard-on with just my words."

Grabbing both sides of Derek's face, Scott pulled Derek into a ravenous kiss, pressing him against the wall. As Scott's intensity increased, Derek felt as if ten days worth of separation was being flushed out of him with this one kiss. He felt his knees begin to give out beneath him, but didn't care. He didn't want this kiss to end.

Reluctantly, they pulled apart, both tugging at their crotches to relieve their straining, and very noticeable, bulges. After readjusting, they figured it was safe to go to class. Mr. Carlton was in the middle of a lecture and the students were taking notes. All eyes rested on them. Derek looked at Beck who, after glancing at the two of them, closed her eyes and shook her head.

"How nice of you two to join us. Did you forget where class was while on winter break?" Both boys knew better than to answer. "Well, since I am feeling well rested, I will forego the detention slips this once, and only once. Understood?"

They both answered in unison. "Yes, sir." Derek was actually pleased that Mr. Carlton had made a point of showing his generosity by not giving them detention. That would undoubtedly be the topic of gossip following class and not the fact that he and Scott had arrived late to class, together, with conspicuously red and swollen lips.

Derek, Scott, and Beck had lunch together and Beck wasted no time launching into a reprimand of both of them. "I'll start with you, Derek, since I've known you longer. You have spent the past ten days as bright and cheery as a dead flower. All of a sudden everything is peaches and cream. I am surprised you don't have emotional whip-lash right now." Derek's face burned as he opened his mouth to protest. Beck raised her hand, "Shush!"

Taking a deep breath, she settled her stare on Scott. "And you. I still love you, but I am seriously pissed at you right now, even though the past ten days weren't your fault. Derek is crazy about you and got it into his head that you didn't want him anymore." It was Scott's turn to flame red as he opened his mouth to protest. Beck raised her hand once again, "Zip it!"

Toggling her head back and forth between the two of them, she looked as if she were watching a tennis match. "Break is over. You're both here. It's time to put all of this nonsense behind us." Shell-shocked, it took Derek and Scott a moment to collect themselves.

Derek wasn't sure whether Beck was truly upset with them or if this was just her dramatic way of telling them that everything was going to be ok. Either way, Derek wasn't used to the feeling of being reprimanded by his best friend and didn't like it. "Uh, ok. Thank you for the thrashing."

Beck took a bite of her burger, her eyes narrow and her body hunched. Finally, she looked up at the two of them again. "You know, this is bullshit anyways. Derek, I have never seen you act so helpless and miserable before, ever. What's with you? It's like you're a completely different person this year." Derek glared at Beck and Scott sat silently, not knowing what to say.

Derek took in a deep breath, trying to calm himself before he said something he would regret. "Is there a problem here? I have never seen you act like such a fucking bitch in all of my life and all of a sudden you are slamming me *and* embarrassing me at the same time."

Scott tried to interject, but both Derek and Beck shot him a warning glance and he quickly closed his mouth and faced his tray. Beck snapped her head towards Derek and pointed directly at him. "Ever since the two of you…" she looked around the room to make sure no one was watching or listening. Lowering her voice, but maintaining a clearly angry tone, she continued, "… started going out, you have been completely absent. I didn't say anything because I knew that you were happy and I have always wanted you to find someone that you could love. But you have never turned into a depressed, wimpy brat just because you couldn't talk to someone for a few days. Get a fucking grip. Grow up!"

Scott couldn't remain silent any longer. "Beck, what the hell is wrong with you?"

Beck turned to Scott, fixing him with a vicious expression. "Why don't you stay out of this? This is between me and Derek right now." Scott closed his mouth and raised his hands in surrender.

Derek had had enough. "Beck, you need to shut up. I don't know what has gotten into you, but if you have a problem with me, we should not be talking about it here in the middle of the cafeteria. You certainly shouldn't be snapping at Scott if you are pissed at me."

"Well, when the fuck else can I talk to you? All you ever do is spend time with Scott and wrestle." Beck's face had become flushed with her frustration and anger.

"Gee, let's think. We have, what, all of our classes together? Maybe you could talk to me then. Or here's a novel idea. How many times do we text each other a day? Maybe you could have texted that you had something you wanted to talk about."

Beck got up. "That's perfect. Get sarcastic. Great defensive move. Be sure to try that on one of your opponents. Maybe you can pin someone with your words. Oh wait, you don't use words. I forgot." Picking up her tray, she stormed off leaving both Derek and Scott stunned, unable to make sense of what had just happened.

Not wanting to discuss the outburst, Derek shoved the rest of his burger into his mouth. Scott, taking the hint, sat silently and waited for Derek to finish eating. When Derek had finished, they got up in silence and headed to their fifth period classes.

As Derek headed to his Latin class, he thought about what had just happened with Beck. Something was off with her. She was dramatic and had a flair for over-exaggeration, but she had never directed frustration and anger directly at him without buffering her rebukes with hugs and an invitation to get coffee or to eat something. This was not like her and it concerned Derek.

That afternoon's practice was grueling. Most of the guys were out of shape from ten days of little to no exercise. At the beginning of practice, Coach had the team gather around him. "We are having a fantastic season boys. We are undefeated and have already beaten one of the schools that we feared could stand in our way of taking the division this year. But, we haven't won yet. That won't happen until the division championships are over. We need to focus, get into the best shape possible, and practice hard. Our meet against Birmingham, the Waltham team, is in three weeks. They have a solid team and they haven't lost any wrestlers from last year." Coach took off his cap and mopped his head. "I am proud of you boys. I know you all have it in you to dig deep and to push yourselves to be your best. Let's get started."

Josh pushed the team hard, spending a great deal of time on sprawls, spins, and sprinting in place. Derek wasn't sure whether Josh's torture-like drills were inspired by Coach's speech or a result of his lingering embarrassment from losing his match against Allistaire. Either way, several of his teammates had to puke in the garbage can outside the wrestling room during that first practice after winter break. The rest were dripping with sweat and panting. Even though Derek had run every day to keep in shape and to quell his growing anxiety, he was exhausted and his muscles felt like rubber at the end of practice.

The hot water from the shower was a relief to his body and Derek spent a long time allowing his muscles to relax from the heat. Once he was dressed, he found Scott. "So, you want to grab a bite to eat?"

Scott looked at him with sad eyes. "I can't, Derek. Remember? My dad said I have to go right home after practice."

Disappointed, Derek tried to mask his feelings. They wouldn't change the fact that Scott was on restriction and would make Scott feel worse than he already did. "That's right, sorry. Let me give you a ride home." Brightening up, Scott grabbed his bag and they walked to his car.

Once outside Scott's home, Derek allowed the car to idle. Scott sat quietly for a moment, and then turned to Derek. His hands were fiddling with the zipper of his bag. "Derek, I know that the past ten days have been tough, but I want to talk about what's going on at home for me right now. Would that be ok?"

"Of course it's ok. You know you can talk to me about anything you want."

Scott remained fidgety, pulling a pen from the front pocket of his bag and clicking it so that the pen head popped in and out. "It's going to be hard for us to spend much time together. The only times that we will be alone are when you pick me up and drop me off. I just want to make sure you understand that it's not because I want to spend less time with you."

After his relief at seeing Scott at school and their affectionate reunion, Derek hadn't considered that their distance from each other would only be marginally reduced now that he was back. "I know. I appreciate you saying so though. We'll figure it out somehow, right?"

Scott took Derek's hand. "I hope so. My dad can make things very difficult for me if I don't give him what he wants. The best thing that could happen is that I bring up my calculus grade quickly. Then things can go back to normal." Scott released Derek's hand and stared at his lap. "I hate that I don't have my cell phone. My dad even said he didn't want me using the internet, so we can't even chat on AIM or anything." Scott punched his leg. "This sucks."

Derek felt his stomach begin to churn. Not only would they see less of each other, but their two main methods of communication were cut off as well. He reminded himself that it wouldn't help things to complain. "Like you said. Once you get your calculus grade up everything will go back to normal." He sounded much more hopeful than he was feeling.

"Right. I really am sorry Derek. It's not fair that this has to affect you too." Scott stared through the windshield with a blank expression on his face.

Scott's misery was written all over his face and Derek wanted to erase it. This was his father's fault and Scott had enough to deal with, without feeling guilty about how Derek was affected by his punishment. "Scott, I know you're not just making up excuses or brushing me off. I'm not going to pretend that this doesn't suck, because it does, but I understand." When Scott didn't look at him, Derek took his hand and pulled him close. Scott looked at him with bleary eyes, brimming with tears that were on the verge of spilling down his cheeks. "Don't worry so much. This is something you can't control. Don't let it rule you. Do what you need to do. If I can help, I will."

Scott's eyes opened as if he had just thought of something. "I said something like that to you on the day of the Lexington meet when we were looking at the water. I forgot all about that."

Derek smiled, knowing full well where this advice had come from. "It was a good message. Don't forget it." Scott needed to remember the water under the bridge. He needed to remember that there was only so much that he could control and not to let the things he couldn't control affect him. Leaning toward Scott, he gave him a soft kiss. When Scott got out of the car, he called after him. "See you tomorrow." Scott waved and shut the door.

Chapter 15

Over the next few days, the temperature dropped significantly with a cold front sweeping in from the north. That, combined with shorter days and the heavy cloud cover, caused a sullen atmosphere to settle in throughout the school.

Derek's routine had shifted once again since they had returned from winter break. He was still picking Scott up before school and dropping him off after practice, but without spending the time with him after practice in his attic, he felt listless. He and Scott had found moments to escape during the day, particularly between the end of school and before practice, but the moments were fleeting and didn't provide enough time for them to really connect the way they had before winter break. More than anything, that was what Derek missed.

To take his mind off things, Derek spent most nights listening to music and mixing songs. Wanting to veer away from the typical dance songs he usually mixed, he began downloading music with ambient, mellower beats and sounds. Groups like Enya and Supreme Beings of Leisure served as his muse.

Derek was listening to a record that contained relaxing beats, which created a tranquil atmosphere, when his attention was jolted from what he was doing by a knock on the attic door. Turning to see who it was, he was surprised to see Beck standing there. He hadn't spoken to Beck since her outburst a few days earlier and their separation felt like an impenetrable wall between them. She looked timid, a look that Derek had never seen on her before. "May I come in? I'm not interrupting you am I?"

Derek turned the volume down on the record player

and walked to the couch. "Come on in. I didn't know you were coming." Beck walked into the attic and hovered around the couch. She was playing with the strap of her purse and wouldn't look him directly in the eye. Both confused and intrigued by this unprecedented behavior, Derek patted the empty space next to him on the couch. "Sit."

Beck sat next to Derek and placed her purse on the floor in front of them. "Derek, I'm so sorry about the other day. I don't know what came over me. I was just so worried about you all through winter break and then, as soon as you saw Scott, your mood shifted so suddenly. It really scared me. I'm not sorry that I'm worried about you, but to attack the two of you the way I did at lunch was inexcusable. And the things I said to you..." Her eyes welled up with tears and a few spilled down her cheeks.

Derek was taken aback. Beck had never issued an apology without having been chided into it before. Even then, her apologies were usually begrudging, followed by *but* and some excuse why her actions had been justified, essentially negating the effect of her apology. "I have to admit, I was shocked and it did kind of piss me off. Why did you do that? Why couldn't you have just talked to me?"

Beck stopped fidgeting with her hands and turned to face Derek, drawing courage from the fact that he was responding with understanding. "I don't know. I wanted to, but something in me just snapped. I had been holding in all of these unexpressed concerns about you. I was trying to help you to feel better over break and none of my efforts were working. Then, as soon as you saw Scott, it was like he turned on a light switch and your mood instantly became cheerful again."

Derek wasn't sure what Beck was getting at. "Are you jealous of Scott? Did you feel like you should have been able to make me feel better and were upset that Scott did?"

"No, absolutely not. I swear that's not it, although I certainly understand why you might think so. Especially since I know which buttons to press to get you to react pretty much any way I want." Derek couldn't help the chuckle that escaped from him. It was true. If anyone knew how to elicit a specific reaction from him, it was Beck.

When he looked back at Beck, she was smiling. It was timid, only half a smile, but she was lightening up. "It's like I have been saying all along, Derek. I'm concerned that you aren't being careful and that you'll get hurt. Maybe I should just mind my own business and let nature take its course. But watching you go from depressed to elated just by seeing Scott, I felt worried and helpless. You can't let any one person have that much influence over you. You have to be able to make *yourself* happy. Friends, boyfriends, family…we can all help you by being there for you as you work through your feelings. But you should be the one who masters your own emotions. No one should have that kind of power over anyone else."

Derek considered what she had said. He was usually a reflective person, so it was surprising to realize that he had done so little of it over the past couple of weeks. "You've been thinking about this a lot haven't you?"

Beck took Derek's hands. "It's all I have been thinking about. But I have been especially regretful since Monday. It's been killing me, knowing that I behaved so badly and not making things right between us, even if it has only been three days. I just needed to make sure I really knew what it was that bothered me so much before I came to you."

Any feeling of frustration and anger he had been harboring towards her for the past few days melted away. He leaned over and hugged her. "Beck, thank you so much for coming over. I hated the small distance that has been between us, even if it was only for a short time. I don't know if I could stand it not having you there as my confidant and partner."

Beck returned his hug, and then held him at arm's length. "You *could* stand it. That's what I am trying to tell you. You don't need anyone in order to be happy. Don't misunderstand, you will never have to go without me being right there by your side, but you don't *need* anyone. Remember that. You can figure your own shit out. Don't let anyone become so central that you lose yourself. Don't forget that the guard you have kept up your whole life can serve a good purpose. It helps you to know that you are the most reliable person that you can count on."

"Wise beyond your years, Beck." Although Derek meant it, he said it with a bit of sarcasm.

"Well, I can't take all the credit. I did call the Psychic Friends Network last night and asked them how this conversation would go."

Derek cocked his head in surprise. "Really?"

Beck smiled, "Oh my God. You are so gullible. No, you moron. Do you really think that I would waste my time or money talking to some washed up, Dion Warwick wanna-be, Psychic Friends Network freak? Give me just the slightest bit of credit."

Derek laughed, happy that some semblance of their old banter had returned. "Hey, help me pick out some sounds from this new record. I'm going for a new feel in the songs I am mixing."

By Friday's practice, the team was back in shape and excited about their match against Waltham in two weeks. If they won that meet, they would have successfully defeated both teams that were potential contenders for winning the division championship. It was motivation to keep them pushing hard.

After practice, Josh asked the guys if they wanted to head into Harvard Square for pizza. He had maintained a serious demeanor in practice, most likely determined to ensure that he did not suffer another loss like he had with Lexington. The core group, Sean, Phil, and Power, immediately said they would go. "How about you, Derek? Scott?"

Scott hadn't told the guys that he was under house arrest, not wanting them to think that he was some wuss whose parents ruled his life. "I can't. I have a big calculus test coming up and I need to hit the books."

Josh shrugged. "Suit yourself. Derek, you coming?"

Derek looked first at Scott, then at Josh. "Uh, maybe. I have to run home first though. Maybe I'll catch up with you guys later." Derek knew that Scott was feeling guilty about not being able to spend more time with him, so he had pushed the topic. Still, he couldn't fathom that Scott's parents wouldn't at least let him out of the house on the weekend. Risking the chance of placing Scott in a worse mood, he decided to broach the topic. "Scott, I was wondering if you might possibly be able to ask your dad if you could go out for maybe a little while tomorrow or Sunday. Do you think that he would say no to that?"

Scott turned to Derek with a sad look in his eyes. "I told you, Derek. When my dad makes up his mind about something, it's final until he changes his mind. He won't let me off the hook, not even for five minutes on the weekend."

"I know, but I just thought—."

"I know what you thought and I'm telling you that he won't allow it. All you're doing right now is making me feel even worse about it."

Scott's comments stung. That was precisely what he

had *not* wanted to do. "Sorry, I just thought I would ask."

Scott's posture softened as he turned to Derek. "No, *I'm* sorry. I know this is hard on you too and it's not fair. You should go to Harvard Square and hang out with the guys. There's no sense in both of us having a ruined social life because of my problems."

"Naw, I think that I'll just head home and listen to my music and continue mixing. I've been experimenting with new sounds."

Scott placed his hand on Derek's shoulder. "You should really go out and have fun. I feel guilty thinking that you are putting yourself on house arrest along with me."

This is not what Derek wanted to hear. "I don't *want* to go out with the guys. I want to go out with *you*." He hadn't meant to sound petulant, but since it was already out, he left it there.

Scott removed his hand from Derek's shoulder. "What do you want me to do Derek? If I ask to go out it will only make things worse. I've already told you. Once my calculus grade comes back up, the restriction will be lifted."

A heated wave of irritation shot from his gut to his head. His words escaped before his brain had a chance to force his mouth to remain closed. "You aren't even willing to try to ask for a break. You're just accepting this like your dad has the right to treat you however he wants." He was sorry the second he said it, but once again, he didn't take the words back.

Scott's eyes flared as he grabbed the passenger side door handle. "You don't know a *thing* about what my father is like. You may not understand why I am settling for my dad's treatment of me, but that's because you have parents who don't expect perfection from you. Maybe if my mom would stand up to him I'd be able to comply with your wishes, but she won't. So *I'm* stuck. *You* don't have to be. Go have pizza with the guys." With that, Scott got out of the car, slammed the door, and walked into his house.

Derek was stunned by Scott's outburst. He knew that he shouldn't have pushed the topic, but he half hoped that his obvious desire to spend time with Scott would at least soften him up a bit. He hadn't expected for Scott to get so angry.

As he drove himself home, he chastised himself for not realizing that Scott had spent time thinking about the differences between their parents. He felt kind of stupid. *How could he not have thought about it?* Derek always knew that his mom and dad were great. His next thought came as a sudden blow. *I've taken them for granted.*

Scott did not have such a luxury. His father was gone most of the time, and when he was around he applied tremendous pressure and imposed harsh punishments. Scott's mother was warm and loving, but would not stand up for him to his father. Pulling into his driveway, Derek was feeling quite guilty about pushing Scott. That wasn't what Scott needed from him. He got enough of that at home. Derek should be a source of relief, not an added stress.

Derek's parents were having dinner in the kitchen when he entered the house. They both looked up when he came in. His father was refreshing his mother's wine glass. "You're home early for a Friday night. What's Scott doing tonight?"

"He has some studying to do for a big calculus test on Monday."

His mother's face took on a perplexed expression. "He hasn't come over all week."

Derek felt his chest begin to constrict. "Well, he's been working on bringing his grade up in that course."

His father began to refill his own wine glass. "I'm sure you boys would rather go out on a Friday night rather than hang in."

It wasn't going to do him any good to pretend that things were ok. All it would do is make him feel guilty. The last thing he needed was to feel another negative emotion. Grabbing a plate from the cabinet, he cut himself a large portion of the lasagna his mother had made and spooned a huge pile of broccoli onto his plate. He looked first at his father, then at his mother, and then began speaking. "Scott got a B- in calculus and his father has told him that he can't go out at all, or use his phone or computer, until he has brought the grade back up to an A. He got A's in everything else, but apparently his father expects him to get straight A's."

As he spoke, he saw his parents' brows crease. His mother watched him studiously, observing his body language. When he finished, she spoke up. "It sounds like Scott is going through a difficult time right now, and has some challenging issues that he is facing at home."

She paused, considering what to say next. "Derek, you *do* know that your father and I are very proud of you and are very happy with your grades. We respect your ability to balance school and wrestling. Your friends have always been good people. We love you very much. There's nothing you could do that would change that." Derek's father's mouth was full so he simply nodded his agreement with what his mother had just said.

Derek felt a lump form in his throat and took a large gulp of water to push it back down. "Actually, I was just thinking about that in the car." His mother clasped her hands in front of her on the table. "No, not that you had concerns about me. What I was thinking about is that you both have been really great. You support everything I do, come to all of my meets, and rarely give me any trouble over my grades."

He turned to his mother, giving her a meaningful look. He placed his hand over hers before speaking again. "This is the house where people always want to come because they know that you will feed them." She smiled.

Derek took in a deep breath and sighed. It was so much easier to think the things that he felt. Putting things into words was always such a struggle. "I guess what I am trying to say is thank you. I always just assumed that parents were basically the same, but I'm beginning to see that they're not. So, thanks for being so cool."

When he finished, his mother's hand reflexively crossed her chest, resting over her heart. Derek could see her eyes become slightly pink and she quickly stood up, taking both her and his father's plates to the sink.

His father looked at him for a moment, and then leaned back in his chair. "I wish you weren't in such a hurry to grow up. It must be all those high school drama shows on the television where all of the kids act like they're twenty-five instead of seventeen. Your mother and I don't expect you to tell us that you appreciate us, son. Your actions tell us all we need to know. You're a good boy. You make good choices. We trust you. That's thanks enough."

Derek felt the lump begin to form in his throat again. His father had never spoken to him about feelings of trust. The sentimental moment was broken by his father's next comment. "Speaking of parents putting pressure on their kids, how are you coming along with your college applications? Deadlines are the end of this month and we didn't spend all summer trekking up and down the northeast for the fun of it."

Derek smiled briefly. *This is the dad I'm used to.* Grateful for the topic shift, Derek laughed. "I'm almost done with the essays and my applications should be ready to go in the mail by the end of next week."

Satisfied, his father got up, gave his mother, who was still standing by the sink, a kiss, then headed out to the living room, patting Derek on the head as he passed.

Derek was almost finished with his dinner when his mother returned to the table. She sat across from him, watching him eat. It was almost like she was watching him like he was a TV special on the Nature Channel. "Derek," she paused, looking as if she were struggling to figure out what she wanted to say. "What you just said to us was very insightful. You are growing up so fast. Too fast." She paused again, looking slightly uncomfortable. "Scott is going through something that you have never had to go through. Give him time. He's a good person." She paused again, looking as if she were searching for the right words to say what she was thinking. Finally she shook her head. "I'm glad you are friends with him. It sounds to me like Scott needs friends right now."

"Yeah, but I don't really know what I'm supposed to do to help him. It seems like whatever I say lately kind of pisses him off."

The look she gave Derek was filled with a mixture of admiration and a bit of sadness. "I love you, Derek. Everything about you makes me proud. I have to admit, you have seemed to grow up so much this past year. It makes me a little sad." Derek looked at his mother, not understanding. "Mothers don't like to see their children grow up. Well, they do, but they don't." Derek was sure that he must have had a perplexed look on his face because his mother started to chuckle. "Listen to me prattle on like a silly old woman. Mothers never stop seeing their children as the little babies they raised. It's difficult to see that you are becoming a man. But you are turning into a good man, Derek. A respectable man."

She stared at Derek for an extended moment, and then cleared her throat. "Well, I am sure that you don't want to sit there and listen to your mother go on about how much she loves her little boy. Would you like some more lasagna?"

Derek wasn't sure what brought on his mother's affirmation of her feelings toward him, but she was right, listening to her talk about how proud she was caused him to shift uneasily in his seat. "No, I'm finished. I think I'll just head up to the attic and continue mixing some of my new songs."

"Ok, dear." With that she picked up his plate and returned to the sink. Tired, Derek trudged up to the attic. It had been a long week and today had been particularly long.

The next day Derek and Beck met up at The Garage in Harvard Square. It was a pitiful excuse of a mall, but it was the only one that was close to their homes and allowed them to people watch. Their favorite spot was a pizza shop on the second level. It was an open space and had tables along the railing looking down on the first level. There was one particular table which allowed them to see directly into the news shop which contained a sizable collection of pornographic magazines. The straight and gay porn mags were in the same section on two shelves next to one another. The two of them liked to play a game where they would choose someone they both thought was cute and predict whether they were gay or straight.

Placing ten single dollar bills on the table between them, they selected their first subject, a man in his mid-twenties with short cropped brown hair and torn jeans. Beck dismissed him immediately. "Too easy. Definitely gay." Derek had to agree and sure enough, after a few minutes of pretending to peruse the auto magazines near the porn rack, he glanced to his side and walked to the shelf with the gay porn.

They continued watching men of varying ages and when they differed on their opinion, would remove one of the dollar bills and place it to the side. When an older man, probably in his forties, entered the store, Derek thought he was straight and Beck was convinced that he was gay. The man walked towards the porn rack and began leafing through various sporting magazines, finally standing between the shelves which contained the gay and straight porn.

Beck leaned against the railing. "Come on. You know you want to pick out one of those gay mags. You probably have a girlfriend or a wife at home who doesn't have a clue about how to suck dick so you *know* you want the next best thing."

Derek laughed, leaning against the railing as well. He saw a ring on the man's wedding finger. "No, what you want is to look at those hot young girls with breasts that are ten sizes bigger than your wife's and who get into sucking toes and butt play."

Beck laughed. "Go on. Get one of the ones with the beefy guys with shaved chests. You like the guys who pretend that they're tops but who are secretly screaming bottoms. You know that you can't resist the idea of those big boys who lust after dick."

Derek tried to will him to the rack with the straight magazines. "Look at those young girls who claim to be eighteen and who are probably twenty-four. You probably want to grab one of those magazines so you can relive your college days when girls' tits hadn't begun to sag and they got wet all on their own without needing any lube."

Beck turned to Derek. "You know, for a gay guy who has never done anything but kiss a girl, you are pretty good at describing woman parts and their functions."

"Shut up and play the game."

They continued to watch the guy until he finally walked over to the shelf with the gay magazines. "Yes! I knew it. He's a big old nellie queen." Several of the patrons in the pizza shop turned to look at her. Realizing she had an audience, she turned to face her onlookers. "Well he is!" The people who had been staring at her replaced their shocked expressions with looks of disapproving irritation, then continued to decide what they were going to order. Beck triumphantly snatched the dollar bill. "First point goes to me."

By the time they had finished the game, Beck had won seven dollars to Derek's measly three. Derek was ready to leave. "Man, I have to work on my gaydar. I can't believe that you can pick 'em out better than me."

Beck flashed him a depraved smile. "It's not you hon, I just channel Judy, Barbara, Madonna, and Cher and it comes to me. It's a gift really."

Derek laughed. "Ok Ms. Diva Thang. Let's spend our winnings on some ice-cream." They left The Garage and walked down the street to Steve's Ice Cream Parlor.

Chapter 16

Derek continued to pick Scott up before school and drive him home, but after their argument, the natural flow of conversation between them had become uneasy. Their time together became strained. It was hard enough to only grab snippets of time together during the day, but with the added tension that was lingering between them, the time lost some of its intimacy and comfort. Derek missed the passion and emotion of their time alone and didn't know what to do to get back to that place with Scott. On top of that, Scott had become visibly stressed, spending study hall and lunch hours working on calculus, preparing for his upcoming test.

Even though he was upset, Derek refused to allow himself to return to the same feelings of helplessness and anxiety that he had experienced during winter break. Falling into the comfortable security of hiding behind his guard, he spent more time with the guys on the team, focused his energy on perfecting his moves during practice, and continued experimenting with the new sound during his mixing sessions. With each distraction, there was one fact that was present in his mind at all times. Scott was pulling further away from him and he was allowing it to happen.

On the day before the match against Waltham, Scott joined Derek and Beck for lunch. Derek didn't know what to make of this since Scott had kept to himself for over a week. Part of him was happy to be near Scott, but his guard caused another part of him to feel nervous and uncomfortable. Beck, in her usual manner, greeted Scott cheerfully. "Hey there stranger. I was beginning to wonder if you still went to school with us. How is everything?"

Scott looked pale and empty. "I just got my calculus test back. I got a C. I studied as hard as I could and I got a C. My dad is going to serve me my head on a platter."

Derek turned to face Scott, forgetting his defenses completely. "Scott, I'm so sorry. I can't believe it. What are you going to do?"

Scott shook his head. "I don't know. I have no idea what my dad will do now that my calculus grade is actually lower. I am guessing that my home prison is going to become maximum security."

Beck slammed her hands on the table. "If I were your mother, I would take his balls and…" Derek shot her a warning glance, trying to communicate through the intensity of his stare that this was not the right approach to take. Beck took the hint and closed her mouth.

Scott smiled bleakly. "It's ok, Derek. Actually, I wouldn't mind hearing what Beck would do to his balls right now."

Seizing the opportunity, Beck continued. "I would take his balls and hold a paring knife at them. Then I'd tell him that if he didn't stop treating you like you were some kind of criminal that I would cut them off and grind them to pulp in the kitchen sink disposal."

Derek cringed at the image Beck had painted. Scott lowered his hands protectively, covering his crotch, but his lopsided smile began to creep across his face. "I appreciate the sentiment, but that was the most grotesque threat against manhood I have heard you make."

True to form, Beck took Scott's statement as a compliment and beamed. "Thank you." To Derek's surprise, Scott started laughing heartily.

At practice, Josh went easy on the team, wanting everyone to feel energized for the meet the next day. As Derek drove Scott home, the tension was unmistakable. The closer they got to Scott's home, the more intense it became. When they finally pulled up to Scott's house, Derek let the car idle and waited to see if Scott was going to speak. When Scott made no move to speak or to leave the car, Derek decided to break the silence. "Well, I guess you are going to have to face the music." He tried to make his voice sound light-hearted, but Scott's face remained solemn. "Try not to let him get to you. You expect him to blow a gasket, so hopefully it won't be worse than you have already prepared for."

Scott nodded his agreement. "I know. I've just been feeling really depressed lately. I feel like I am under a rock that is trapping me and I can't figure out how to free myself." He looked at Derek. "I know I've been distant. I just can't seem to get out of my own head. Even though I studied hard for the calculus test, if I were to tell the truth, I couldn't concentrate on studying at all. I haven't been able to concentrate on much of anything lately. I feel like I'm going a little crazy."

Derek wanted to reach out and touch Scott. He wanted to hug him closely and tell him that everything would be ok and that he would be there for him for anything that he needed. He *wanted* to say these things, but his guard tugged at his gut, reminding him that if he wasn't careful, he would get hurt. "Scott, I know it has been tough for you, but it will pass. Maybe right now things feel overwhelming, but things pass."

Scott sat for a moment longer then leaned towards Derek and gave him a peck on the cheek. It was just a little kiss, nothing passionate or intimate. Derek wanted to grab Scott and lock them together in a kiss that expressed how he felt. That gave Scott all of the love in his heart. He wanted to grab Scott by the shoulders and force him to see what Derek was able to see so clearly. That his father didn't know shit and certainly didn't appreciate how incredible he was. He wanted to do these things, but he didn't.

Scott maintained eye contact with Derek for a moment. As Derek watched him, he thought he could see longing behind the surface of his eyes; a slight trembling of his exterior that indicated a deeper longing trying to get out. But then the moment was broken as Scott reached for the handle and let himself out of the car. A voice cried out inside of Derek's head. *Call him back. Don't let him walk away from you.* Ignoring the voice, he remained silent and watched as Scott let himself into his house and closed the door behind him.

The next day was tense. Ever since Scott had brought him to the Foot Bridge the day of the Lexington meet Derek had become calmer on the days of their meets. Scott, on the other hand, had become increasingly fretful on meet days, even more so than on a typical day since his return from Iowa.

As the team loaded onto the bus to head to Waltham, Scott took a seat by himself in the back, placing his book bag next to him. This was an unspoken sign, understood by all of the members on the team that someone wanted to sit alone for the ride.

Derek joined Josh and Power near the front of the bus and they talked about their opponents from the previous year. They had been able to watch a few Waltham meets prior to their scheduled meet and were relieved that most of the members of the Birmington team had remained at the same weight class as the year before. In fact, their general wrestling style seemed unchanged. Derek figured it made sense. *Why mess with something that was working so well?*

Derek's opponent was Kevin Charles, also a senior. He had won the district championship for their weight class the previous year. They were fairly evenly matched, although Kevin had been stronger than Derek and was able to out-power him. Derek hoped that his weight training from the summer and from the past few weeks would help to balance their strength.

The Waltham auditorium was packed. While there were still more spectators supporting Birmington, the crowd supporting Brampton's team was much larger than it had been for the Lexington meet. Derek assumed that people wanted to come and show their support against Waltham since they had already beaten Lexington. If they won tonight, they stood a good chance of taking the division.

Once again, Derek saw his parents sitting on the bottom bench of the nearest bleacher. His mother bought two cases of bottled water, the smaller-sized bottles of Poland Springs, and had a tray filled with appetizer-sized meatballs.

Shannon was also sitting next to his parents and smiled when he walked over. "Derek, it's so nice to see you." The fact that Shannon and his parents both knew why Derek and Scott had not been able to spend time together hung over them like a storm cloud threatening to unleash rain at any moment. It caused their interaction to be slightly forced.

Derek's mom put her arm around his shoulder, refraining from giving him a kiss. Somehow she knew that he would tolerate her affections, but that it would bother him more than usual under these circumstances.

When Scott walked over, Shannon gave him a hug. Derek's dad said hello and shook his hand and his mother let go of Derek's shoulders, placing it around Scott's. "We've missed you, Scott. Good luck today." Scott smiled but looked sad.

Once both teams had warmed up, the captains went to the center of the mat to shake hands. Then the meet began. The first four matches each lasted the full three periods. Derek only half watched the matches, constantly looking back at his parents. His mother and Shannon were deep in conversation, each with worried creases wrinkling their foreheads. By the time it was Derek's turn to wrestle, he had worked himself into a small frenzy. His four teammates from the lower weight classes had all won, although not by pins, so the score was twelve to zero in favor of Brampton.

Derek walked to the center of the mat and faced Kevin. With each step towards center mat, he shed the distracting thoughts that were interfering with his concentration. Thoughts of Scott, of his mother and Shannon talking, and of his worries about losing to Kevin last year. When he took neutral position, he was centered and ready to wrestle.

The ref instructed them to shake hands and blew his whistle. Derek shot, faster than usual, for Kevin's leg and captured it, hoisting it into the air. Stepping in front of the foot Kevin still had on the mat, he brought Kevin down and secured control. The ref awarded him his two points for the takedown. Kevin tried to use his strength to stand up, but Derek found that he was able to maintain control and leverage, keeping Kevin securely in his hold. Kevin tried a few other defensive moves, but Derek allowed his instincts to guide his actions and he countered them, maintaining control. While he was strong enough to keep Kevin from over-powering him, he was unable to maneuver him to expose his back to the mat.

Entering the second period, Derek was ahead, two to zero. He began the second period on the mat in referee's position with Kevin on top of him. When the ref blew the whistle, he mustered all of his energy and executed a perfect escape move. The ref awarded him one point. Using his skill and speed, Derek took Kevin down and was awarded another two points. As in the first period, Derek was unable to turn Kevin to his back, but he did not lose control of him either.

In the third period, Derek was ahead five to zero. Since Kevin had taken the top position in the second period, Derek had to take the top position in the third. This was Derek's least favorite position because he could not rely on his speed to gain points. He envisioned the move he would use to turn Kevin's back to the mat. When the ref blew the whistle to begin the period, he shot his arms to grab Kevin's ankle and knee and shoved with all of his weight, forcing Kevin to fall from his position on all fours to his side. Kevin struggled, but was unaccustomed to wrestling past the first period and Derek could tell that he was growing tired. *Thank God I spent so much time running. I definitely have better endurance than he does.*

A surge of confidence shot through him. He had worked out all summer and had run all year. He knew his moves and executed them well. He had the spirit to dig deep, willing himself to push through sore muscles filling with lactic acid and lungs screaming for more oxygen. This was his year and the realization gave him a tremendous boost of energy.

Working his arm into position to secure a half-nelson hold, he slowly and steadily rolled Kevin over, earning three more points for exposing Kevin's back to the mat. Kevin fought and arched onto his head, but Derek felt his fight weakening quickly. With the last reserves of his energy, Derek tightened his hold and squeezed, forcing both of Kevin's shoulders to the mat. All he had to do was keep him there for three seconds. The ref started his count and after three waves of his arm, slammed the mat. Derek had won with a pin. It had taken nearly all of three periods, but he did it. Brampton was awarded six team points for the pin and was now ahead eighteen to zero.

Cheers floated towards him from his team and from several of the bleachers that were occupied by Brampton students and parents. When he walked off the mat, his team hoisted him in the air, and congratulated him.

Brampton won the next three matches, so when it was time for Scott's match, they were ahead twenty-seven to zero.

Derek tried to catch Scott's attention before he walked onto the mat, but Scott did not look his way. Tony Liu was his opponent and had also won division the previous year. Derek knew that this was going to be a tough match. When the ref blew his whistle, Tony took Scott down quickly. During the rest of the first period, he maintained control of Scott, turning him to his back twice. Watching Scott wrestle, Derek sensed that something was missing. Scott did not have the same determined look on his face. He seemed to be losing energy faster than usual.

Going into the second period, he was losing eight to zero. As Derek had in his match, Scott began the period on the mat in referee's position with Tony taking the top position. He quickly escaped and took Tony down earning one point for the escape and two points for the takedown. Scott was unable to secure a hold to turn Tony to his back, but he did not lose control of Tony for the remainder of the period.

Entering the third period, the score was eight to three with Tony in the lead. Tony began on the mat with Scott on top. He escaped quickly earning himself a point. The score was now nine to three. And then Derek saw the change. Determination crept into Scott's eyes. Circling Tony, Scott looked like a panther stalking its prey. After about thirty seconds, he went for the takedown and successfully controlled Tony on the mat earning him two points. The score was now nine to five.

With only forty-five seconds remaining in the match, Derek could barely keep himself seated at the side of the mat as he watched. *Please Scott. Get the points you need.* Scott managed to secure a hold on Tony forcing him first onto his belly and then slowly rolling him to his back. Although Scott earned 3 points for exposing Tony's back to the mat, he was unable to pin both of Tony's shoulders down for three seconds. When the final buzzer rang, Scott had lost nine to eight.

The Birmington team jumped up on their bleachers and started screaming. With only two matches left, there was no way they were going to win the meet, but this was the first win for their team and their reaction was as if Tony had trampled Scott into the ground. Scott shook hands and the ref lifted Tony's arm as the winner. Sulking off the mat, Scott plopped down to the side of the rest of the team as Josh walked out for his match.

Both Josh and Power pinned their opponents and the final score for the meet was a crushing thirty-nine to three. An explosion of excitement rippled through the team and the Brampton spectators. People rushed to the side of the mat and everyone began hugging everyone else.

Once things had settled down, Derek looked for Scott but could not find him. Looking over to where his parents were sitting, he saw that Shannon was not there either. He walked over to his parents who excitedly hugged and congratulated him, but pulled back when Derek didn't respond with the enthusiasm they expected. When he spoke, his voice was filled with sullen disappointment. "Where's Scott?'

His mother looked at him, her face drawn in concern. "Once the meet ended, he left with Shannon." Derek's heart sank. His mother placed an arm around his shoulder. "Would you like a ride home with us honey."

"No, I think I'll head back on the bus. I'm guessing it's going to be an awesome bus ride after this win." After his initial wave of disappointment, Derek was sure that he had summoned the will to sound and appear cheerful. Even so, his mother was looking at him with the same worried expression as before.

His father saved them both from having to address the issue. "I bet you're right son." He placed an arm around Derek's shoulder, giving him a half hug. "We'll see you at home. That was some match, Derek. After the way he trounced you last year, it was very gratifying to see you pin that sucker."

Derek's face blushed. "I'm not sure whether that's a compliment or not, but thanks...I think."

His father laughed and patted him on the back. "Always wondering what others think aren't you son? For the record, it was a compliment." His mother gave him a hug which was tighter than usual and held on for longer than Derek would have expected.

Derek's father touched his wife's arm. "Honey, you're going to have to let go if he plans on making it home at all tonight. Half of his team is already headed out." She released him and gave him a kiss on the cheek.

As expected, it was a boisterous, celebratory ride back to school and, for the ride at least, Derek was able to push thoughts of Scott out of his mind.

When Scott got into Derek's car the next morning, he was unusually quiet. Sitting next to him, the silence made the gap between the two of them unbearable. They had been so close and now they were two feet apart and may as well be two miles apart. Pulling to the side of the road, Derek turned to Scott. "Are you ok?"

When Scott looked at Derek, his irritation was unmistakable. "What are you doing? We have to get to school."

"We have time. I'm worried about you, Scott. You haven't been yourself for a while. We haven't been ourselves for quite a while. I miss us. Don't you?"

Scott looked out the passenger side window, laying his

hands on his lap. After what felt like an hour, he spoke. "Yes, I miss us. But what does that matter? It doesn't change anything. It doesn't change my situation."

It disturbed Derek when he realized how relieved he was that Scott missed their time together. *When did I begin doubting that?* "I know it doesn't change your situation, but I hate that we have been so distant from each other."

Scott pulled his stare away from the window and turned his head to face Derek. He bit his lower lip, which, although they had not been intimate with each other for weeks, still sent chills through Derek's body and caused his cock to stir. As Scott looked at him, Derek could see the inner dialogue taking place. Scott's eyes began to water, but then he took in a breath and contained his rising emotions. "I don't know what you want me to say."

Derek hadn't expected that response. "I want you to say that you miss me and that you still want me. I want you to say that it's killing you as much as it's killing me that we have to spend so much time apart. I want you to kiss me." His voice cracked with his last statement and he felt his eyes begin to burn.

Scott's lips began to tremble and Derek was sure he saw desire in his eyes. Holding Derek's gaze, he raised his hand. Derek held his breath, waiting for the moment of connection. Yearning for the sensation of Scott's hands touching him. Scott's hand was a mere inch from his face, and then he pulled it away and placed it in his lap. "Maybe I do want all those things Derek, but do you have any idea how much shit I am dealing with right now? My dad is worse than ever. My grades are beginning to drop. I lost the match last night. I'm not able to spend any time with you. Now you're pressuring me to give you something I can't give you?" Tears were streaming down his face and his voice had risen so that he was almost shouting. "What makes it worse is I wish I *could* give you everything that you want."

Derek was dumbstruck. Scott had just told him everything that he wanted to hear. At the same time, he was saying that despite feeling everything that Derek wanted him to, it made no difference. While Scott sat next to him, not making any attempt to stop his crying, Derek felt his own eyes fill with salty tears that began to drip out of his eyelids forming hot droplets on his pants. "Maybe you can talk to your mom and see if you can get any time to get out. I'd be happy with a couple hours on a Saturday if that's all I could get."

Scott's entire body flared up in anger. "You don't get it do you? I can't handle everything that's going on anymore. Everything that used to come easily to me is falling apart. Maybe you're able to handle the fact that you're in your first relationship, but maybe I can't. Maybe it's the reason my life sucks so much right now."

Derek's heart constricted in his chest. "Y-You think that us being a couple is the reason that things suck for you right now?"

Scott's lips tensed into thin white lines. He looked at Derek first with regret and then, as clearly as if someone had flipped a switch, Scott's emotions went dark and he was completely unreadable. "What I'm saying is that I think I need time to myself right now. I need to get myself back on track. Having other people around isn't going to help me do that. We've been trying to pretend that things will get better between us, but right now, I don't see how that can happen."

Derek began to control his breathing, mentally telling his muscles to relax. Checking for holes in his guard, he attended to the spots that hurt the most and began to surround them with armor. His head, his heart. Both were completely shielded before he spoke again. "Are you breaking up with me?"

Scott wiped his eyes. "No. I don't know. I'm just saying I need some space."

Derek pulled the car back onto the road without uttering another word and continued the rest of the drive to school. *Well, this is what I get for letting my guard down. I get dumped. Never again.*

Chapter 17

When they arrived at school, Derek was in a haze. He replayed the conversation he had with Scott over and over in his mind. He couldn't believe that they had grown so close and then moved so far apart over the course of a few months.

Beck, sensing the awkwardness between them, remained silent, not knowing whether her antics would ease or exacerbate the situation. In second period pre-calculus, Derek felt his cell phone vibrate. When he placed it on his lap and opened it, there was a text from Beck. *Spill. What is going on?*

Derek didn't feel like rehashing the conversation. It didn't feel real. *Think Scott and I just broke up.*

Beck stared at Derek with earnest concern. She placed her hand on his arm. *So sorry Derek. Are you ok?*

Derek felt a lump form in his throat and his eyes began to burn. Stealing himself, he swallowed a few times and rubbed his eyes. Once he felt he had control over himself, he opened his notebook and wrote the date on the top of the page. *I'm fine. Everything's fine.* He didn't dare turn to face Beck for fear that her sympathy would push him over the edge. Her worried expression burned a hole in the side of his face, but he refused to turn to face it. There was no way that he was going to let anything in that might touch his mind or his feelings. Not right now when they had just been ripped to shreds.

Beck opened her mouth but decided it would be better to leave things well enough alone for the moment. Opening her notebook she wrote the date on the top of a new page as well.

At lunch, Derek joined the guys on the team who

were still ecstatic after their big win against Waltham. Students kept coming to their table congratulating them and letting them know that they would be at division to cheer them on. Beck had chosen to join the team with Derek for lunch. Looking around the lunch room, Derek couldn't find Scott anywhere. He immediately felt a sense of disappointment, but pushed the thought from his mind.

The second half of the day continued much as the first half had, Derek going through the motions of his classes, but keeping his brain activity to a minimum. Every time he thought about Scott and their conversation that morning, his emotions swelled and he had to work harder each time to push them back.

Last period history was particularly difficult since it was the only other class he shared with Scott and he didn't have Beck there as a buffer. Scott had moved from his normal spot, sitting at the side of the room and wasn't looking at him. Derek tried not to look at Scott either, but every few minutes he found that he was staring at Scott and had missed what the teacher had been saying. Each time he pulled his eyes from Scott, it was like tearing off skin or picking a scab that was meant to help him heal.

It wasn't until practice when Coach sat the team on the mat that his thoughts were finally able to stop drifting towards Scott. "I can't begin to tell you how proud I am of you guys. First, I want to congratulate you. Second, I want to state one thing I know with absolute certainty. Waltham is just as good as they were last year. They have the same team members and wrestled with just as much skill. You are the ones who have changed. You have become tighter and more focused as a group. As individuals, you have each improved tremendously."

Derek considered Coach's words. He was right. The Waltham team hadn't changed. They had. The parallel to his own life hit him hard. He had changed too. He wasn't the same person he had been last year.

"This season is clicking boys, and in three weeks, when we go to division, we stand a very good chance of winning the title of division champions. For those of you who have been on the team for the past three years, that would be an incredible way to finish your high school careers." For the past three years he had also solidified his protective shell, but this year he had allowed it to weaken. He had let someone else through his coat of armor and had felt like a champion.

"It will be something you will always remember, even if you never wrestle again after this year. We need to continue to push. Nothing is guaranteed until division is over." That's where the coach lost him. He didn't want to push. Pushing is how he got himself into trouble and it was why he was feeling so miserable right now. His internal reverie was broken by the team's cheer.

Josh worked them hard that day. He took them to the weight room after warm-ups and had each of them design a three-day workout circuit. They had been split into three groups and would be working out together. One group began with upper body muscles, another group began with lower body muscles, and a third group devised aerobic exercises to build endurance. They would be able to complete five cycles before the division championship.

Even though it wasn't as difficult to see Scott at practice, it still hurt knowing that Scott was right there. Looking at him dressed in clothes that revealed the body that Derek had come to love touching and kissing, reminded him of what they no longer had and those were the moments that he needed to distract himself. A number of times, during lulls in the practice, he would look over at Scott, but Scott remained aloof and would not return his gaze.

After practice, Derek walked towards Scott, hoping that they would walk out to his car together, but Scott grabbed his bag and headed out of the athletic building. Following him, Derek tried to catch up, but Scott was practically running and Derek realized that he was going to walk home. *Fine, be that way.* Getting into his car, Derek blasted his radio and drove home, anger surging through him like bolts of lightning. If this was what he should expect from trying to open up to feeling love and emotion, it wasn't worth it. It had been far easier and safer to hide behind his protective defenses. He promised himself that he would never allow himself to become vulnerable again. No one would cause him to feel as miserable and empty as Scott had made him feel. The promise was that much easier to keep since Scott had secluded himself from everyone. He sat by himself in classes, ate lunch on his own, and remained silent during practices.

Over the next couple of weeks, Derek became more and more withdrawn, but he made sure he still appeared cheerful when he was around people. Practices were the only time when he actually felt it was safe to push his defenses aside. Concentrating on his body, the interplay of his mind and his muscles, improving his technique, were things that he could focus on and do without emotion. These were physical things that he could improve upon alone. It was simple mechanics. *Put this arm here. Move my leg this way. Next time lower my body a couple of inches.* Even Scott's presence wasn't enough to distract him from his focus during practices.

On Monday, the week before division, Beck asked Derek to eat lunch with her in the senior lounge. It was usually empty during the senior lunch period and would give them a chance to talk alone. Not liking the serious tone in her voice, Derek agreed hesitantly. Once they had grabbed their lunches, they headed to the senior lounge and settled into two seats by the window. Derek took a big bite out of his sandwich and watched the snow lightly dance through the air, drifting to the ground and forming a thin white blanket over the grass and fallen twigs. It was a peaceful scene.

Beck sat silently, looking out the window as well. As she chewed her food, she rubbed her nose, a sign Derek had learned over the years meant that she was considering how to begin a difficult conversation. "Derek, I have been really worried about you." Another scratch to her nose. "Not just worried. Disturbed."

Derek turned to face Beck. He knew something like this was coming, but was surprised at the conviction in her voice. "What are you so worried about? I've told you a million times. I'm fine."

"I know you have. And, by all appearances, you seem to actually be fine. But I know you, and I don't think you are fine at all." Beck pressed her lips together, taking in an audible breath through her nose before continuing. "I'm not worried that you're sad, or depressed, or obsessing. Actually, I'm worried for exactly the opposite reason. You're too controlled. Too calm. And not sad, depressed, or obsessing at all." She took a sip of her milk. "I can't believe that I'm going to say this, since all year I've been telling you to be careful, but I'm worried that your defenses are going to ruin all of the progress you have made this year." Derek didn't understand and his face must have revealed his confusion. "Okay, let me try to explain it a different way. I am still concerned that you need to be careful, but for entirely different reasons than earlier in the year."

Derek was genuinely interested to see where Beck was going with this and put his sandwich down. "Beck, what are you talking about?"

"At the beginning of the year, you became immediately infatuated with Scott." At the mention of his name Derek tensed and Beck remained silent to see how Derek would react. "Please, Derek, let me say what I have to say. If you don't want me to I won't, but I really need to tell you why I'm worried about you."

Derek's shoulders slumped in defeat. He couldn't deny his best friend anything when he knew she clearly needed it. "Ok, fine."

Relieved, Beck continued. "At the beginning of the year I told you to be careful because I saw you opening yourself in a way I had never seen before. Well, I had seen it, but only privately with me. But I had never seen it in public, let alone at school. I was worried that you would move too fast, read too much into things that I didn't know were there in Scott, and ultimately hurt yourself, making this year a terrible experience for you. I was worried that if you got hurt by exposing yourself to ridicule the first time you showed a sign of interest in another boy, you may never be willing to open yourself up to those kinds of feelings again. Are you following my line of thinking so far?"

Derek dutifully summarized her statements. "I was whipped. You freaked because you thought everyone would find out I'm gay. So you told me to be careful."

Beck shook her head. "Okay, I'll allow the oversimplification, but only because I have a bigger point to make. I think you get that I had specific reasons for telling you to be careful at the beginning of the year. But now, I am even more concerned about you than I was before."

Derek looked at Beck with genuine confusion. "I don't understand. You wanted me to be careful. You said I needed to keep my defenses up. I didn't and look what happened. You should be happy that I figured out that you were right before anything really damaging happened."

Beck sighed. "That's exactly what I said. And it's what I truly believed. But I don't think I do anymore." She placed her hand on Derek's leg and waited until he was looking directly at her. "Ever since that morning when you and Scott had your fight...broke up I guess... your guard has come back stronger than ever. It's like a force field you have built around yourself, preventing feelings from getting in or out. That's not good, Derek. You need to feel this. You need to let yourself hurt. You love Scott and if you don't allow yourself to feel angry and sad and hurt, I'm afraid that you may get used to protecting yourself from feeling things whenever the going gets tough."

Derek understood what she was saying, but didn't want to face it. To face that truth would leave him exposed. To consider that his behavior now which was the only thing holding him together could have a long-term impact on his ability to feel in the future was too scary an idea to consider. Not while he was still so miserable. "What? Are you trying to say that you *want* me to be hurt and sad?"

Beck was unfazed by Derek's choice to selectively choose the most negative aspect of what she had just said. In fact, Derek noticed that a small smile had crept over her lips. "No Derek, of course I don't want you to be hurt and sad. But I do want you to feel! I want you to remember how wonderful it felt to be with Scott. I want you to remember that your heart became fuller than I have ever seen it. Allow yourself to cry. Hell, punch walls for all I care. But don't bottle your feelings up and pretend they aren't there. Whether things work out between you and Scott or not, *you* are the one that I love. You're too good a person to close yourself off now that I have seen how wonderful you are when you open up. If it's not Scott, it will be someone else who will win your heart and cherish you the way you deserve. I don't want you to be closed to that when it comes along because you are afraid of feeling like you do now."

Derek's mind replayed the year in fast-forward. He

remembered first seeing Scott, the weeks of trying to figure out if Scott was gay and whether he could possibly return his feelings, their first kiss, their runs together, the attic…the Foot Bridge.

The image of the Foot Bridge brought his inner movie to an abrupt halt. Scott's words at the Foot Bridge had been a turning point for Derek. That moment had embodied the combination of Scott's ability to express his thoughts and feelings, and the strong, confident person that Derek had fallen in love with. It was when he realized that Scott was more than a physical body for him to share experiences with. He was someone who saw the world as Derek saw it, with optimism and naïve idealism.

At the same time, it was the moment that Derek realized that the differences between the two of them were what made them such a perfect pair. Scott's self-assurance and his ability to put his emotions into words, was the perfect balance to Derek's rational stability. Derek had the foundation of having lived in one place and having parents who were proud of his accomplishments rather than constantly pushing for a perfection that he would never attain. Scott had the confidence to be himself. If it hadn't been for Scott, Derek never would have lowered his guard and allowed himself to experience everything that he had with Scott.

What started as an image in his mind of Scott and the feelings he and Scott had shared, turned into a feeling of what he and Scott no longer shared. Like a knot was tied around his heart, it tightened minute by minute. He imagined Scott's lips against his and the arousal that he felt each time Scott smiled his crooked grin or bit his lower lip. Their shared dedication to wrestling and the sense of pride at a move executed perfectly or a match fought for and won. The alignment of their thinking, despite the different ways they expressed themselves; Scott with words and Derek through music. And, like a wave washing over him, he began to drown in the knowledge that he couldn't have that with Scott anymore.

As these feelings bombarded Derek one after the other, his heart began to beat faster and his breathing became shallow. His lungs constricted, limiting his ability to take in air, and his vision became blurry. His eyes began to sting as he felt a burning wetness in them, and then streaming tears as they poured down his cheeks. He hadn't noticed that Beck had moved, but became suddenly aware that he was being held tightly. Allowing Beck to pull his head to her chest, he rested against the warm softness of her body as he was racked by sobs. Beck rocked him, whispering, "I'm here. I'm here." Until his crying had subsided.

When Derek got home from practice, his parents' car was not in the driveway. Entering the house, he found his dad sitting at the kitchen table. "Hey, Dad. Where's Mom?"

His dad looked up when Derek entered the kitchen. "She went out with one of her girlfriends tonight. I was thinking we could go grab a bite to eat. Your choice. What do you say?"

"Sure, sounds good." The day had been draining for Derek. Having an easy evening with his dad who rarely engaged him in serious discussion seemed like the perfect remedy for his overwrought mind. Grabbing their coats, they headed to Derek's car. "Hmm, why don't we go to Bisuteki?" Derek thought that watching the chefs chop and demolish food before his eyes on the stove-top tables would be the kind of aggression that would make him feel better.

"Good choice. Your mom will be upset with the amount of salt I'm about to eat, but she's not here right now. Let's go." His father smiled, enjoying this passive form of resistance against his mother's insistence on healthy eating and obeying the increasing demands of his doctor.

Their table was full and the chef put on a good show, tossing shrimp tails into his hat with his knife and chopping onions into perfect rings, stacking them together and sending flames shooting towards the ceiling. They talked about Derek's college applications and the schools he wanted to attend. Derek was hoping to remain local, but did not want to live at home once he began his freshman year. His top choices were Boston University, Northeastern University, and Tufts. Each of these colleges provided easy access to the city, but they were close enough so that he could come home for his mom's cooking whenever he wanted.

His father became excited as they discussed college life. "It's the best time in your life, son. No responsibility besides studying. Your first taste of freedom. Tons of kids figuring themselves out all together in one location. You know college is where I met your mom right?" Derek had heard the story of how his parents had met countless times, but he enjoyed hearing it each time it was told. "I was this cocky kid majoring in economics. Your mom majored in English. My crowd dreamed of making their first million by the time we were twenty-five and your mom's crowd dreamed of romance and writing love stories which would be turned into screenplays for movies and television. We were two groups that never mixed.

"But one night, in a bar during our senior year, I was drinking beers and playing darts with some of my friends. One of them asked me to get another round. When I walked up to the bar, there she was standing behind a couple of larger boys who were ordering drinks themselves. She was standing patiently waiting for a space to open at the bar and looking a bit frustrated. I found the scene to be quite amusing and had a sudden urge to help her order her drinks. I was never one to walk up to the ladies, but for some reason, I just walked right up to her and said, *Looks like these guys don't notice that a beautiful woman is waiting to get a drink. Let me help you out.* She was suspicious of me of course. Even *I* realized what I said had sounded like a corny come-on line, but she allowed me to elbow a path to the bar. I stepped aside, allowing her to order her drinks, and then helped her to bring them to her table where her girlfriends were sitting. She invited me to join them and I was very nervous, but I decided *what the hell* and joined them."

"What about your friends? Weren't they pissed that you ditched them?"

Derek's father laughed. "The only thing I can remember from that evening after I met your mother, is your mother. We talked and talked and talked. She was charming and her laugh…it was like an angel's song. I think I fell in love with her right then in the bar that night."

"But your friends. They must have been pissed or worried." Derek couldn't comprehend just leaving your friends like that. It would draw so much unwanted attention and drama.

His father considered Derek's question. "Well, I suppose when I was in high school, I felt as you do now. But you'll learn, son, that there are some things that are far more important and rewarding than keeping your friends happy. Finding your love definitely ranks at the top of that list."

Derek imagined his parents, only a couple of years older than he was right now, meeting each other and falling in love. Then he thought of Scott, remembering the first time he saw him in English class and his immediate attraction to him. He wondered why it couldn't have been that easy for the two of them. "Dad, after you met Mom, did you guys know right away that you were going to get married?"

Derek's father laughed. "Oh, God no. We had our share of ups and downs just like everyone else. I was very focused and driven with my courses. My dad expected me to join his stock trading firm once I graduated and put a lot of pressure on me to focus on graduate school. Your mom was much better at enjoying life. She became quite frustrated with me on a number of occasions. There was even one point where she broke things off with me."

Derek was shocked. "Really? Neither of you ever told me that before."

"Well, it didn't really matter. In the end, I smartened up and realized that a lifetime of happiness was more important than a lifetime of luxuries that only money can buy. When I stood up to my dad, telling him that I wouldn't be joining his firm after college, he was furious, but your mom was elated. I proposed to her two weeks later and she accepted. My dad eventually came around. Years later he actually told me that he was proud that I had the courage to stand up to him the way I did. That was just after you were born and he was thrilled to be a grandfather."

Derek smiled. "Wow, that's amazing. I wish you had told me this before. I had no idea."

His dad patted his shoulder. "Things have a way of working out, son. You just have to be patient and you have to follow your heart. That's why your mom and I have been so happy together. We didn't allow other people to dictate our choices. We chose what was best for us and it has taken us to where we are now…happily married with a terrific kid who is about to head off to college. Quite a ride I must say."

They ate the rest of dinner talking about colleges and

about the division championship that coming weekend.

When they got home, the car was back in the driveway. They walked into the house and his mother was sitting in the living room reading. "Did you boys have a nice evening?" His mother glanced first at his father and then at him. Derek could see a hint of edginess in her eyes, which she quickly masked with a smile.

His dad walked over to his mother and leaned over, giving her a lingering kiss on the lips. She blushed. "Yup, dinner was great."

"Where did you guys go?"

Derek walked over and kissed him mom on the cheek. "We went to Bisuteki. It was fun."

His mother shot his father a disapproving glance. "Henry! Bisuteki? I leave the house for one evening and off you go, like a child, to a restaurant I would never approve of. How much soy sauce did you use?"

His father laughed. "Enough."

As his parents bickered, Derek felt a warm feeling of comfort. He walked up to his room to get started on his homework. Once finished, he listened to his iPod and fell into a calm and restful sleep for the first time in weeks.

Chapter 18

Derek woke the next morning, free from the physical and mental weariness he had grown accustomed to. Hopping out of bed, he took notice of little things like the hot water on his skin when he took his shower or the smell of breakfast in the air as he walked down the hall towards the kitchen. Having been so absorbed in his problems, it came as a shock to him that he had ignored the things he had always appreciated. Small details invigorated him: the cloudless day; the crisp, blue sky; the biting winter chill.

At school, he snuck up behind Beck and grabbed her by the sides. She let out a high-pitched squeal and wheeled around. "What the...Derek, I almost kicked you in the..."

"Nuts. Yeah, I'm sure." He gave her a big hug. "Let's go to class."

"You're in a cheerful mood today. Did your parents finally put their foot down and send you to a shrink to put you on Cymbalta or something?"

"Nice, Beck." Derek linked his arm with Beck's as they walked down the hall. "No, I didn't go to a shrink. I just had a good day yesterday. First a friend knocked some sense into my head and then my dad took me to an awesome dinner."

Beck squeezed Derek's arm. "Well, remind me to send your friend a box of chocolates for waking the dead. I'm sure she would love them."

"Who said a girl knocked sense into my head? Sheesh Beck, so presumptuous." Stopping by their lockers to put their things away, they then headed to English class. Scott no longer shared the back row with them, choosing an isolated seat to the side of the room. He was already seated when they entered.

Throughout English, Derek kept glancing in his direction. Over the past few weeks, he had made a point of avoiding contact with Scott so it surprised him when Scott made eye contact with him as well. At first, Derek would glance away, but as the class wore on, he allowed himself to linger in his gaze for longer periods of time. Scott's body language revealed a mixture of sadness and regret, but Derek detected something else, specifically in his eyes. Derek couldn't quite put his finger on what it was.

The snickering of his classmates jolted his attention back to the lesson. "Earth to Mr. Thompson," said Mr. Carlton.

Derek snapped his head towards his teacher. "Huh?" A new round of giggles erupted from his classmates.

"I was asking you about our book, A Separate Peace."

Derek's cheeks flushed crimson. "Uh, I'm sorry, could you repeat the question?"

Mr. Carlton shook his head. "I'm sure you are probably focused on the division championship this coming weekend, but while in school, please do try to remember we teachers count our victories in our students' academic achievements."

"Yeah. Of course. I'm sorry." Why is Mr. Carlton making such a big deal out of this? So I spaced out for a second.

"My question was, why do you think Finny refused to believe Gene when he claimed responsibility for causing him to fall out of the tree?"

Derek considered the question for a moment. He had asked himself the same thing when he read that part of the book. He identified with both Finny and with Gene. Finny...the outgoing and carefree friend keeping the peace at all costs. Gene…the brooding and reserved loner keeping all his thoughts and feelings closed off. They were two sides within himself. The brooding side constantly urged him to put up his guard. To avoid risks. The carefree side, the side that Scott had brought out in him, pushed him to take chances; chances which led to one of the greatest rewards of his life…and one of the greatest heartaches. His obstinate refusal to allow himself to continue to be hurt by Scott was Gene. His entire high school wrestling career was Finny.

Scott was Finny through and through. Honest, brave, daring. Only recently, since Scott's father had come crashing down on him had Scott begun to display some of Gene's characteristics. *Maybe everyone has a little of Gene and a little of Finny in them. Maybe everyone needs a little of both in order to really live.* Ideas raced through his mind, connection upon connection. His response was directed at the teacher, but meant for someone far more important.

"I think that Finny refused to believe Gene caused his accident because, in his own way, Finny loved Gene. He believed Gene was someone who *could* let go of his reserved nature, but was afraid to give himself a chance. If Finny accepted Gene's confession, Gene would have become as crippled mentally as Finny had become physically. Finny wanted to believe in Gene, not end their friendship. I think Finny put his needs aside, deciding Gene's were more pressing. He wanted Gene to realize his own greatness. The first time Finny broke his leg and Gene visited him in the infirmary, he hinted at his suspicion that Gene had somehow been responsible. The interaction left him with terrible guilt. The second time Gene visited Finny, this time at his home, and confessed to causing the accident, it was Finny's second chance to make things right between him and his best friend."

Derek stopped talking and looked over at Scott, not

caring whether his abrupt pause drew attention. Scott had been his Finny. He had drawn him out of his shell and helped him to become fuller and more alive. Now it was his turn to be Scott's Finny. Scott needed to remember how wonderful he was. Not seeing himself clearly, he needed to see his worth through someone else's eyes... Derek's. "Finny ended up making the ultimate sacrifice which finally opened Gene's life to what it could be."

The class was silent after Derek finished his answer. Derek held Scott's gaze, the expression of awe unmistakable.

"That, Mr. Thompson, was a very insightful answer. Does anyone wish to comment or add any thoughts?"

After class, Beck walked with Derek to their second period class. "That was a beautiful answer you gave in class today. Was it, by any chance, life imitating literature?"

Derek allowed a small smile to cross his face. "You know I was talking about me and Scott."

"So you are saying you want a second chance to give Scott what he needs so you can maintain the relationship?"

Derek stopped. "Not exactly. What I think I am saying is I realize Scott's needs are more important than my own right now. I want a chance to tell him I finally realize I have more supports in my life which help me deal with adversity than he does. I was wrong to put pressure on him when he has nowhere to turn while sorting through all the shit on his plate. As much as I don't want to lose what we have...had, I love him too much to continue to make things hard on him. Maybe I need to let him go so he can get through whatever he's going through right now."

Beck's brow creased. She wasn't sure what had caused such a complete turnaround in Derek. "You figured this out in one day?"

Derek laughed. "No, I think I've known it all along. Yesterday just pushed me to finally see it. Thank you for pulling me aside at lunch, Beck. I needed to cry and to let myself begin to feel again. I'm not going to lie. Being around Scott and not being able to touch him is torture. Hell, we aren't even talking. But I love him and pretending our problems don't matter is pure bullshit." The weight of the past few weeks slipped even further off Derek's shoulders.

At home, Derek went to his room to drop off his jacket and his bag before heading to the kitchen for dinner. He was surprised to find his mother standing at the entrance of his room when he turned around. "Honey, I'd like to talk to you." She looked serious, but not angry. "Your father had to work late. Tax season. He won't be home for quite some time."

A slight twinge of panic shot up Derek's spine. Derek sat on his bed. "Sure, Mom."

His mother walked across the room and sat on the bed next to him. She clasped her hands and looked at the posters on his walls and the books and trophies on his shelves, the dirty laundry strewn about the floor. "You really should put your clothes in a hamper. You'll ruin them if you walk all over them."

Derek laughed nervously. "You wanted to talk to me about my dirty clothes?"

His mother placed a hand on his cheek. "No, of course not." She sat silently on his bed for a few minutes not saying anything. The air in the room became thick with anticipation. Finally she sighed. "The other night when you and your father went to dinner, I got together with someone."

"Yeah, Dad said you got together with one of your

girlfriends."

"Yes, I did meet up with a new friend…Scott's mother." Derek's heart skipped a beat. "She called me and asked to talk. She's worried about Scott. May I share with you the contents of our conversation?"

Derek couldn't form words. The list of possible topics his and Scott's mother could have talked about made it difficult to breathe. "S-Sure."

His mother patted his knee reassuringly. "We had a good conversation, Derek. You shouldn't be worried." He understood she was attempting to calm his nerves, but it didn't work. "She told me Scott's been lonely and depressed ever since winter break. She explained about his father, his demanding expectations, and about the punishments he inflicts. I told her you had already shared some of this with me and it seemed to make her feel more at ease to talk freely. She's experiencing terrible guilt, constantly forcing him to replant roots and make new friends. Whenever he begins to settle in someplace, those roots get pulled out from under him and he must start all over again. I can only imagine how she must feel because if I had done that to you…well, I simply wouldn't."

Derek wasn't sure where this was going. "How does any of this relate to me? I don't understand why Shannon decided to call you and talk to you about all of this. It's not like the two of you are friends. You only talk to one another at meets."

His mother had anticipated this question. "True. But when we talk it's usually about you and Scott." Derek's heart skipped a beat. "I first suspected she was worried at the Waltham meet." Derek recalled how distracted he had been seeing his mother and Shannon engaged in deep conversation.

His mother continued. "Derek, I think the reason she called *me* is because of *you*." Derek didn't know how to respond. *Does she know about us?* "One of the things that's comforted Shannon is knowing you and Scott are close. She said he's never become so comfortable in a new place so quickly. He's seemed happier than he's been in many years. Since his father prohibited him from any social activities after school and on weekends, she's watched him spiral into a dark depression. She's scared and didn't know what to do, so she called me. I think she was hoping I might be able to help her to figure out how you and Scott could spend time together again."

Derek's head snapped to face his mother. "What did you tell her?"

"First I asked her some questions. Like whether she had communicated her concerns to her husband. She said Ronald is under a great deal of stress."

Derek interrupted her. "Who's Ronald?"

His mother looked confused. "Scott's father."

"Oh. He only introduced himself to me as Mr. Thayer."

"I see." His mother grimaced. "Anyhow, I asked her if she had talked to Scott about what was troubling him. Apparently, he was *very* forthcoming." Derek's gut clenched. "He told her it was unfair his father was never around, yet assumed it was all right to treat him like a slave. He feels alienated and alone. He even expressed his anger at *her* for not fighting on his behalf. Her guilt, I think, is what pushed her to talk to me."

"He said all of that?" A twinge of embarrassment tugged at the sides of Derek's mind, realizing he had worried Scott would talk about him rather than his own problems. *When did I become so egocentric? The world doesn't revolve around me.*

"Oh, he said much more." Derek froze, the concern returning despite the internal scolding he had just given himself. "He said he had never been as upset about moving as when his parents moved him here to Cambridge, forcing him to miss out on his senior year. Meeting you made his anger disappear immediately. He said he's never had a friend like you. He was happy about the move after your first day of school…until winter break. His father's punishment is like forcing him to move all over again, but this time, he's facing his new friends even though he can't spend any time with them."

His mother's hands began to shake a little and her lips began to tremble. Derek placed his hands over hers in an attempt to comfort her. "Don't mind me, Derek. I'm a silly, emotional woman at times and I can't help but feel for the pain of others. Shannon didn't say so, but I got the sense she cares for you very much, Derek. As a mother, I believe the reason she cares for you is because you make her son happy. I think," his mother stopped speaking again, words becoming difficult for her, "I think that Scott cares about you very much too. Someone who has been forced to lose people over and over never learns to trust anything can remain stable. But Scott had begun to trust you would be someone who wouldn't disappear. I think Scott blames his father for having to lose you as a friend."

Derek's emotions flared within him and he couldn't contain his words. "Lose me as a friend. He hasn't lost me as a friend. He's the one who shut me out. He's the one who said he wanted his space and asked me to stop picking him up before school and dropping him off after practice." Derek's eyes began to sting.

As he spoke, his mother silently listened, watching him carefully. Once he finished, she allowed a couple of minutes of silence to fill the room. "You care about him don't you?" Derek didn't respond. "Honey, I've watched you grow up. When I held you as a baby and listened to your happy giggles, I knew I had brought a bright and cheerful person into this world. You've brought happiness, joy, and pride into my life. But as you've grown, I've watched you build walls around yourself. Your father and I talk about it often. But you've had lots of friends, done well in school, and stayed out of trouble, so we just accepted your brooding as one aspect out of many in your personality and didn't consider it something to worry about. I think that was a mistake on our part."

Derek's mother took his hand and waited until he faced her and was listening. "You keep everything bottled up inside of you and your only outlets are running and wrestling. Sometimes people need other people so they can get things off their chest. As a young man about to head off to college, I think it's time for you to face some grown-up facts. Your happiness will not be gained by keeping things in and trying to be who you think others expect you to be. I'm not saying you should be selfish or shouldn't consider the feelings and needs of others. You aren't capable of disregarding others. When you keep your feelings in, it can be harmful and unhealthy."

Derek's body began to quiver, and tears began to roll down his cheeks. His mother allowed him a moment to gain control of himself, and then continued. "Derek, I'm going to ask you a very difficult question, but it's a question that must be asked, and it has to be asked now." She paused and her struggle to find the courage to speak was transparent. "Derek, are you gay?"

Derek wasn't surprised by the question, but the fact that it had been asked out loud left him paralyzed. His hands and arms started shaking and his stomach tumbled about, threatening to erupt. Every fear he had held about revealing he was gay bombarded his mind at once: his fears of rejection, disapproval, hatred, and alienation. All of them started circling in his brain. All he could draw the strength to say was, "Yes."

His emotions burst within him as his whole body shook and he began to cry in earnest. His mother grabbed him tightly, holding him close. He lost a sense of time as they sat, hugging and crying together. Finally, Derek began to regain control of himself. He first stopped his trembling and then, slowly, stopped crying. After a few more minutes of resting in his mother's arms, they drew apart. "How did you know?"

His mother smiled, her eyes red and swollen and her cheeks shimmering with her tears. "Oh sweetie. You may keep a lot of things to yourself, but some things you simply can't keep from a mother. We have a way of knowing things. I suppose it's because I carried you in my body for nine months and stayed home to raise you. I've had my suspicions for years now, but this year, you lit up. Something came alive in you after you met Scott and I just knew. What I didn't know was how to ask."

A comfortable silence fell between them, giving Derek a chance to process their conversation. To his surprise, instead of dread or mortification, relief flooded through him. "I've been too scared to tell you. I was afraid you might not love me anymore."

His mother's lips began to quiver, but she stoically swallowed back her emotions. "Derek, nothing in this world could *ever* cause me to lose one ounce of the pride and love I feel for you. I won't lie, the fact you feared losing my love hurts, but although I call you a young man, you *are* still a boy. You are *my* boy and I will always love you. I'll have to adjust and accept that some of the hopes and dreams I've had for you won't come true, but this is not a bad thing. Nothing about you is bad. We'll work on adjusting to this together, as a family. Some of my dreams will remain the same. I still want you to find someone to love and who will love you. For some of my other hopes and dreams, like you experiencing parenthood, we'll have to see what happens with those. All parents want their children to be happy and healthy. Our needs are simple in that regard."

Derek couldn't believe his mother was ticking off each of his fears one by one, like she had a checklist of everything he had ever worried about. He leaned in and hugged her again. "I love you so much, Mom."

Hugging him back, a few of her tears spilled onto his shoulder and soaked through his t-shirt. "I love you, too."

Sitting back to lean against his headboard he looked at his mother. "Does Dad know? Have you talked about this with him?"

She smiled. "No, I don't think so. Men aren't as observant as women. Even a man as wonderful as your father has his limitations. Men see what they want to and can create explanations for things they don't quite understand to make them fit the picture they want to see. But, when you are ready, you *should* tell your father. I can be with you when you do. Like I said, we will grow with this as a family and we will all continue to love one another. Remember Derek, just like with me. Your father will *never* stop loving you."

Derek contemplated her words then let out a huge yawn. "I'm completely drained."

She smiled and stood up. "Why don't you lie down and rest. I'll come and get you when dinner is ready."

Derek lay back, replaying the conversation with his mother. Ever since he had come out to himself and to Beck, his greatest fear had been telling his parents. They loved him, but he wondered if they would become uncomfortable or distant. It had forced him to keep secrets and was when he began to pay attention to the guard he always kept up.

This conversation bore no resemblance to the one from his imagination. He always thought *he* would be the one to tell his parents, sitting *them* down and making a grand proclamation which would then send them reeling into tears and confusion. He had never anticipated coming out would be something that was initiated by his mother.

Rather than forcing a wedge between him and his mother, the conversation had brought them closer. Knowing he had underestimated his mother caused a wave of guilt to sweep over him as more tears streamed down the sides of his face and onto his pillow.

After a few minutes, his tears dried and the lump in his throat dissipated. He stared at the ceiling and turned his attention inwards. Everything was still ok. The world hadn't burst out in flames. His relief was magnified when he realized he had been holding in a tremendous amount of stress for a long time. The big secret was out and his mother still loved him unconditionally.

The smile that pulled at the corners of Derek's mouth caused his cheek muscles to strain. His life had changed dramatically this year and he had opened up to experiences he had spent a lifetime hiding from. He drifted into a restful nap proud that he had come out the other side, maybe a bit bruised, but in perfect working order.

Chapter 19

No longer carrying the weight of his troubles on his shoulders, Derek looked toward the division championship with excitement. He knew he could win, and now, with a clear mind, he could focus on wrestling without distraction. *The only thing that would make this perfect is if Scott were here to share this moment with me.*

The school buzzed with the excitement of the upcoming tournament. Flyers appeared on walls, the wrestling team was bombarded with good wishes, and classes were interrupted by daily announcements counting down the days to Saturday. The school even rented a shuttle to run back and forth between Brampton and Newton High, where division would be taking place.

Despite the chaos and excitement around him, Derek remained calm and confident. So much had happened in the past two days to change his outlook on everything. He had spent so much time maintaining a cool exterior and bottling up his feelings that the only thing he was able to do was concentrate on wrestling. His new sense of lightness made him want to skip through school. Of course, his natural tendency to avoid behavior that would draw attention to him hadn't changed. That would probably never change, but he finally understood that using his guard was good, as long as he struck the right balance between risk taking and reserve.

The only lingering distraction that kept Derek from being completely happy was Scott. It became increasingly difficult to draw his attention away from Scott in the English and history classes they shared. Each time he peered into those blue-green eyes, he couldn't shake his regret at Scott's pain, evidenced by his slumped posture and the dark circles under his eyes. Derek tried to summon the courage to talk to him several times during the week, but couldn't bring himself to do it.

At Friday's practice before the division championship tournament, Coach sat the team on the mat. "Today will be a short practice. I've spoken to your teachers and you've been excused from your weekend homework. Please don't make a big deal out of this because it isn't fair to the other students and won't help the other coaches to negotiate special treatment for their teams when they are in a position to win a championship. Today we'll just warm up and practice basic moves. Our journey together has built team spirit. Each of you plays an important role in the overall success of our team, but for the next two days, you need to focus on your own matches. You need to dig deep and make a decision…are you a champion or not? I already know the answer, but my opinion doesn't matter when you're on the mat. Good luck and I'm proud of you."

On Saturday morning, the team gathered in the athletic building parking lot at 7:00 AM to board their regular bus. The shuttle bus was already packed with students. When they arrived at Newton High thirty minutes later, they were amazed by the sheer size of the auditorium. Eight wrestling mats covered the center of the room surrounded on all sides by bleachers. The sixteen schools with the best overall records from the regular season were competing.

One of the refs walked to the center of the auditorium with a microphone, calling for the crowd's attention. "Before we begin the first round today, I would like to explain how the next two days will commence. Today will consist of two rounds. In the first round, sixteen wrestlers in each weight class will be reduced to eight. In the second round, those eight wrestlers will be reduced to four. Tomorrow there will be three rounds. The first will be semi-finals. Next, the wrestlers who do not win will wrestle to secure third and fourth place for their weight class. The finals will take place last, determining the champions. Once the top four places at each weight class are determined, team points will be tallied. First place wrestlers earn four team points, second place wrestlers earn three team points, and so on. The schools with the top three overall team scores will be recognized. The champions will receive a school trophy and banner. I want to wish everyone good luck."

By the end of the day, seven of the eleven wrestlers on the Brampton team progressed to the semi-final round: two wrestlers in the lower weight classes along with Derek, Frank, Scott, Josh, and Power. Only five wrestlers from the Lexington team moved on along with eight wrestlers from the Waltham team. Waltham held the advantage because they had more players guaranteed to earn team points, no matter whether they came in first or fourth. To win, most of the Brampton wrestlers would have to come in first or second in their weight class.

The sun was still high in the sky when Derek got home. Restless and excited he decided to go for a run. He would only hurt himself and his team if he allowed his nerves to get the best of him. Heading towards the river, he began thinking about wrestling, but pushed his thoughts aside.

At the Foot Bridge, he stopped and leaned against the railing, looking down over the water. It seemed angry, creating small whirlpools where it rushed past the cement legs. This water wanted to flow and nothing was going to stop it. A few feet past the bridge, the whirlpools reintegrated and the water's surface returned to one mass of raging, tumultuous motion.

Derek wondered what the water would say if it could speak. *I'm going to get where I'm heading. A temporary obstacle is not going to stop me.* If someone told the water it could no longer flow, it would have laughed and continued its journey, only mildly hindered from its goal.

An image of Scott entered his mind and, along with his observation of the water, something clicked into place. Scott was the water and the bridge legs were the obstacles he had faced. Mr. Thayer was just a bridge leg. Derek laughed at the image, but only for a moment. *Mr. Thayer may be the bridge leg, but Scott hasn't found his way around him yet.* He was still an obstacle that kept Scott from being the person he was meant to be: a happy and daring person; a person who rose above the stresses which caused most people to freeze; a person who appreciated the things others never noticed. Derek wanted Scott to find his way around this bridge leg, his father, and get back to the roaring flow of continuing his journey downstream. *But what can I do to help him?*

The next day the whole team showed up at the athletic building for the ride to Newton High. The auditorium was much less crowded than the previous day. Most of the wrestlers who had not advanced to semi-finals and a few of the schools which had been completely eliminated chose not to come. A partition had been erected to split the auditorium in half with two mats on either side. This gave spectators more room to crowd around and watch the final matches of the tournament.

One of the two Brampton wrestlers in the lower weight classes made it to the finals. Derek won his match fairly quickly. Frank's match took a bit more time, but he won as well.

The team crowded around to the mat to support Scott when his name was called. Scott walked out onto the mat. His opponent was Fred Master, a wrestler from the Newton High team. Scott and Fred took neutral position in the center of the mat, shook hands, and began wrestling.

The match started out well. Scott shot forward, grabbing Fred's leg, and dropped him to the mat scoring two points for the takedown. He secured a hold on Fred and rolled him to his back, earning three more points for back exposure. Fred managed to arch off his back and roll to his stomach. The remainder of the period consisted of Scott attempting to get more back points.

Scott led five to zero entering the second period. Fred knelt in referee's position on the mat with Scott on top of him. The whistle blew, and Fred executed a picture perfect reversal, gaining the top position and earning two points. Scott struggled to regain control of the match, but each time he stepped up to try to escape, Fred would bring him back down to the mat. Finally, Scott managed to escape, earning one point, but Fred immediately shot to Scott's legs and took him down once again, earning two points for the takedown. It surprised Derek how evenly matched the two were since Scott had defeated Fred easily during the season. Fred grabbed Scott's arm and Scott lost his balance and fell to his side. Seizing the opportunity, Fred secured a half-nelson hold and rolled Scott to his back, earning three back points. Fred squeezed, pushing both of Scott's shoulders to the mat. The ref started counting, but Scott arched onto his head and turned to his stomach. The fifteen seconds remaining in the second period dragged on unmercifully, but finally the buzzer rang. The score was now seven to six with Fred in the lead.

Scott looked tired when he took his position to begin the third period. Derek summoned a lungful of air and shouted above the crowd and his teammates. "Scott, come on! You can *do* this! Dig deep!" Scott looked up and locked eyes with Derek before kneeling down to his starting position. "You're awesome Scott! Finish this match. Think of the Foot Bridge!" Through his peripheral vision, he sensed some of his teammates turn to stare at him but he didn't care. All he cared about was Scott making it to the finals. Not because he wanted the team points, but because he wanted Scott to finally overcome the obstacles he had been facing.

Scott bit his bottom lip, still looking at Derek, and then nodded his head. Taking his position, the ref blew the whistle and the third period began.

The shift was clear as day. Something had turned on inside Scott. Quickly reversing Fred, Scott earned two points. He shot his arms across Fred's body, using his weight to knock Fred onto his side. Fred struggled back to a kneeling position, but each time he did, Scott knocked him back down. This continued for a minute and a half of the two-minute period; Fred fighting to a kneeling position and Scott knocking him back down. With twenty seconds left, determination set in Scott's face. He drove Fred down to the mat, gritted his teeth, and squinted his eyes in a look of pure fight. He dug his feet into the mat, pushing all of his body weight against Fred and slowly worked his arm around Fred's head to secure a half-nelson hold. With ten seconds left on the clock, Scott slowly rolled Fred onto his back. Scott couldn't secure both of Fred's shoulders to the mat, but he did earn three back points. The buzzer rang and Derek jumped to his feet, cheering louder than anyone else. Scott and Fred shook hands and the ref raised Scott's hand as the winner. He had won eleven to seven.

Scott walked off the mat panting and sweating, but clearly pleased. The team made a path, patting him as he passed by. He headed to the outskirts of the room to cool down, his chest heaving from the effort of his match. Shannon and Derek's parents walked over to Scott and congratulated him.

Derek wanted to walk over as well, but the silence between them had gone on for so long he didn't know whether Scott would welcome him. Deciding he didn't care if he got rejected, he grabbed Scott's towel, water bottle, and sweatshirt, and walked over to where Scott, Shannon, and his parents were standing. "Great ninth inning push. Congratulations!"

Scott smiled, his lopsided grin spreading across his face. Derek hadn't seen that smile in over a month. His blood rushed south and he was glad he had put jeans on over his singlet.

"I didn't think I was going to be able to do it, but when you said all that stuff before the third period I...I don't know...I knew I would win." He peered directly into Derek's eyes, pausing for a moment before speaking. "I appreciate it. I needed a kick in the ass. Oops, sorry Mom."

Shannon laughed and placed an arm around his shoulder. "I think I have used the term once or twice in my life." She wrinkled her nose and sniffed a few times. "I forgot how bad you smell after your matches." She removed her arm but remained by his side.

Scott turned crimson. "Mom, oh my God, I can't believe you said that."

Shannon turned beet red. "Oh, honey, I'm sorry I didn't mean to hurt your feelings."

Scott shook his head. "You *didn't* hurt my feelings. You embarrassed the *hell* out of me."

Derek's mom laughed, making an exaggerated show of leaning over to take a whiff of Derek and exclaiming that he too smelled rather unpleasant.

Derek gave her a glare, handing the towel and water bottle to Scott. "You want to go into the hallway to cool off? The air is much cooler outside of the auditorium."

Scott nodded as he took the towel and dried his skin, still covered with a sheen of sweat, then got up and followed Derek out of the auditorium. The air was at least fifteen degrees cooler in the hallway and Scott shivered. "I grabbed your sweatshirt too. Here."

When Scott took the sweatshirt from Derek, their fingers brushed together. Putting the sweatshirt on, he glanced at Derek. "Thanks." His voice was quiet, unsure.

A number of wrestlers, student spectators, and parents roamed the halls focusing on their next wrestling match or speculating about whether they thought Cambridge or Waltham would win division. Derek wanted to be alone with Scott. "Come on, let's go upstairs and find somewhere private we can talk." Scott followed Derek up a set of stairs at the end of the hallway. Alone on the second floor, they stood silently facing one another in a hallway lined with lockers on one side and windows on the other.

Derek sat on a window ledge which was deep enough so it could also serve as a bench. His pulse quickened as he searched for the courage to begin speaking. "Scott, I wanted to talk to you. Actually, I have been wanting to talk to you all week, but I've been…afraid."

Scott faced him and Derek could sense the guilt beneath the surface. "I'm sorry. I don't want you to be afraid to talk to me."

"I was afraid you would tell me to leave you alone, or to go to hell or something." Derek fiddled with his hands which were resting in his lap. When he looked up, Scott's expression had shifted from guilt to sadness. Derek took a deep breath and continued. "Yesterday, after I got home, I went for a run. I stopped on the Foot Bridge and realized a few things." *I realized that I still love you but am willing to put my feelings aside if it's what you need from me. I realized you are the most incredible person I have ever met and I hate that your father has had such a horrible effect on you.* He wanted to say these things, but they would only distract from what he really wanted to say. "I wanted to apologize to you." Scott's eyes widened and he began to protest, but Derek pushed on. "I was being completely selfish and unfair pushing you into talking with your parents about going out. I wanted to spend time with you and didn't consider your needs. I was supposed to be someone who relieved your troubles, not someone who added to them."

Scott started to speak again, but Derek cut him off. "No, please, let me get this off my chest." Scott fell silent. "I can't imagine what it must have been like for you to have to move around so much. When I met you at the beginning of the year you were brave, self-assured, and lighthearted. You brought things out in me that I had kept locked away and I liked it. You changed me in a way that opened me up. It scared me, but I can't remember ever being happier. I'm not just talking about kissing and getting off, I'm talking about love. You made me feel like I was the most important person in your world. When things changed between us, I became depressed and withdrawn. I couldn't stand that we weren't together like we had been. I wanted to hold you and kiss you and to keep moving forward, but we couldn't and it hurt. I thought if I put up my guard I could protect myself from becoming vulnerable again and it worked for a while, but I couldn't continue doing it. I won't go back to the person I was before I met you. You've changed me and it's definitely a change for the better."

Derek swallowed, his mouth running dry. "Could I have a sip of that?" Scott handed the water bottle over, and Derek took a big gulp. "What I'm trying to say is you gave me something, and when you needed me to give you what you needed, space and understanding, I couldn't do it. I'm sorry for that. I want you to know how much you mean to me and how much I hope you find your way back to the happy and carefree person you are." *And if you will have me back, I will be the happiest person in the world.* "Maybe things won't work out for us and it won't be either of our faults. That sucks, but at least I got to know you and to love you. I want you to be happy Scott, whether it's with me or not." Derek inhaled, surprised to find his breathing had become shaky.

Scott stared at Derek, not saying anything. Derek tried to sense what Scott was thinking, but there was so much going on in Scott's eyes and in his body language Derek couldn't get a read. "Well, I guess I should let you get back to the auditorium. You know you can beat Tony. Don't stand in your own way. You *are* a champion. Go onto the mat knowing you're a winner. I sure as hell know you are." Derek held Scott's gaze, then headed back towards the stairs.

Derek didn't make it five steps before Scott spoke. "You don't get to say all that and then just walk away." Derek froze and slowly turned around, expecting to be confronted with anger. When he faced Scott, he saw no trace of annoyance. Scott took a step closer to Derek before speaking. "*I'm* the one who should be apologizing to *you* Derek. You opened yourself up to me. You allowed yourself to take a chance on me and I failed you completely. I allowed my dad to force me into a punishment I didn't deserve, and didn't fight for myself at all. It's the story of my life with him. I accept what my dad decides and believe I can't do anything about it."

Derek started to protest, but Scott held up a hand. "I listened to you. Now you're going to listen to me. I lost myself over the last month and in the process I lost you too. That's not your fault Derek, it's mine. I'm the one who pushed you away. Maybe I did it by forcing you to get angry and frustrated. Maybe I created a situation to fool myself into believing you were being selfish. I needed someone to be mad at and you were the only one to lash out against. But the real loser here is me.

"You say I brought things out in you. What you don't realize is you have brought things out in me as well. You welcomed me as a friend since the first day of school. You introduced me to Beck and to the guys on the team. You shared your music with me. You made me believe, for the first time, that I could count on someone to be there for good. On top of everything, you made me like being gay. You accepted me just as I am and loved me for it. No one has ever made me feel so stable and secure."

Scott took another step towards Derek. "I've been miserable ever since winter break, but my dad is not the main reason why. I've gotten used to my dad being the way he is. That needs to change, but it's *so* not the point right now. I was miserable because I knew I hurt you. When you shut off from me completely after you drove me to school and I said I needed space, the best part of me slipped away with you. I've done nothing but think about you and miss you. I've wanted to get down on my knees and beg you to take me back, but was afraid you didn't want me anymore. I still love you, Derek. I never stopped."

Derek's whole body flooded with happiness and emotion, his words barely audible, as tears began to spill down his cheeks. "I still love you, too."

Scott took two steps closer to Derek. "What I'm trying to say is I want you back in my life. Not just as my friend, but as my boyfriend. Everything is better when I can share it with you."

Derek's muscles began to go limp and his chest began to heave. He was sure he was going to fall over at any moment. He hadn't seen Scott close the gap between them, but was thankful he had. As his knees began to buckle, two strong arms wrapped around him, preventing him from crashing to the ground. Allowing his body to sink into Scott's embrace, all other sensations faded away, and Scott's arms wrapped tightly around him was the only thing he cared about.

Derek had no idea how long they stood holding one another, but when they finally pulled apart, Derek stared at Scott's face and saw pure affection through the tears streaming down his cheeks. They both reached for each other at the same time and their hands tangled.

Laughing, Scott raised his hand to cup Derek's neck in his palm. Curving his fingers so they caressed the back of his neck, he drew Derek towards him, bringing their mouths together in a gentle, lingering kiss. Scott placed his other hand on the side of Derek's head as the intensity of the kiss increased. Their mouths opened and their tongues ventured into each other's mouths, reclaiming the feelings and tastes they had been deprived of for so long. Eventually, Scott's grip on Derek eased and their kiss returned to a sweet and gentle expression of love.

Pulling apart, they faced each other and Derek peered into Scott's blue-green eyes. He had forgotten how beautiful they were and suddenly realized why...the spark of mischief and seductiveness had returned. To his surprise, even though Derek's cock already strained at full mast, it grew even harder. He took Scott's hand and placed it over his heart. "Look what you do to me. My heart is jumping out of my chest."

The glint in Scott's eyes danced as he lowered his hand to Derek's crotch. "Mmmm...I'm glad that I still do *that* to you." He held Derek at arm's length. "Let me get a good look at you." Assessing him as if he were on display, Scott couldn't help but giggle. "Besides your bloodshot eyes, your red and swollen lips, and..." Scott dropped his eyes, then raised them once again, one eyebrow cocked, "...that enormous package you are sporting, I'd say you're fairly presentable."

Derek laughed in earnest. "I think I'll sit here for a moment until I calm down a bit.

Scott took Derek's hand, placing it over his own crotch. "Maybe we should both sit for a while to calm down."

It didn't take long for their mothers to find them, when they finally returned to the auditorium. Derek's mother looked concerned. "Where have you two been? The second round of matches is almost over." Her gaze bounced between the two of them, a quizzical look crossing her face. After a second, the questioning expression shifted to one of understanding. "Oh...*oh!*"

Shannon looked utterly confused. "Well, answer her. Where have you been?"

Derek's mother cut in before either of them could answer. "Often the boys who make it to the finals take a break during the second round while the wrestlers who have matches compete for third and fourth place. I can't believe that slipped my mind." She shot Derek a knowing glance.

Derek looked at his mother with gratitude. "How did Josh and Power do?"

"Josh and Power both won their matches. It's so exciting, six of the seven Brampton wrestlers moved to the finals after the first round. Lexington only has two and Waltham only has four."

Shannon still looked confused and opened her mouth as if to ask another question, but Derek's mother grabbed her by the arm and dragged her away.

Scott turned to Derek. "What was *that* all about?"

Derek glanced at Scott. "My mom knows about me. Now I guess she's figured out about *us*."

Scott panicked, and then relaxed, the tension flowing out of his body. "Okay, I'll admit, I'm a little freaked out, but I can deal with it." Derek wanted to hug him, but refrained. Instead, he walked to his bag to prepare for his final match.

The Brampton wrestler who had competed in the semi-finals lost his match. Three of the Waltham wrestlers had taken third and one had taken fourth. This put Brampton at a disadvantage going into finals. There was one member from the Brampton team who had his final match before Derek's and he lost. What made it worse was he lost to a Waltham wrestler.

Derek had already wrestled Kevin from the Waltham team earlier in the year and had pinned him which boosted his confidence going into this match. Neither of them had to work too hard to make it to the finals, so they both had a good deal of energy. When the match began, he scored a quick takedown and turned Kevin to his back, earning back points. The first period ended with Derek in the lead five to zero.

In the second period, Derek began on the mat with Kevin on top. He quickly escaped and took Kevin down to the mat. Derek waited for the burn and ache he normally experienced at this point in his matches, but it never came. *I can do this. I beat him once already this year.* At the same time, Kevin's ability to resist Derek weakened. *I am stronger and have better endurance.* Taking advantage of Kevin's diminishing energy, Derek knocked Kevin to his side and rolled him to his back. Kevin arched onto his head, attempting to roll back to his stomach or to escape, but each time he arched, Derek tightened his hold. *Kevin is wasting his energy. It's time to end this.* Squeezing with all of his strength, Derek restricted Kevin's ability to move and slowly secured his shoulders to the mat. The ref counted to three and slammed the mat.

His teammates screamed his name in a chant-like fashion, splitting it into two distinct syllables. *De-rek. De-rek. De-rek.* He heard his parents and Shannon shouting "He won! He won!" Walking to the center of the mat, he shook Kevin's hand and the ref raised his arm as the winner. He was the division champion for his weight class.

There were several matches before the next Brampton wrestler, Frank, had his final match. Derek walked over to his parents and Shannon who gave him a hug and congratulated him. His mother had a tear running down her cheek. "I'm so proud of you honey. What a way to finish your high school wrestling career." Scott walked over to join them and his mother released Derek, pulling Scott into a big hug, squishing his face to her breasts. Scott looked mortified, but allowed the gesture. Derek had to bite his lip to keep from laughing.

When Frank took the mat, Derek and Scott walked over to watch. "Scott, go prepare yourself. You're wrestling Tony. Last time you wrestled him your head wasn't in it." Scott brooded for a moment remembering that he and Derek had been in a dark place at that time. "But," Derek added, "now there's no reason for you to be distracted."

Scott smiled and leaned close to Derek's ear. "Well, I *could* be distracted if I think of what you and I did upstairs."

Derek fixed him with a serious glare. "Then don't think about that right now." Scott pouted, causing his bottom lip to become even more prominent. Derek leaned closer to Scott. "You know, when you do that, I want to nibble on your lips."

Scott's grin widened as he lifted his eyebrows in a suggestive manner. "You promise?"

Derek shook his head. "I'll do more than that if you beat Tony."

Frank lost his match to a Waltham wrestler. The next match was Scott's. He walked to the center of the mat and stood in neutral position facing Tony. The ref blew the whistle, and both Tony and Scott lunged for each other's legs. They missed and ended up facing each other from a standing position once again. Tony shot down to Scott's legs, successfully grasping one and brought Scott to the mat. The look of frustration and defeat which Derek had seen during Scott's semi-final match against Fred was nowhere to be seen. Instead, there was an expression of fierce determination. He quickly escaped Tony's hold and faced him from a standing position once again.

Scott's feet began to move quickly as he fought for arm control. Tony kept shifting his view from Scott's arms to his legs. Scott moved a leg to expose it only to pull it back just as Tony was about to go for the takedown.

Finally he allowed Tony to gain the inside control of his arm.

"No!" Derek screamed. "Get inside control."

Scott must have heard him, but he allowed Tony to keep inside control. He started forcing Tony to circle with him, watchful of any offensive moves Tony might make. Faster than Derek could register, Scott shot his free arm to take the outside grip of Tony's free arm, bent his knees, and shoved his hips forward and up. Tony lifted off the ground and his feet began to swing upwards. With a sideways tug, Scott torqued Tony and used the motion of the throw to direct Tony's back to the mat, landing squarely on Tony's chest. Quickly hooking his legs and squeezing his arms, Scott had a secure hold.

Derek jumped to his feet, actually losing contact with the ground for a moment. "Holy fuck! The suplex." His teammates, Coach, and a few parents turned to look at Derek with horror. He slapped his hands over his mouth. The only person who seemed amused was Scott. Derek swore he could see his crooked smile trying to force its way through his gritted teeth.

Scott squeezed tighter on Tony's arms and, using his legs for leverage, arched his back as far as it would go. The ref counted to three and slammed the mat. Scott had won and was the champion for his weight class.

Josh and Power both won, but Derek and Scott hadn't watched those matches. They were talking at each other simultaneously, speaking at least eighty words a minute reviewing how Scott had achieved the perfectly executed suplex.

Once Power won his match, the ref who had announced the scoring procedures the day before returned to the center of the auditorium. "We will take a ten minute break to tally the scores and to allow the teams to convene before we announce the winners of this year's division championship." No one needed to wait for the ref to know who had won. Everyone had already done the math. With four first place, two second place, and one fourth place wrestler, Brampton had earned twenty-three team points. Waltham had two first place, two second place, three third place, and one fourth place wrestlers which only earned them twenty-one team points. Brampton was the division championship team and both Derek and Scott were the champions of their weight class.

Chapter 20

The next morning Derek woke up especially early. He got ready for school and bustled out to his car, driving to Scott's house.

When Scott came out he ran to the car, hopped in, and kissed Derek for several seconds. "This is a surprise. I didn't ask you to pick me up."

Derek grinned. "If you want I'll let you out and you can walk."

"Not a chance." He took Derek's hand. "Drive." Derek made no move to start the car. Scott shot him a puzzled glance. "What's wrong?"

Derek gave Scott a serious look. After a moment, he said, "I can't."

Scott gazed at him with concern. "What do you mean?"

Derek sighed. "Well," he paused for dramatic effect. "You have my hand and I kind of need it to put the car in gear."

Scott let go of Derek's hand and shoved him. "You shit! You scared me." As Derek put the car in gear he began to laugh.

When they arrived at school, hundreds of students congregated outside the front doors and in the lobby. Banners had been raised overnight and it appeared that a streamer machine had vomited everywhere. The members of the wrestling team were huddled together in the center of the lobby. They couldn't take more than two steps before someone stopped and congratulated them or patted them on the back. It took Derek and Scott about twenty minutes to walk up the stairs and down the hallway to their lockers. Finally, first bell rang and students began to dissipate from the halls. Derek and Scott headed to English and took their seats. When Beck entered the room and noticed the two of them sitting next to each other, she raised a single eyebrow, peering from one to the other. Satisfied her eyes weren't playing tricks on her, a wide grin spread across her face and she walked over to sit with them. "So, I am guessing this means..."

"Yup," said Scott.

"Good. I was about two days away from taking both of your nuts and..."

Scott placed two fingers over Beck's lips, silencing her. "Just this once, I'm begging you, don't threaten my nuts." He flashed a grin at her, widening his eyes and pretending he had the power to hypnotize her into compliance.

Beck glared at him, a thin smile ruining her effort to appear irritated. "M'k. Pine. Uh wnt." Scott and Derek both looked at Beck, not understanding what she had said. She dramatically lifted her hand, allowing her wrist to go limp and pointing her finger towards the ones Scott still had covering her lips. Scott removed his fingers. "I said, *Ok. Fine. I won't.* But only this once."

They ate lunch together and Beck attempted to listen as Derek and Scott kept interrupting each other telling her what had happened on the second floor of Newton High. Although it was the world's most difficult story to follow, she somehow managed to keep quiet until they finished.

As they got ready to leave for their fifth period classes, Josh stopped by the table. "Hey Derek, Scott, Beck. I'm having a bash at my house on Friday night to celebrate our win, and the fact that Friday's the last day before February break. Derek, you can't mix this party. You need to be free to celebrate with everyone." He didn't wait for a response, running to catch up with a few of the guys from the team.

After school, Derek dropped Scott off at home, feeling a slight twinge of disappointment as he watched him walk up the steps to his front door. He wished things had returned to the way they had been before Scott's punishment. What he wouldn't give to get Scott alone in his attic right now. After the last couple of months of not spending any time with Scott, Derek forced himself to accept the situation without complaint.

When he got home he found his mother sitting at the kitchen table. He knew she had figured out what he and Scott had been up to at Newton High, and he also knew it made her uncomfortable, but he wanted to wait a while before discussing his love life with her. She said they would figure things out as a family, so Derek saw no reason to rush into a discussion about his sexual practices right now.

"Honey, I wanted to talk to you for a minute." Dread settled onto Derek's shoulders like a weight and he sat down at the table, waiting to find out what his mother wanted to say. "As you know, your father has been working long hours since it's tax season. He and I are going away for a few days to relax and have some down time. We plan on leaving on Friday afternoon and coming back on Monday morning. We'll leave you money for food and for going out to enjoy the beginning of your break."

"Yeah? That sounds good." The weight lifted. *That's not what I expected to hear.* He had to work to keep the rising excitement out of his voice. "You two deserve to get away once in a while." He gave his mom a kiss on the cheek and walked towards his room. Once there, he shut the door gently, then did a silent happy dance. His celebration was short lived when he remembered Scott was still under house arrest. Hatred for Scott's dad flared up in his chest.

He flopped down onto his bed, grabbing his English book and beginning his homework. He was in the middle of his Latin homework when his mother came to his bedroom door. "Honey, you have a visitor." Derek wondered who would stop by unannounced and his breath caught in his chest when he saw Scott standing in his doorway. Derek's pleasure bubbled up inside of him and his mouth spread into a wild grin. His mother would have to be a moron not to know exactly what he was thinking…and she was *no* moron.

"I'm fixing some chicken for dinner. I'll let you boys know when it's ready." She lingered in the doorway for a moment. "Um, I'd like for the two of you to leave the door open." Her cheeks pinked, clearly uncomfortable at having to make this request.

"Mom!" Nothing more needed to be said for Derek's embarrassment to be clearly known.

Derek's indignation seemed to snap his mother out of her discomfort. "Or the two of you are welcome to spend time in the living room. I have no problem with you closing this door if you're out there." The pink had left her cheeks as she locked Derek in an unwavering stare.

Derek softened his demeanor. "No, keeping the door open is fine."

She glanced back and forth between the two of them, maintaining a serious expression on her face. Derek had never seen her so parental before. As she headed towards the kitchen, Derek swore he heard a soft giggle. *Wow, she is some cool shit!* Turning his attention to Scott, he ran to the doorway to make sure his mother wasn't lingering, then ran to Scott and wrapped his arms around his neck. Scott returned the embrace and they kissed. "What are you doing here?"

Scott sat down on Derek's bed leaning against the

headboard. Derek sat cross-legged towards the foot of his bed facing him. "After you dropped me off, my mom told me she wanted to talk. She had made fried chicken, which I found odd because she only makes it when she has something big to tell me. I half expected she was going to announce another move." Derek's body stiffened. "Relax, we're not going anywhere. She told me about the conversation she had with your mom. I listened as she poured her soul out, apologizing every third sentence for failing to stand up to my dad. She even started crying at one point and I almost lied, saying things hadn't been all that bad."

Derek gave him an incredulous stare. Scott leaned forward and placed a hand on Derek's shoulder. "Calm down. I said I *almost* lied." Shifting his grip to the back of Derek's neck, Scott pulled Derek in for a short kiss, then released him and leaned back against the headboard.

"So, she's going on and on, telling me how understanding I've been about the moves and the punishments. And then she hits me with the big news. She told me my punishment was over and I could go out again. I asked her when dad had decided to let me off the hook and she said he hadn't. It blew my mind. She said that even though he hadn't changed his mind, she didn't care and was going to…what were her exact words…oh yeah. *Handle things.*" Scott shook his head, a thin smile crossing his lips. "She told me I didn't deserve the way I had been treated and I had never given them any reason to be disappointed in me. She said this was between her and dad and I shouldn't worry. I did of course, and said maybe I should stay home until she actually talked to him, but she told me to get my unpunished ass out of her house and to go and enjoy the day. She actually suggested I come over here. I've never seen her so assertive and in charge before."

"Well, I am glad she was, and I'm happy you're here."

Crawling on his hands and knees, Derek edged closer to Scott. He tilted his head to the side, like a panther listening for sounds in the forest, trying to get a sense of his mother's location. He heard her open the oven and pull the tray out. *Must be basting the chicken.* Secure in the knowledge she wasn't about to walk into his room, he continued slinking towards Scott who had placed an expression of mock fear on his face. Derek placed his hands on Scott's ankles and pulled, flattening him on the bed, and then continued crawling over Scott's body until he was straddling him. "I have some good news for you, too." His voice dripped with lust.

Scott was becoming hard, grinding his hips against Derek and pressing their crotches together. The friction caused Scott's breath to quicken.

It took Derek a moment to regain his train of thought. "I have some really good news for you." He leaned down and kissed Scott on the lips, evoking a light hum from him. Lowering his head, his lips and tongue traced Scott's jaw, until his mouth rested against Scott's neck. Shifting between kissing and licking, Derek's own excitement intensified as Scott writhed beneath him.

Scott struggled to keep his voice contained to avoid drawing the attention of Derek's mother. "Derek, if you don't stop…I'm gonna—"

Derek silenced Scott by running his tongue in circles over the sensitive skin of Scott's neck, slowly working his way upward until his mouth was next to Scott's ear. "My mom just told me I'm gonna have the house to myself for the weekend." Derek didn't know whether Scott's gasp was from the stimulation or from what he had just told him.

Scott grabbed Derek and toppled him over onto his side, causing a book to fall onto the floor. "Your parents are going away for the weekend?" A glint of excitement sparkled in his eyes.

"Everything okay in there?" Derek's mother called from the kitchen.

"Yes, Claire," Scott said, "I tossed a book at Derek's head. He's being a pain in the butt."

"All right, then. Smack him once for me too." They listened to her light giggling for a moment.

Scott smiled, but his expression became serious as he rolled Derek onto his back, resting his weight on his elbows and forearms as he peered down into Derek's eyes. "That *is* good news. So what are you planning on doing with this house all to yourself?"

Derek smiled and lifted his head to kiss Scott. Scott playfully pulled his face out of reach. Derek pouted. "Isn't it obvious what I'm planning?"

Scott leaned down and caressed Derek's neck with several short and gentle kisses. "No, I must be dense. Why don't you spell it out for me?"

Derek pouted. "So you're looking for an explicit invitation?"

Scott grinned wickedly. "Uh huh."

"Okay, fine." Derek tried to sound petulant, but couldn't manage it. "Will you come over and spend the weekend with me?"

Scott's response was answer enough. He leaned down and closed his mouth over Derek's giving him a hungry and passionate kiss. Scott lifted his head so he could gaze at Derek, whose eyes were shining with warmth and caring. "I really love you, Derek."

Derek pulled Scott into a strong embrace. "I love you, too. So much."

The remainder of the spring flew by. Snow melted, and with the arrival of warmer weather and fresh greenness, a constant stream of students could be found outside during lunch and study hall periods. The wrestling team had been celebrated in an all-school assembly shortly after their victory and the banner which announced Brampton as division champions hung in the lobby of the school. It would be moved to the athletic building once school ended to hang with the other championship banners Brampton had been awarded over the years.

Things had been tense in Scott's home since his mother had put her foot down and overrode his father's punishment, but Shannon made sure Scott experienced none of the stress between her and her husband. As a result, Scott had once again become vibrant and full of energy.

Despite his fear of getting caught, Derek spent his free time furtively exploring the school with Scott for places to have some privacy. They had discovered several locations where they spent their unscheduled time conducting themselves in a manner most unbefitting a Brampton student.

Derek and Scott had both received their acceptance letters to Boston University in April and, although they had been accepted to many other colleges, decided they wanted to stay close to home, albeit for different reasons. Derek wanted to stay in Boston because of his family. Scott wanted to remain because he had moved around enough and his experiences over the past year in Boston had turned it into a home to him. Their number one reason for choosing to go to Boston University was because it was the only place they both applied to and got accepted.

Numerous parties filled the remaining months of school, Derek mixing for most of them. A few became the focal point of gossip over the spring because parents had returned unexpectedly to find their homes crowded with the entire senior class. Those unfortunate students, whose parents had caught them, suspiciously fell off the social radar for the remainder of the school year.

Graduation day was bright and sunny. The student council officers from the lower three grades set up the decorations along the football field and lined up the chairs for the graduating senior class. As custom dictated, the lower grade student council members attended graduation. The senior class usually selected a gift for the school, presenting it to the junior who would serve as the president the next year.

The seniors sat alphabetically by their last names, so Derek and Scott sat next to each other, Derek walking across the stage right behind Scott. As each student received their diplomas, their families stood and cheered, mothers tearful and fathers holding them. The seniors were beaming and ready to put high school behind them; excited to begin their new lives as college students. A big reception after graduation took place on the soccer field next to the football bleachers and families gathered to eat and socialize. The entire affair lasted about two hours.

Over the next couple of weeks, several smaller graduation parties took place, parents having to coordinate with one another so their parties didn't overlap. These end-of-year parties were a big deal and no one wanted to miss a single one. Derek's parents threw his party the weekend following graduation. The wrestling team had been invited along with Beck. All of the fathers drank beer and surrounded Henry by the grill, offering their suggestions about grilling technique. The mothers gathered on the porch or in the kitchen chatting about their children and their summer plans.

Derek gazed around his yard and laughed at how 1950's it all seemed. He was distracted by Scott and Beck who appeared at his side. "Can we talk to you for a moment?" Scott had been the one to speak, but they both had conspiratorial grins on their faces. Derek paused, distrustful of the expressions on their faces.

Reluctantly, Derek allowed himself to be led through the kitchen, down the hall, and up the stairs to the attic. "Okay, you have to close your eyes." Beck spoke this time.

Scott stood behind Derek covering his eyes before they entered the attic. Derek heard something sliding across the floor. He also heard his mother and Shannon's voices as they entered the attic as well. Finally, Beck spoke up. "Okay, I think it's ready. You can let Derek see again."

Scott removed his hand from Derek's eyes. The sudden brightness of the room blinded him for a minute. When his eyes adjusted, he saw it sitting in the middle of the room with a huge red bow on top. The TASCAM M-164FX 16 Channel Mixing Board with Digital Effects Derek that he had wanted to buy when he, Scott, and Beck had gone to Best Buy at the Copley Place Plaza. "Oh my God. I can't believe it." Derek walked over to the mixing board and ran his fingers over the controls. "Mom, did you get this?"

His mother shook her head. "Nope, this is from those two."

Derek turned to Scott and Beck in disbelief. "I can't… This is too much. I can't *believe* it."

Scott and Beck exchanged amused glances, and then Beck walked up to Derek. "Well, we could always bring it back."

Derek stood protectively between Beck and his new mixing board. "No way. This is awesome. But I didn't get you guys anything." Derek's mother and Shannon, clearly only wanting to see Derek's reaction, said they needed to return to the party and left the attic. Beck's grin spread from ear-to-ear. "So you love it?"

Still in shock, Derek spluttered a reply. "Yes, I love it. Thank you both."

Beck gave Derek a hug. "Good. I'm glad." She gave him a small peck on the lips. "Now, what I want for my present is acting lessons. Here." She pulled out a neatly folded piece of paper from her front pant pocket. "I want to take acting classes which will be offered through community college. My parents say the tuition to Brandeis is graduation present enough. Well, that and the car they bought me so I could come home. I'm still convinced they bought the car more as a gift to themselves. My mom still hasn't stopped crying about me moving away from home."

Derek smiled. Only Beck would find a reason to complain about receiving a car as a present. "Sure. I'd be happy to pay for your lessons as your graduation gift."

Beck's face lit up. "Excellent, because I've already filled out the application form. All you have to do is write a check and—"

Derek gave her a hug, making sure his embrace forced Beck's mouth against his shoulder. "No problem Beck." The class would only cost $100 and he still had the $300 that he had saved up to buy the mixing board. She hugged him back, apparently unaware his action had been motivated by a desire to shut her up.

"Okay, well, I'll leave you two. Don't stay up here too long or I'm gonna send up the sex police." She turned to face Derek. "That would be your mother, in case you didn't know." Derek gave her a heated glare which clearly conveyed the message *Shut up and leave already.* She smiled and left the attic, giving Scott a high five as she passed him.

Once they were alone, Derek rushed to Scott's side and gave him a huge hug. "Thank you so much. I love it." Scott hugged him back. "I can't believe I didn't get anything for you."

Scott held Derek at arm's length. "You really *are* clueless aren't you?" Derek's face must have reflected his shock because Scott's crooked grin crossed his face and he shook his head. "You have given me the greatest gift, Derek. You love me. You want me. You make me incredibly happy."

Derek didn't know what to say. "But that's not a gift, it's—" His words were cut off by Scott's mouth. He allowed himself to be drawn in, his chest being squeezed until it molded against Scott's body. Derek opened his mouth, allowing Scott full access to him and their tongues danced and intertwined.

With one hand tightly wound around Derek's waist, Scott's other hand gently touched the side of his face, savoring the heat radiating from Derek's skin.

A tingling sensation shot up Derek's spine as Scott's thumb caressed his cheek as they kissed. His crotch began to grow and expand. "Mmmm."

After a few minutes, the kiss shifted from needful intensity to languid sensuality. Finally willing himself to pull out of the kiss, Scott continued holding Derek in his arms, allowing their bodies to sway gently. "Derek, you are my gift. End of discussion."

Tightening his arms around Scott and savoring the feel of their bodies together, he knew Scott meant what he said. He looked up and sealed his lips against Scott's, allowing him to enjoy his graduation gift a little bit longer before they returned to the party.

About the Author

D. H. Starr is a clean-cut guy with a wickedly naughty mind. He grew up in Boston and loves the city for its history and beauty. Also, having lived in NYC, he enjoys the fast pace and the availability of anything and everything. He first became interested in reading from his mother who always had a stack of books piled next to her bed. Family is important to D. H. and his stories center around the intricate and complex dynamics of relationships and working through problems while maintaining respect and love. His favorite books tend to fall in the genres of science fiction, fantasy, paranormal, and coming of age.

To learn more about D. H. Starr and his books, please visit his website at www.dhstarr.com if you are 18+.

To view his young adult work and resources, visit www.dhstarrYAbooks.com.

CPSIA information can be obtained at www.ICGtesting.com
Printed in the USA
242637LV00001B/1/P